Island Bound

By

J.D. Gordon

2/03

© 2002 by J.D. Gordon. All rights reserved.

No part of this book may be reproduced, stored in a retrieval system, or transmitted by any means, electronic, mechanical, photocopying, recording, or otherwise, without written permission from the author.

ISBN: 0-7596-9351-X (e-book)
ISBN: 0-7596-9352-8 (Paperback)
ISBN: 0-7596-9353-6 (Dustjacket)

This book is printed on acid free paper.

1stBooks - rev. 10/7/02

Chapter One

Clear January sunlight pierced the dusty air of a shabby one-bedroom apartment in a small town just west of Chicago. Police officers and firefighters in dark uniforms scurried back and forth from the vehicles outside toting paramedic equipment or busily scribbling on paperwork splayed across a battered coffee table. Two men, Eddie Gilbert and his temporary partner, Donny Frazen, examined the spectacle in the coat closet. There, with a khaki trench coat to the left and a stained leather jacket to the right, hung the stiffened body of a middle-aged man. His face was blue, and his eyes stared emptily at a spider web in the corner of the doorway.

"First time out today and we have to deal with a hanging," Eddie muttered to no one in particular. "I'm thinking this isn't going to be a good day."

"Well, I can easily say this guy's day didn't start out too well either - hanging himself with a bungee cord," Donny remarked scornfully. He tapped the rubber of the bungee a couple times with his finger and said, "Look, poor bastard couldn't even tie a proper noose. A failure in life, a failure in death."

Some police officers, paramedics, and firefighters found it necessary to indulge in a blackened sense of comedy in order to cope with the stresses of working as emergency personnel, but Eddie didn't particularly care for comments like that. Then again, he didn't particularly care for the guy who made it, either. Donny had to be one of the biggest assholes on the department. He was the kind of guy who always had to be right, even if he was wrong, like some kind of wanna-be lawyer. Sometimes he even fucked up his patient care, but he would argue with any one who found fault with him until his opponent caved in and let him have his way.

Eddie hated having to work with Donnie, but he was able to tolerate him because he knew the arrangement would only be temporary. His usual partner, Hank Brickman, had taken some time off to relax with his wife and her family at their weekend home in Green Lake, Wisconsin. Wisconsin in January - Eddie thought a person would have to have a few screws loose to think Wisconsin would be a nice spot for vacationing in the wintertime. As for himself, Eddie couldn't wait to escape from the evils of Chicago's winter fury. In just a few days, perhaps even before Hank returned from Wisconsin, Eddie would be far away from snow, sleet, and the ruthless winds that chilled his bones.

Eddie needed some time away from work for a while. For the past few years, he had allowed himself no time to unwind. He spent his summers working on one of the cruise boats operating out of Chicago's Navy Pier, and during the school year, he spent his days off from the fire department working as an athletic trainer for the football and baseball teams at the local community college, well known as the College of Dupage. He often did side jobs for some extra cash, and whatever spare time he had left he devoted to boating safety courses with the Coast Guard. Keeping that kind of schedule, Eddie began to feel he'd lost touch with the adventurous, carefree guy he used to be.

It was all going to be worth it, though. Ed would need the extra money and the knowledge he had gained through the Coast Guard courses and his experience on the cruise boat to make his dream vacation a reality. He rented a convertible Mitsubishi Spyder, which he would drive all the way to Key West Florida, making stops along the way as needed. Once he arrived at the Southern most point of the continental United States, Ed would exchange the car for a small, motor-powered yacht with no crew. That was the way he wanted it; he craved the excitement of knowing that his survival depended on himself alone, that there would be no one to help him if he ran into trouble. He would cruise the Caribbean for a few weeks, but after that, he had no plans. He just wanted to travel and see what would happen.

There was just one place Eddie felt certain he would visit, and that was a nice little town that went by the name of Memphis. One of his childhood chums would be there to meet him for the weekend, and Eddie knew the two of them would have a great time. There's no place like Memphis for listening to some good music, dining on some good food, drinking some good beer, and meeting some beautiful, absolutely top-notch women. Eddie and his buddies used to drive down to Memphis every year for the Blues on Beale Street festival, and they had some wild times there, feeling young and happy. Eddie hoped that he'd be able to recapture some of that old youthful excitement on his vacation because lately he'd been feeling like he was stuck in a predictable, mundane routine.

"Anyone find an I.D. for this guy?" asked Terry, one of the police officers.

Eddie snapped out of his reverie and started to examine the corpse in the coat closet. He noticed a white sheet of paper crumpled in one of the man's hands. He must have been hanging there for quite some time, and Eddie found it difficult to remove the paper from the hand's death grip. He finally succeeded in wresting the paper from the body and quickly scanned the print, trying to find an explanation for the sad situation.

"Well, there's no name. This is an apology for his son and daughter, telling them he's sorry for doing such a shitty job of caring for them while they were growing up."

"Hey, I found something over here!" eagerly exclaimed a young rookie cop named Derek. "It's a life insurance policy. The guy's name is Giles Henderson, and there's a lot of paperwork here: medical bills, credit card statements…"

Jerry, a sergeant from the police department, approached the desk to shuffle through the information. The sergeant was a levelheaded, bear-like guy. Even at fifty years of age, he could wipe the decks with most of the cops on the police department. Eddie once had occasion to go boozing with the guy, and he discovered that Jerry could not only soak up alcohol like a sponge, but he was a real lady-killer as well. Young women flocked to him like flies to honey, but he never took them up on their offers. After he had gently turned away one of the women who made a pass at him, he would lean over to the guy sitting next to him and remark, "If I hadn't been married for the past twenty years, I would definitely scam on *that*."

"Wow, the guy was sixty-grand in debt, and he was just laid off from his job the other day. Says here he was a forklift driver for the United Cable Corporation, whatever that is."

"That's here in town," Jerry remarked authoritatively. "They manufacture the copper wire for use in telephone systems." He paused and thought out loud, "I wonder why they canned him?" He turned to Derek and barked, "Rookie, since you dug that up, you get to fill in the report and call the coroner. I'm going to get some lunch."

"Lunch? You just ate breakfast two hours ago," Eddie laughed. "You're getting old, and that behavior is going to catch up with you some day."

"Fuck you, Eddie; I'll still be able to kick your skinny ass," Jerry replied, letting it be known that he wouldn't take that kind of lip. Still, he playfully punched Eddie in the shoulder and said, "Hey, have a good sabbatical. After today, I'm off for the next week, so I won't run into you again."

"I'll send ya a post card, and I'll wrap it around a fresh-made piña colada."

At two hundred pounds and five feet, ten inches, Eddie certainly was no skinny ass. Eddie liked Jerry, but still, he could never understand how people in his line of work could let themselves get so out of shape. The life of a comrade or citizen, or even his own, could be on the line.

"Hey Derek, when the coroner calls, let me talk to him right away, O.K? We can't leave until we transfer information." Eddie was ready to follow Jerry's lead and get some lunch.

"I wonder if this moron thought his family was going to get the life insurance money. Didn't he know you don't get shit if you knock *yourself* off?" Donny added another one of his colorful editorials to the situation.

Eddie rolled his eyes. "Have you always been an asshole, Donny, or just while I've known you?"

"Pretty much," he replied frankly, then added, "I particularly like being an asshole around you though, Edwardo."

"Well, at least you're honest."

While waiting for the coroner to call, Eddie couldn't help studying the form of Giles Henderson. He had been a short, slight man, and the wrinkles around his mouth bore witness that he'd not spent much of his life smiling. His face was frozen in the same shocked expression he wore at the moment of his death, and it seemed that at the very last, the peace he sought in suicide still managed to elude him. It wasn't the first time Ed had seen the body of a person who committed suicide, but he still wondered each time he looked into one of those dead, distraught faces how people could let their lives get so out of control. Ed believed firmly that no one should ever feel the need to do what Giles did to himself. Paramedics get suicidal subjects all the time, but usually they are just troubled individuals looking for attention. That had not been the case with Giles. Here was a man who truly wanted to accomplish the gruesome task. He strung himself up with a bungee cord around his neck, the other end lashed to the coat bar. Eddie surveyed the body and noted that if he had changed his mind, all he had to do was stand up.

Ed figured Giles had done it late the night before. He would have to communicate this to the coroner, although the coroner really just needed to know if there were any signs of foul play.

Ed's thoughts were interrupted by the sound of a telephone ringing.

"Ed, it's the coroner. Derek said anxiously. "You wanted to talk to him right away?" Derek didn't seem to be too comfortable being in the same room with a dead body. His eyes kept darting back and forth from his paperwork to the closet, as if he expected at any moment the body would come after him like a zombie in the movies. He was new on the job, and Eddie could easily see that he'd never needed to call the coroner's office before.

"You O.K. Derek?" Eddie asked with concern.

"I'm fine, Ed. This is just my first time doing this on my own." Derek tried to sound self-assured, but his voice betrayed how shaken he was.

"That's cool," Ed said as he grabbed the receiver.

The coroner's name was Warwick, and Ed remembered speaking to him on other occasions. He was a nice enough guy, but he didn't spend too much time shooting the breeze with him. He was hungry, and he just wanted to get the job wrapped up so he could get back to the station for some lunch. The coroner released the paramedics from the scene, and Ed handed the phone back to the police officer.

"Derek we're outta here," Eddie said. "You gonna be O.K., man?"

"Yeah, I'll be fine," Derek answered, obviously relieved that he would be leaving soon, too.

Ed and Donny returned to their ambulance and reported back to dispatch.

"Central from ambulance ten, we are in service and on the air. Close the call," said into the radio.

A voice on the radio crackled, "O.K., ambulance ten, you're in service and on the air."

The two drove in silence to the grocery store to purchase the meals for the day, and after Donny pulled the rig into the parking lot, Eddie ran inside to pick up some ribeye steaks to cook on the grill. The steaks were always on sale, and that was why Eddie purchased them, not because he himself was fond of steak. In fact, he hardly ever touched meat since the age of twelve when he saw a thick, disgusting vein from a breaded pork chop wiggling off the side of his fork. Eddie stopped by the produce section and grabbed some red potatoes and Brussels sprouts, even though everyone in the firehouse called Brussels sprouts "fart balls."

Back at the firehouse Ed began to prepare the day's lunch. He had long ago appointed himself the official chef, and since then he had made it clear that no one else was allowed in the kitchen while he cooked. In fact, no one argued over the issue because Eddie prepared damn good grub.

Ed developed an interest in cooking as a child, when he used to hang out in his grandma Gambino's kitchen on holidays. He loved to watch his grandmother prepare huge trays of Italian delicacies such as lasagna, sausage, fresh-made ravioli and a number of other dishes. He helped her to cut vegetables, or sometimes she would put him in charge of a pot on the stove with the task of stirring it every few minutes. When the family at the table greeted the food with praise and eagerness, Eddie used to stand by his grandmother's side and just beam with pride. As an adult, Ed still marveled at the happiness a simple thing like a good meal could bring people.

The firefighters paid ten bucks a day for lunch and dinner, whether there was time to eat it or not. Like a big family, the firefighters congregated around the table for meals because it was the one time of the day when all of them did the same thing at the same time.

While Ed was peeling potatoes in the kitchen, Steve Anderson poked his head through the door and said, "Hey, you daydreamin'? What time is lunch?"

"It'll be ready when it is ready," Ed replied. He didn't like to be pressured when he was cooking.

"What did you have out there?"

"Hanging. Looks like a definite suicide," Eddie stated grimly.

Steve frowned. "Just the kind of call you want before you leave on vacation, right?"

"All the more reason to go," Eddie shrugged.

Steve had been working with the fire department for about fifteen years. Since he had seniority, he got first pick of duties. Steve chose engineering, a crucial position in any fire department. It was his task to make certain that all firefighters called to a burning building would be supplied with an ample amount of water. Lives depended upon Steve, because if the men lost water pressure at a critical point in a job, they would be powerless to stop the blaze. Steve did well in his work, but it wasn't because of its weightiness that he chose it. The Salt Creek Fire Department only responded to twenty or thirty fires a year. That meant that Steve spent most of his time at work watching television and sleeping.

"How long are you going to be on vacation?" Steve asked conversationally.

"I'm outta here for six whole weeks."

"Six weeks!" Steve responded with surprise. "What the hell are you going to do in six weeks?"

"A lot of traveling…"

Ed began to describe his vacation to Steve, telling him everything about the boat he planned to rent. Steve stepped into the kitchen and hoisted himself up onto the counter, periodically helping himself to slices of raw potatoes as Eddie cut them. His voice took on a serious tone, and he said, "You packin' heat?"

"Packin' heat? You mean, am I bringing a *gun* with me?"

"Exactly," Steve said, looking Eddie in the eyes and not cracking a smile. "I'm serious. Really, it could be dangerous out there by yourself."

Eddie laid his knife down. "Are you crazy? I'm going on a vacation, not a killing spree. What do I need a gun for? And stop stealing my potatoes," he scolded. "I won't be by myself the whole time, anyway. My buddy in Tampa is going to go out on the boat with me for awhile."

"Well, don't come crying to me if somebody murders you out there," Steve warned, taking a couple more hunks of raw potato and hopping down from the counter to get some salt out of the cabinet. "Who else is going with you?"

Eddie sighed heavily and shook his knife at Steve. "Really, I mean it. Can't you wait until they're cooked? They're gonna taste much better if you'll just hold on a minute."

Steve let loose a huge, naughty grin. He couldn't say anything, though, because his mouth was full of raw potatoes.

"I'm not really sure who I'm gonna meet up with. A couple of my buddies are going to try and meet me periodically, but nothing's set in stone."

When everything was ready, Ed picked up the receiver for the loudspeaker and banged it hard on the fire extinguisher a few times. A gong-like sound reverberated throughout the fire station, announcing chowtime to all the men. Ed placed everything on the table as the rest of the shift filed into the kitchen for lunch. Meanwhile, the overhead speakers released unsettling noise pollution into the kitchen.

"Ambulance ten, you are to respond to a boy with his head stuck in the mailbox at 123 South Harvey Lane. Time out 12:32 hours."

Eddie's empty stomach complained as he tore it away from the plates of steaming food on the table. "It never fails, late lunch again, damn it. How does a kid get his head stuck in a mail box, anyway?" He asked himself. "You comin' Donny?"

"Yeah, I'm coming," Donny replied with disgust.

Eddie knew interruptions were all part of the job, but why did they always have to happen just as lunch was ready?

Donny and Eddie jumped into the ambulance, hit the lights, and pulled out of the apparatus bay floor and onto the concrete apron. Ed flipped the siren button to wail as Donny maneuvered the ambulance onto the street. Traffic was heavy, and Donny had to move into the left-hand lane and into oncoming traffic. As the two paramedics sat silently, Ed thought about his usual partner, Hank. When the two of them were working together, there was never silence; the two of them would converse all the way to the call. Quite often, they turned up the radio until it was way too loud and sang heartily to a good tune. Unlike Donny, who responded to the violence of the job with cynicism and inappropriate humor, Hank and Eddie chose to keep their apprehensions to themselves. Eddie knew that even though Hank belted out the tunes with gusto as if he hadn't a care in the world, his partner was just as worried as he was about what they might find when they arrived at the scene. Would they arrive in time? Would a child die on the way to the hospital? It became second nature for them to deal with these ideas in the back of their heads, even while laughing and singing all the way to the emergency.

Donny pulled the ambulance to the left side of the road, and Ed took the opportunity to size up the situation. There were four people standing around the mailbox: three women and one man. In the man's arms rested the legs and torso of a young boy. Like some modern-day rendition of ancient Egyptian gods with heads of jackals or wildcats, this boy had a big blue mailbox in place of his noggin. Ed stepped out of the ambulance and approached the group, stepping over a mound of snow at the end of the driveway. As his feet sunk into the slush and he almost slipped on the ice, he thought that it was yet another reason to take a long vacation in warmer regions. His aggravation vanished, however, when he saw the comic side of the ridiculous scene before him.

"Just what exactly happened here?" Eddie asked, hands on hips and a warm smile on his face.

Ed asked what the boy's name was, and one of the women offered, "Michael, but he goes by Jake. He's seven." She looked very worried and tried to comfort the boy by stroking one of the arms that poked uselessly out of the mailbox.

Donny positioned himself next to the man holding Jake in his arms, ready to take over the load.

"I just sent him out to get the mail," the worried woman explained, "and he didn't come back, and he didn't come back…I never imagined he'd gotten his head stuck in there." She dabbed at her nose with a crumpled paper towel.

"Hey Jake, how did you manage to get your melon stuck in there?" Eddie shouted into the mailbox from the side.

Jake responded, but Ed couldn't understand him. The only evidence of Jake's answer were muffled sounds of attempted speech. Eddie thought of the old Peanuts cartoon in which the adults' voices sounded like this: "Wa wawawa wawa waaa."

"Hold on Jake, we'll have you out of there in a jiffy," Eddie attempted to reassure the boy, whose wiggling feet expressed more than his incomprehensible voice.

Ed retrieved a pair of tin snips from the ambulance, and as Donny held the boy's now shivering body, which was dressed only in pajamas and large furry slippers, he carefully snipped away the metal surrounding the boy's head. A short while later, Jake was free.

Jake held his arms out for the woman with the paper towel at her nose and began crying.

"Now's not the time to start crying. You've been rescued!" Donny argued.

Eddie approached the woman with the boy in her arms and said, "You must be Jake's mom?"

The women nodded yes.

"We would like to take Jake into the ambulance and give him a quick check-up to make sure every thing is O.K." Ed explained. The mother wanted to know if Jake needed to go to the hospital, but Ed informed her that transportation to the hospital was entirely up to the parents.

"Well, is he alright?" she asked with a great deal of concern.

"Jake's quite a trooper, and he seems fine, just a little shaken up."

The woman gave her son a scrutinizing stare and stated, "I don't think he needs to go to the hospital. We'll be all right."

"Not a problem, but I'll have to ask you to sign a liability release form."

The form was supposed to protect the department from any lawsuits concerning the abandonment of patients. Ed explained the process to the boy's mother and told her if any problems arose, she should call the fire department again or take Jack to the emergency room. Jake's mom signed the required documents.

As she returned the forms to Ed, he noticed for the first time that the woman was quite attractive. "What's your name, ma'am?" he asked, working his hero appeal to its limit. The mother's name was Rebecca Johnston.

"Any relation to Doc Johnston from the hospital?" he asked.

"He's my husband," the woman said proudly.

"Oh, I see." Ed was a little flustered, but he concealed it well. "That's great. Doctor Johnston's a great guy."

"Yes," the woman said, clutching the doctor's son in her arms. "I know."

Back in the truck, Donny razzed Eddie. "Oh no!" he said. "You weren't trying to put the make on Doctor Johnston's wife, were you? I know you weren't trying to do *that*. What did you think, son? The woman's got a child in her arms. Didn't you think she just *might* have a husband to go along with it?"

Eddie laid his head back in the seat and shut his eyes, trying to tune Donny out. "Shut up, man."

"Ummhmmm, 'That's great. Doctor Johnston's a great guy.' That's a real great cover-up, too, Ed. And you were just as smooth as molasses," Donny chuckled as he turned the huge wheel of the truck around a corner. "I like that."

"He is a great guy. Really." Eddie tried to defend himself, but he knew Donny caught on to his tactics.

The rest of the afternoon was uneventful. Ed spent the rest of the day tying up some loose ends, calling his neighbor and to ask if she would come over every couple of days to feed his fish and collect the newspaper. Then he started working on some clerical tasks around the department. He was having a hard time keeping his mind on his work, though. After all, screening emergency medical reports was not exactly the most exciting part of the job. While he worked, Eddie's thoughts drifted to his upcoming vacation. This was going to be a long one. Where was he going to put all of his stuff in the tiny car he rented? He needed a lot of gear for his boating expedition, but space for luggage was going to be limited.

Eddie also reconsidered Steve's comments about bringing a gun along. The idea might not be bad one. Ed had a couple of firearms that he kept locked in a case under his bed, but the idea of bringing one along on the vacation seemed like it would be asking for trouble. On the other hand, he had read in the newspaper less than a week ago about a family of tourists killed at a rest area by a psychotic maniac. He began to think that he shouldn't go on his vacation defenseless. He would occasionally venture into areas that were far from civilization, and it was true that much of his time would be spent alone. Eddie thought about some of his favorite movies, and he concluded that if the main characters in them had only had a gun, everything would have been much better for them.

Eddie's battalion chief stepped into the room.

"Have you got everything ready to pass on to Scott?" he asked.

"You betcha, I'm working on it right now."

Scott was the firefighter that was going to screen the runs while Ed was away. Eddie stopped his battalion chief before he left the room.

"Timmy, what time ya' want dinner?"

"Any time is fine, as long as it's before bed time. What are we having?"

"Ribeyes, smooshed tots, and fart balls."

"No steak for you though, right?" questioned Timmy.

Eddie pursed his lips in thought. "Maybe. I haven't decided yet."

"Well, just hit the extinguisher when it's ready," Timmy said. Eddie could see that he was hungry, but he was also considerate of Eddie's timing.

Eddie wrapped up the paperwork and headed to the kitchen. He set up the grill on the patio outside, and he even allowed some of the other men to join in the dinner preparations. Soon, there were great piles of beefsteak heaped on the table, and everyone dug in with great appreciation for Eddie's expertise in the kitchen. Steve called Eddie's attention as he took a big bite of mashed potatoes with garlic and said. "Yeah, you're right, man! I should've waited for the real stuff!"

While the rest of the crew was cleaning up the mess from dinner, Ed retired to the comfort of the Laz-y-Boy recliners in the day room. One of the benefits of being the cook was that Eddie never had to wash a single dish. He settled comfortably into the chair and left the remote on a rerun of a canceled sitcom.

After the clatter of the dishes in the kitchen had begun to diminish, another fireman, Rick Donaldson, dropped his two hundred and eighty-pound girth in the recliner to Eddie's left.

"Rickster, easy on the chairs, man, these things gotta last our whole careers."

Ed was making a reference to the fact that the fire department wasn't big on supplying the firefighters with luxuries beyond the basics in life. Most of the items purchased were acquired from the funds of the Salt Creek Fire Fighters' Association. Although this organization now had become just a social club, its roots lay deep in the history of the fire department. The association had once been the actual fire department when it was first established in 1932 as a private, volunteer organization. When the fire department became a free-standing, taxing, government agency, the firefighters at the time placed the leftover money in an account for current and future members of the fire department to use for various items and events. The money usually went to retirement funds, holiday parties, and simple items such as flashlights, dinnerware, sweatshirts, and pens. However, someone along the line had wisely decided to invest in a couple of Laz-y-Boy recliners, which then became the most envied seats in the fire department.

Rick was one of the department's rookie firefighters, and he constantly told stories about being a lean, mean, fighting machine for the Marines during the Gulf War, always concluding them by smacking his generous gut and claiming that he was in a lot better shape in his younger years.

Ed had spent some time in the military as well. After graduating from high school, he enlisted as a medic in the Navy Reserve. He had always liked the water: ocean, sea, lake, or whatever it was, as long as it was water. By the time Ed completed his basic and advanced training and was informed that he would be assigned to an infantry unit, he realized it was too late to change his decision. His recruiter forgot to explain that the Navy provided the medical personnel for all the marine infantry units. Eddie was surprised to discover that he was going to be assigned to a platoon of Marine infantry, but he didn't mind much; the military benefits funded his college tuition.

After Ed's military training he attended Elmhurst College where he learned the ins and outs of athletic training for various sports teams. Eddie had accepted a position with the University of Illinois in Champaign as a trainer in the athletic department when Salt Creek contacted him and offered him a position. Ed applied and tested with the fire department on a whim and graduated from his training as a firefighter alongside his partner, Hank. He figured the fire department could interrupt his work, but he never really expected to be called upon. However, when Ed received the call, he accepted. He packed up his

Island Bound

belongings and started foraging for a place to live within the town limits of Salt Creek.

The expense of living there forced him to find part time work in addition to his duties as a fireman. At first, Eddie had been happy with his career and living in Salt Creek, apart from the unpleasant winter conditions. Now, he had begun to feel too confined and settled. As he thought again of his upcoming vacation, he contentedly kicked back in the recliner and dozed off.

He was startled to consciousness when the alert tones informed the crew that they had another run.

"Salt Creek Fire, respond to the report of a burning car at 262 Pleasant Circle Road. Engine Company 234, you're due. Salt Creek dispatch is clear at 22:21 hours."

The sounds of a diesel engine invaded the atmosphere of the day room, followed shortly by the sound of the engine's siren and air horns as company 234 ventured out into the cold January evening.

Ed was just slipping under the covers as the alert tones erupted once again. Ed and Donny glanced at each other with confusion as the voice on the other side of the speakers announced that all Salt Creek units were required to respond to the structure fire at the same address.

The two men moved out on to the apparatus floor to ready themselves for the call. Before jumping into the ambulance, Ed and Donny dressed in their turnout gear, which consisted of several different pieces of flame and heat resistant items. Ed set his stocking feet into the bottom of the knee-high rubber boots and then pulled up his protective pants. Following the pants came the hood, jacket, and tool belt. The rest of the equipment would be applied when they arrived at the scene.

As the two pulled on to Pleasant Circle Road, Eddie noted a large plume of black smoke rising into the air. The other companies had arrived on the scene as well and began spilling from the vehicles to await instructions from the officer in charge. Ed noticed the first company had already stretched a hose across the home's lawn and into the garage. The fire was already spreading into other areas of the home.

Ed and Donny reported their arrival to the officer in charge and moved to the compartment in the back of the ambulance where their air packs and masks were stored.

"Ambulance ten, this is command. Pull a second line and enter through the front door. Another company is entering from the garage, so keep your eyes open." The officer communicated to the companies with a portable radio.

Donny looked at Eddie and said, "I think someone neglected to tell us that the car was located *inside* the garage." The burning car of the earlier call had ignited the roof of the garage, and from there it had spread throughout the whole house.

Ed grabbed the nozzle of the pre-connected hand line and pulled the hose from its bed. Then, he and Donny stretched the line to the front of the house. The family stood on the lawn, shivering in the cold air and watching the scene unfold with concern. Another officer was trying to move them to the warmth and safety of the ambulance.

Flames jumped from the roof of the porch while dark smoke exited the front door. To the right of their position, firefighters were scrambling up a ladder onto the home's roof, carrying with them an assortment of axes and power tools. They would employ these items to breech an opening in the roof that would ventilate the house, an important process in improving the environment inside for the firefighters.

Eddie secured his grip on the nozzle and stood firmly to control the line as the pressure increased. Donny signaled for the engineer to charge their hose line and settled in behind Eddie to help maneuver the line onto the porch and into the building. As the hose came to life, the two men approached the porch. Ed opened the nozzle and applied the stream to the roof, creating white steam and sizzling, popping sounds as the cool water clashed with the heat, smoke and fire.

Ed and Donny walked onto the porch and dropped to their knees in front of the door. Flames whipped from the picture window just left of their position. Ed pushed the door open and crawled into the home where heat and thick, stifling smoke enveloped the fire fighters. Through the plastic lens of his air mask, Ed could make out the form of a doorway with the bright flickering glow of his opponent, the fire, in the corner of the room. They moved deeper into the structure, and the heat increased with each movement forward.

Ed opened the nozzle one more time and directed the stream at the fire. The intense heat was replaced by a heavy mixture of steam and smoke. The two crawled deeper into the structure, only to bump heads with another company entering from the garage.

"Are you all clear?" another firefighter inquired with a muffled voice.

"All clear on our end." Ed displayed a thumb up.

"All right, command wants us to pull out and prepare for overhaul."

"What about the second floor?" Donny asked.

"The truckies got it."

Thumbs up. Ed and Donny retreated from the building.

Outside the building Eddie and Donny sat on the edge of the fire engine while another firefighter replaced their air tanks. With his mask off, Ed inhaled the scent of the house fire mixed with the crisp air of the winter night, surveying the events unfolding around him. Spectators stood just behind the police officers who were trying to keep the area safe and secure. The firefighters stood around in groups, smoking cigarettes and joking while they awaited specific orders for overhaul. Light smoke drifted through the maze of strobe lights the fire vehicles and equipment emitted with an eerie glow.

After the command for overhaul, the fun was over. Although the blaze had been extinguished, the firefighters needed to enter the home once more to search for smaller, hidden fires. This activity was accomplished by poking holes in walls, tearing at the ceiling, and finding hot spots. Afterwards, they would roll the hoses for cleaning and return the tools and equipment to their proper locations.

After cleaning and replacing the hoses, Ed glanced at his watch. They had been out of quarters for six hours now, and only four hours remained of his last shift before his vacation. When they got back to the station, Ed walked into the bunkroom and laid down, hoping to catch a few hours of shuteye.

As Ed was stretching himself out upon the bed, the tones rang for what Ed hoped would absolutely be the last call. Although exhaustion was setting in, Ed jumped out of bed, dressed, and met Donny at the ambulance. The address of the call was familiar.

"Donny, you know this place?"

"Sure," Donny said, "That's Bob Warner's house."

"Exactly," Eddie said with satisfaction, "this should be a quick one."

Bob Warner, an elderly, heavy man affected with Parkinson's disease, was what paramedics refer to as a regular customer. Typically the firefighters were called upon to help him to the bed or washroom when his daughter, who lived with him and took care of him, had a difficult time moving him from point A to point B. Tonight, however, Ed and Donny entered the house and found Bob stretched out on the floor of his bedroom with blood streaming down the side of his face.

Bob's daughter explained that he had been trying to get out of bed when he fell and bumped his head on the TV. Bob greeted the paramedics with a warm smile.

"I think I'm going to have to go to the hospital this time."

"Yeah, Bob, it sure does look that way," Eddie said as he and Donny cleaned his wound. Ed was relieved to see that his injury did not appear to be serious.

The paramedics placed Bob on the stretcher and wheeled him to the ambulance.

"Bob, just in case you don't remember, I'm Eddie. I'll be up to sit with you after I contact the hospital. If you need something, just holler."

Ed called the hospital to report the incident and let the staff know they were coming. Then, as promised, Eddie moved up next to Bob for some small talk because he liked to hear Bob's war stories. He had participated in several campaigns during the Big War and had even been a part of the D-day invasion. Bob's job had been to parachute behind the German defense lines, and, as Bob put it, make as much trouble for the enemy as possible. On previous occasions when Eddie had been summoned to help Bob, he had heard fascinating tales about his assignments in Africa and Italy as well.

"You ever heard of the 82nd Airborne Division?" Bob asked.

Ed nodded, and Bob let his bandaged head fall back on the pillow. His eyes took on that far away look that people get when they examine the past. Always good-humored, Bob humphed ironically and remarked, "You know, I spent two years fighting in that division, and I never received a scratch." He read the surprise on Eddie's face and added, "Now, my own television set has done me more harm than any Nazi with a machinegun."

The two of them laughed under the sound of the ambulance's siren. After a few moments, Bob commented, "I was a prisoner of war, though. In a German prison camp."

It was clear that Bob was an old hand at telling stories. He stopped as though it was all he had to say, waiting skillfully for Eddie to display his interest.

"You were a prisoner of war? What was it like?"

"Oh, the daily routine was that some officer would bark at us to wake up a few hours before dawn. It was cold there, and they herded us like cattle into railcars that didn't exactly have first-class accommodations, if you can imagine. Then, they would transport us to various undisclosed regions to repair damaged rail lines. It was hard work, and it seemed like I would never be warm again." Bob paused and turned his eyes to Eddie again, saying significantly, "There were others, of course, who had it much worse than I did."

After a few moments, Bob continued, "I wasn't there long, though - just four months."

Eddie asked, "Did the war end?"

"No." Bob smiled proudly.

"What happened, then?" Eddie really was curious about why Bob had only been there four months. He wondered if the Germans had worked out a prisoner exchange with the American forces, which would have meant that Bob was an important man during the war.

The old man declared, "The Germans couldn't put a leash my neck. I escaped twice, but the first time didn't work out too well. I didn't have much of a problem getting out of the camp, but when I got to the next town, somebody turned me in." He glanced at Eddie and asked, "Can you guess who it was?"

Eddie shrugged and took a wild guess. "Hitler?"

Bob's face broke into a wide grin, laughing so heartily that his belly shook. "Hitler? You think it was Hitler who caught me?" Bob lost control again.

"Who was it then?"

"It was the town mayor. But maybe I should change it to Hitler the next time I tell the story. That might be more interesting."

Eddie noticed that they were getting close to the hospital, and he didn't want to wait until the next time Bob called 911 to find out how he had escaped from the camp. He prompted, "So the time it worked, what happened? How did you do it?"

"Well, after the first escape attempt, I was afraid to use the same route I had used before because I knew the Germans had figured out how I did it. Every night for two weeks after they took me back to the camp, I scratched my chin and tried to plan another escape. I just couldn't stand to be cooped up behind barbed wire, especially when I knew that the Germans might decide to kill me at any minute. I just couldn't think of another way to get out of the camp. As luck would have it, though, I was blessed only one month later with an Allied bombing run. I took advantage of the confusion and found escape route number two. After my first escape, some of the other guys helped me out with some information about a nearby safe house that was inhabited by the French Underground, and I was able to make it there unseen. It was a close call, though, because the Germans sent the hounds after me when they noticed I was gone."

Eddie was annoyed that they were pulling into the emergency drive-up at the hospital, and he just had to hear the end of Bob's escape. As he unloaded the stretcher from the ambulance, he asked, "What happened then?"

Bob wanted to finish the story too, so he picked up his pace. "I found the safe house and the French personnel. They smuggled me through some dark tunnels camouflaged into the floor in the back of the house, then they put me in a van and dumped me beside the English Channel. They told me they had done all they could, but I was on my own from that point on."

"How did you make it across the Channel?"

"I ambushed a fishing boat, of course."

Eddie shook his head in amazement. "That's quite a tale Bob. I wish I could hear about how you got a hold of the boat, but looks like we're at the end of the line." Eddie watched the nurse wheel Bob down the hall. He was amazed that this frail old man who could hardly get to the bathroom by himself had once escaped from a German prisoner of war camp. Shaking his head, he returned to the ambulance.

"Donny, I'm gonna be a minute; I have to do some shopping."

"You mean *plundering*, don't you?" Donny called from the ambulance.

Paramedics weren't supposed to take hospital supplies for personal use; that would be stealing. However, Ed figured the hospital wouldn't miss the items he planned to borrow, and furthermore, he promised himself he would return anything he didn't use after his vacation. Taking with him the stretcher Bob had just vacated, Ed headed to the supply closet.

He wheeled the stretcher from the ambulance into the closet and closed the doors. After examining the contents of the shelves that held everything from bedpans to syringes, he began placing items on the stretcher. The stretcher was his cover - Ed didn't really want to advertise his thievery. He assembled the ingredients for a top-of-the-line first aid kit, including two one-liter bags of normal saline IV fluid, IV tubing, prep pads, needles, bandages, dressings, rubber tourniquets and a variety of medications, then he piled the blankets over his stash and headed back to the ambulance. He looked innocent as he pushed his shopping cart down the hall, except that the blankets were a little too lumpy.

Donny and Ed jumped back into the ambulance and reported to dispatch that they were back in service and returning to quarters. During the drive back Donny and Ed made small talk and stopped at a Starbucks for a couple of lattés.

Donny backed the ambulance into its appropriate parking space in the firehouse, and Ed walked towards the stairs leading to the battalion chief's office. He placed the run on his desk, glanced at the clock on the wall, and noticed the time was 7:28 am. He had only two minutes left before the official start of his vacation. Ed moseyed down to the bunkroom and put his sheets and blankets into his locker.

Eddie walked out onto the apparatus floor where several firefighters were smoking and telling jokes. Eddie bummed a cigarette off one of the guys and said, "I'll see you guys in six weeks."

Chapter Two

Light Keeper's Island sits just across the bay from Tampa. It takes its name from its history; at one time, a lighthouse stood in the center of the island, and the only people who lived there were the keeper and his family.

A two-lane suspension bridge connects the island to Tampa, and a boat ferries back and forth a few times daily. Except for private boat owners and exceptionally talented swimmers, the bridge and the boat represent the sole means of transport to and from the island.

Some of the South's richest families maintain residences on Light Keeper's Island. They enjoy its exclusive atmosphere as well as its pleasant location in the bay so close to downtown Tampa. In addition to these fine attributes, Light Keeper's Island features excellent security. The bridge and the boat arrive at the same part of the island, and before visitors, maintenance men, or any other people are permitted to set foot on the island's soil, they must present a pass from someone who owns property there.

One of the most luxurious condominiums on Light Keeper's Island stood near the center, and it was built like a fortress. Rising twenty stories into the sky, it formed a box around an atrium at its center. All the units in the building came with two balconies, one facing the outside while the other overlooked the atrium, which boasted an abundance of plant life, pathways, and even a small restaurant and bar for the privileged enjoyment of the building's residents. The inner balconies served a double purpose in that they also provided access to the building's bank of elevators. The two levels beneath the atrium housed the residents' automobiles. The building offered twenty-four hour valet service, and as soon as residents pulled into the underground garage, they relinquished their cars to the attendants who would then wash and vacuum the vehicle in order to prepare it for its next use. Twenty-two stories higher, on the top floor of the building, Bruce Klein owned a summer residence.

Bruce Klein stood out among the other residents as one of the most wealthy and prestigious. After the Vietnam War, he had joined up with his old friend, Harold Keith, and the two of them built an enterprise they called K&K Transportation. Their business flourished and provided the two men with extremely deep pockets. Within ten years, K&K enjoyed the distinction of being one of the largest shipping companies on the water. Besides owning half of a multi-million dollar corporation, Bruce Klein played an active role in Florida's political scene.

His daughter, Jennifer, rarely saw him because of all the time he spent in government and personal business. When she was five, her mother visited her gynecologist and learned that she exhibited all the signs of late-stage breast cancer. One year later, she was dead. When that happened, Bruce used his work to escape from his sorrow, and a parade of high-priced nannies, boarding schools, and psychotherapists stepped in to replace Jennifer's parents.

At the age of twenty-three, Jennifer faced the unsettling fact that she was due to be married in two week's time. She flew to Tampa and crossed the bridge to Light Keeper's Island, hoping to spend some time with her father. Bruce had promised her he would drop everything for two whole days so that they could spend time together before her wedding, but Jennifer was skeptical when he telephoned her three months in advance to arrange the meeting. She knew the winter months were always the busiest for him, and he hadn't always been the most reliable person in her life. In the end, she decided to take him up on his offer because it would be convenient to stay on Light Keeper's Island just before the wedding. She and her four closest friends in Tampa had been planning to take a trip together in celebration of her last two weeks as a single woman.

She wasn't surprised when she let herself into the condo and found an apologetic note in her father's scrawl on the table by the door.

"My Dear Little Girl," her father wrote, "You're going to kill me, but something happened in New York. I just couldn't get out of it. I'm so sorry, but I won't be able to make it home until Thursday. Can our plans wait until then? P.S. Have a good time without me the next couple of days. My secretary got you two tickets to the opera. Maybe you could go with Dex? They're in the mailbox. Love you, Sweetie. Dad."

Stapled to the note, Jennifer found five hundred dollars. "That's just like him," she thought to herself. She figured she wouldn't see him until her wedding day, if he even showed up for that, because Thursday was the same day she had planned to leave for her bachelorette trip.

She went to her bedroom and put a Harry Belafonte CD into the stereo. As his voice drifted out of the French doors and onto the verandah overlooking the bay, she put her suitcase on the bed and sat in front of her vanity mirror, searching her reflection. It was a trick one of her therapists had taught her to use when she felt confused by her own feelings. That had been thirteen years ago, but Jennifer still used it every time she felt upset.

She wasn't troubled about her father running off to New York and breaking his promise to her. She had long ago learned not to depend on him. She noticed the wind on the bay had messed her hair, so she took a brush out of the drawer of the vanity and began to straighten it. Her troubled thoughts began to organize themselves as she pondered the familiar strength of her mouth.

"O.K. Let's deal with each of these problems in order," she said, pretending that she was her old therapist and her reflection was herself. "What's the biggest thing on your mind?"

"I guess it's…" her reflection shook her head in slow motions to the right and left, puzzling over her problem. She scratched her chin distractedly. "It's because I'm getting married in two weeks, and I don't look or feel a bit like those

Island Bound

women in the bridal magazines at all. They all look so happy and excited and hopeful."

"You do realize, however," Jennifer pointed out to herself, "that those women are not really getting married in two weeks like you. They're professional models, and they're paid a lot of money to look happy because that sells wedding dresses, right?"

Jennifer's reflection nodded in agreement.

"But that doesn't make you feel any better, does it?" Jennifer continued.

"No, because something keeps telling me that it's all wrong to marry Dex. I have that exact thought every time I wake up in the morning. And when I think about it, I get a nervous, sick feeling in the bottom of my stomach," the reflection confided, wrinkling her forehead in sincerity.

"Are you afraid it's not going to be a successful marriage?"

"That's just it, though. It's doomed to be successful. We get along great, and we're very close friends. It's just that everybody expects it so much." The reflection ran her fingers through her hair and messed it up again, then continued, "I swear to God, I think if I don't marry Dex, the delicate fabric holding the world's universal principles together would just be torn into two big impossible pieces."

"Nonsense. You're exaggerating. Your family and friends want this wedding because they think *you* want it. You're not going to rip the universal fabric, believe me. The real issue here is whether or not you love Dex enough to spend your life with him," Jennifer told herself.

"Well, I wouldn't say that I don't care for him, but he's not exactly my Prince Charming, either. I don't get goose bumps when he says my name or anything."

Jennifer leaned back in her chair thoughtfully. Finally, after much thought, she looked herself sternly in the eyes and declared, "Jennifer, my professional opinion is that you are one seriously screwed-up girl, and the best thing you can do is run off to Italy and join a convent."

Jennifer couldn't stand to take herself too seriously for too long. She was able to hold herself back long enough to make her reflection protest, "But I'm not Catholic!" Then she collapsed on the surface of the vanity in laughter.

Dex, or Dexter, was of the family that lent the second "K" to K&K Shipping. Jennifer and Dexter were born two weeks apart and practically grew up as brother and sister, attending school together, taking joint family vacations together, and eating Christmas dinner at the same table. Dexter had asked Jennifer for her hand in marriage when the couple finished college in June. As soon as she accepted, Jennifer began to look for ways to get out of marrying him. The first option would be to skip town and stand Dex up at the alter. Among her friends and family, that decision would be about as popular as Chernobyl among environmentalists. Alternatively, she could be a good little girl and follow through on her promise. In the end, Jennifer decided to do nothing. If fate wanted her to marry Dex, marry him she would. On the other hand, if it wasn't meant to be, it wouldn't happen. There was no sense in worrying about it.

Jennifer slipped into a floral sundress that fell just above her knees. After applying lipstick, grabbing her purse, and slipping on a pair of leather sandals, she grabbed the phone and called the valet, asking the attendant to bring her car to the front entrance of the building. Jennifer and her maid-of-honor, Katie, were meeting for lunch to discuss the details of the bachelorette trip.

Jennifer twisted the knob on the front door, making sure the lock was set. Always a little careless, she had a bad habit of leaving the door unlocked. This time, she remembered and even made a point of checking it a second time, just to be certain. While walking to the elevator, Jennifer glanced down into the courtyard of the building.

*

In the lowest level of the parking garage that provided spaces for one of the high-rise office buildings located in Tampa's downtown business district, a tall, handsome, and well built individual sat behind the wheel of his recently acquired, luxurious 2001 model Lincoln LS. A black briefcase lay on the passenger's seat. The man took the briefcase onto his lap and popped the lock, then sifted through the case's contents. Inside were a laptop computer, cellular phone, a wallet, and various documents relating to the transfer of titles of high-priced Florida real estate. A leather cardholder contained business cards printed on Hammermill paper with "Law Office of Aurther E. Streder" placed attractively in the upper left-hand corner. A Tampa address was supplied as well with several contact numbers for the office, cell phone, and pager. After removing the documents from the brief case, he used the space to stow a small, air-powered dart gun, a syringe, two brown medicine vials, and several packages of individually wrapped sterile surgeon gloves in addition to the soiled ones he was now wearing. The man adjusted his Italian tie, slipped the keys into the ignition, and brought the vehicle to life. The smooth sound of Natalie Merchant filled the car's interior.

The vehicle's driver placed the cardholder in the breast pocket of his tan, linen Armani suit and took out a handsome sterling silver comb monogrammed with the letters L.A.C. He glanced at his reflection in the Lincoln's rear-view mirror, noting that his recent activities had not affected his dark, slicked-back hair. He put the comb back in his pocket. Then the man examined the wallet he had discovered in the briefcase. It contained several credit cards and other identifications for Aurther Streder, as well as seven hundred dollars in cash. The man removed the money and placed it in his pants pocket. "Nice little windfall," he mumbled to himself.

Island Bound

As the man cleared his throat and pulled out of the parking space, Aurther Streder, crumpled in the Lincoln's trunk, took his last breath.

The vehicle's V8 engine accelerated rapidly as the vehicle began its trip across the bridge leading to Light Keeper's Island.

The Lincoln's occupant reached inside his suit coat and the adjusted the holster containing a 9-mm Glock handgun. A Glock was his weapon of choice, and he took pride in his proficiency with it.

The man pulled into a parking spot that was reserved for visitors. A sign was posted in front of the guest parking spot that directed nonresidents to the security office to gain access to the condominium.

The man grabbed the briefcase and headed for the security office. He had been instructed not to cause a scene at that time, but he figured the issue wouldn't come up. He didn't expect to have any problems breaching the building's security.

Kendall Parks, a retired police officer from Boston with bushy white eyebrows and a shrewd mouth, had recently taken a job as a security officer on Light Keeper's Island. After leaving the force, he and his wife moved to Florida to escape the northern winter climate. He spent the first few years of retirement fishing, traveling, and doing whatever he wanted to do. One day, he looked at his life and realized how stagnant it had become. He needed to work, just to keep his mind occupied.

One winter while attending a Bucs verses the Bears football game, Kendall met another retired officer from Chicago. After the game the two retirees downed several beers together at a location close to the stadium. During the conversation, the other ex-police officer began to tell Kendall about the security forces on Light Keeper's Island.

"Oh, yeah, it's a real cush job," the man assured Kendall. "It's just perfect for guys like us. That island is real pretty. And you don't have to do any heavy stuff. The pay's real generous, too. Let me give you the name of the guy you should speak to." With some difficulty, Kendall's companion pulled a tattered notebook out of the back pocket of his trousers and a stubby pencil out of his breast pocket. He scratched something on the paper and handed it to Kendall.

Kendall eyed the paper. He saw the name and phone number of the man he should contact for the job, but his new friend had written something else at the bottom of the paper. Kendall asked his companion curiously, "What's this? Bertie's Chow House?"

"I just wrote that down for you in case you take the job over there. It's a really nice little place right on the bay, and what you should do, if you take the job over on the island, is stop at Bertie's before you get on the bridge. You can get yourself a nice lunch over there real cheap. I wouldn't buy food on the island, 'cause it's too expensive." The man smiled wisely at Kendall as if he'd just disclosed the ultimate trick to beating the whole system.

"Why, thank you. That's real considerate," Kendall smiled.

"Don't mention it. But if you go there, you ought to tell them Mac sent you, alright?" the man said.

The next day Kendall applied for a position and started working early the next week as a security officer in the parking garage of a ritzy high rise condominium. It felt good to be on the job again, and Kendall was anxious to impress his new employers. He took care over every detail and made sure nothing escaped his sharp old eyes.

One day, a guy pulled up in a brand new Lincoln. Kendall could tell just from the look of him that he was a jerk. He wore fancy clothes and acted like he was God's gift to parking garages.

"Good afternoon," the man said with a big, fake grin on his face. "I'm here to see Ms. Jennifer Klien."

"You got a pass?" Kendall asked suspiciously.

The man made a show of searching through his pockets and finally said, "You know, it's a funny thing. She gave me a pass just last week when we made the appointment to meet this evening. Now," he gave Kendall a perplexed smile, "I just can't seem to find it. It's strange, because I was just sure that I..."

Kendall wasn't going to take any crap. He'd heard it all before. "Look, Mister, I'm sorry, but I can't let you in unless you got a pass."

"Maybe this would work instead," the man suggested, handing Kendall a business card.

Kendall checked it over but shook his head, "Nope. Sorry. You gotta have a pass."

The man reached into his pocket again and pulled out a one-hundred dollar bill. "Perhaps this might persuade you to allow me to keep my appointment with Ms. Klein?"

Kendall shook his head again, "Nothin' doin,' buddy. I told ya before. No pass, no appointment. I don't want your money. The best I can do is call Ms. Klien and let her know she has a visitor."

The man got angry, shot a hateful glance at Kendall, and raised his voice to a level of tense frustration. "If that's the best you can do," he spat, "no thanks. I haven't got the time to fool around. I guess I'll just e-mail the documents she needs."

The man turned and headed back to his car. As an afterthought, he warned Kendall, "You can be sure that your manager will hear about how you interrupted an important appointment this evening between me and Ms. Klein."

Kendall shook his head in disgust as the Lincoln pulled out of the garage. "What a jerk," he said as he munched on some take-out from Bertie's.

After a few minutes, he saw Jennifer Klein herself hurrying to her car and wondered if he had been wrong to not let the guy see her.

He called after her, "Ms. Klien, don't drive off so quick. You just had a visitor."

Jennifer stopped and approached Kendall's guardroom.

"First of all, Kendall, just call me Jennifer," she told him. She hated for older people to call her Ms. Klein. "Don't be so formal. I had a visitor, you said?"

"Yep. He said his name was Aurther Streder, and he told me he was your attorney. He said he had an important meeting with you this evening." Kendall fished in his pocket to find the note. "Here's his card. I didn't let him in, 'cause he didn't have a pass."

"That's bizarre," Jennifer said, "I wasn't expecting anyone. Did you try to call me?"

"No, but I told him I would try. He just turned and walked away and said he would be in contact later."

"Well, it really doesn't matter. I've never heard of him. He probably has something to do with my father."

Jennifer said good-bye to Kendall and then positioned herself in the driver's seat of her 1999 Jeep Wrangler. The forecast called for rain later in the day, so Jennifer asked the valet to leave the top up. Jennifer slipped the lawyer's business card into her purse and made a mental note to mention it to her father the next time she spoke with him. By the time she turned off the bridge and onto the road leading to the center of the city, she had already left the incident in the back of her mind.

Jennifer found street parking close to the restaurant Katie had chosen. As Jennifer crossed the street, she glanced at her watch and noticed that she was running almost thirty minutes late. Katie would just chalk it up on her list of times that Jennifer had arrived late for appointments.

As Jennifer neared the entrance to the cafe, a handsome young man was exiting through the main door. There was a black BMW with the passenger door held open by the cafe's doorman. The man glanced in Jennifer's direction, and the two shared a brief moment of eye contact. Jennifer didn't recognize the man, but during their brief encounter, the man stopped for a moment as if he was going to speak to her. He hesitated a second, winked at her, then handed the attendant a twenty and sat down in the BMW's passenger seat. The attendant responded with an enthusiastic "Thank you, Sir!" and secured the vehicle's door. Jennifer noticed the vehicle's driver glance back in her direction and shake his head. The BMW waited a moment, then moved into the traffic of the Tampa roadway.

Jennifer didn't recognize either the man or the vehicle. The attendant opened the door to allow Jennifer entry to the cafe. The way the man had looked at her seemed odd to her, but having no reason to let it worry her, she soon forgot it altogether. The entire incident was left behind when a young blonde woman sitting at the bar attracted Jennifer's attention.

"Hey Katie, how long have you been waiting?" Jennifer asked anxiously, afraid that Katie would chastise her for being late.

Katie removed a Virginia Slims cigarette and a lighter from her purse. The metal in the lighter struck the flint, creating a flame. She inhaled the smoke from the nicotine stick and placed the pack of smokes and the lighter on the bar in front of her.

"I've been here for about five minutes. I knew that if I wanted to eat lunch at one, I should tell you to meet me at twelve-thirty."

As Jennifer sat down, the bartender approached the women, vigorously shaking a shiny, cylindrical container. The cafe specialized in four-ounce martinis mixed under the scrutiny of the cafe's guests. Jennifer could hear the ice and the liquid shifting about. The bartender stopped his motion in front of the two and reached down below the patrons' line of sight. In a flash, the bartender placed a tall, frosted cocktail glass on the bar, and a light green liquid escaped from the top of the shaker as the bar man tipped it skillfully. When the glass was full he dropped in two skewered cherries, allowing them to be submerged in the frothy liquid.

"Let me know when you're ready to order ladies," he told them.

Katie winked at the bartender and exhaled a cloud of smoke.

"We'll probably have a few drinks before ordering." Katie turned towards her closest friend. "I hope you don't mind, but I told him to just bring the drink over when you sat down."

Jennifer smiled at Katie with friendly reassurance and lifted the glass to her lips. The ice-encrusted edge of the cocktail glass stuck to Jennifer's lower lip momentarily, then was replaced by a comfortable, slippery sensation as the sweet liquid concoction entered her mouth.

"Mmmmm, that hits the spot." Jennifer sighed. "Thanks, Katie. Let's talk about this party."

"It's really going to be more of a bachelorette vacation," Katie corrected hesitantly, not wanting to give away the surprises she had planned for Jennifer. "What's Dexter got going on for his bachelor party?"

"I haven't the slightest idea. To be honest, I haven't talked to Dexter in about three days."

"Is there a little trouble in paradise?" Katie asked leadingly, always a gossip-hound.

Jennifer stared absently at her drink for a couple of moments. "Well, maybe. I'm just not sure. I know I'm looking forward to getting away for my bachelorette vacation, as you call it."

The seating area of the cafe began to fill with the afternoon's business crowd, and the lunch bartender told the girls the floor staff was short for the day and advised them they would receive better service at the bar. Katie remarked saltily to Jennifer that if they stayed at the bar, he would receive a better tip as well.

Katie proceeded to ignite another cigarette and ordered another round of drinks, even though Jennifer had just dented the first drink. Katie was the wild child among Jennifer's group of friends, which consisted of three other girls. She had other friends, of course, but these four girls had grown up together. Some may have attended different colleges or chosen different paths of life, but when the chips were down, they all ended up in the same place.

The sounds of the busy city and a warm, salty bay breeze drifted in from the cafe's balcony. The girls enjoyed the meal, each other's company, the booze, and the afternoon. Katie described the plan for the vacation between courses and the small talk which erupts whenever two long-time girlfriends unite. The afternoon ended with Katie slurring her words and collecting a phone number from the bartender.

"Two days till takeoff, right Katie?"

"Yep, Jen, that's about the size of it."

Jennifer returned home to complete her day. Her afternoon consisted of lying on the island's private beach where she enjoyed the buzz produced by the afternoon's cocktails. Her mind drifted as she settled into a comfortable nap.

Chapter Three

An icy, tall glass filled with sparkling Pellegrino, the juice of three lemons, and a tablespoon of sugar sat sweating atop a large, mahogany desk. The desk seemed out of place within the spacious interior of the office suite. The suite boasted fifteen-foot high arched ceilings painted in a dull light cream color. Between the archways, Casablanca ceiling fans stirred the soft Caribbean air creating a comfortable climate for the room's occupants. The floor's construction was of white oak, while the walls of the room consisted of paned windows and whitewashed ornamented columns to support them. A covered balcony stretched out behind the mahogany desk overlooking a manicured lawn covering at least six acres. In the distance the sea tumbled between large mountains and into a calm lagoon.

On top of the mountains Blackwell Crow was still able to make out the old British artillery compounds. During the British Empire's period of colonization, the sites were employed to protect the island and the lagoon specifically from sea invaders. Four large, dormant cannons still existed among the ruins of the guard towers, gates, and barracks. After discovering the site, Blackwell had spent much of his time exploring the ruins. It was this setting he had chosen as the spot for the new location of the Crow family business.

Crow Enterprises consisted of a variety of businesses and had been conceived originally during the 1700's by Stevenson Crow, one of Blackwell's great-grandfathers. The business, in less gentle terms, could also be called piracy.

Stevenson Crow was a Lieutenant with the British Navy assigned to a forty-gun frigate stationed in the Bahamas. Stevenson was the vessel's first officer, and as such, he carried the responsibility of command any time the ship's captain was absent. Stevenson had been a lieutenant for several years - in fact, several years too long. He was passed up for promotions due to political reasons.

One hot summer day the frigate entered into combat with a Spanish ship of war, and Stevenson's frigate was out-manned and out-gunned. During the course of the battle the ship's captain was mortally wounded after one of the Spanish ship's broadsides, and Stevenson took command of the ship. Under Stevenson's valiant command, the tide of battle turned. When the confusion of the fight faded, Stevenson was in possession of the Spanish warship and sixty-five prisoners, including the Spanish captain. After repairing the damage on both ships, Stevenson returned to the Bahamas with his prize and the report of his first action while in command. This time he was sure he would receive his promotion due to his valor in combat.

Stevenson never received his promotion. The next day his commander handed him orders to report for duty on the same ship, at the same rank under a new captain. The frustrated Crow gathered crewmen that would be loyal to him, stole the captured Spanish warship, and returned to sea. Stevenson spent the rest of his years as a scoundrel, pirating ships in the Caribbean. He was never caught. On the contrary, he found great success, and the business was handed down from generation to generation in the Crow family. Over the years the business slowly transformed into a legitimate enterprise.

In Blackwell's time, the company was worth millions. Its markets included plantations of tropical fruits, tourism, hospitality, pearl cultivation, and yacht brokering. However, under Blackwell's control, the family business returned to less desirable areas of trade.

Blackwell was standing in the doorway leading out to the covered verandah. He watched as a perfectly refurbished 1922 model Crisscraft docked in the lagoon below. A tall man in a light suit with slicked-back black hair was at the driver's seat. The Crisscraft was Blackwell's favorite. With the polished wood and brass and the low rumble of the inboard engine, anyone could see the boat was built with luxury as well as performance in mind. One of the dockhands secured the craft to the dock, and the dark-haired man disappeared on one of the garden paths.

Blackwell entered the private washroom just off the main room. He straightened his tie and combed his light brown, thinning hair. Blackwell's hairline began to recede about ten years ago when he was forty-five, and he thought it gave him a distinguished air. Blackwell's days in the gym and on the water provided a well-built, healthy frame, although he was rather short. His height always motivated him to work hard in every aspect of his life so that no one could reproach him for it.

Blackwell moved to the desk and refreshed himself with a long drink from the Pellegrino, then sat at the desk, waiting. After about ten minutes, Lester Crow stepped into the room. Lester was Blackwell's adopted son as well as his muscle man. Blackwell raised Lester from infancy, providing him with an aristocratic education. Teachings included traditional course work at the best private schools supplemented with instruction from ex-Special Forces members picked from the world's best militaries. All that was accompanied by daily physical conditioning and martial arts training.

"Were you successful, my son?"

"I made visual contact but did not apprehend the subject. The opportunity for physical contact never presented itself. Your instructions included not causing a scene," Lester replied.

Blackwell tapped his fingertips thoughtfully on his desk and agreed, "Yes, I did include that with my instructions. The girl will be falling into our hands soon enough. Then we'll see what Bruce Klien has to say."

"She will be in the Caribbean next week," Lester said, taking a hand-rolled Cuban from the humidor on his father's desk. After clipping the end Lester placed the Cuban between his lips and ignited the tip. He collapsed into a chair facing Blackwell and mentioned meditatively, "Father, maybe we should let her enjoy her wedding, then pick her up."

"We will take her whenever the opportunity arises," Blackwell replied firmly.

Taking a few puffs, Lester addressed his father once again, meeting his stern glance with assurance.

"What are your instructions now?"

"Assemble your team and travel to Antigua. A vessel named the El Presidente will arrive there in two days. From Antigua the vessel will travel to Saint Thomas. I want that vessel."

"Do you have the required information?" Lester asked.

Blackwell handed his son a manila envelope secured at the top with a small brass clip engraved with the monogram C.E. The envelope contained vital information concerning his next mission. Lester opened it and removed the information. The intelligence report included statistics regarding the El Presidente, specifying the current amount of crew, passengers, and weaponry onboard.

The El Presidente was a 1925 motor yacht. Most of the ships constructed in that period had wooden frames, and as Lester examined the photographs, he noted the beautiful lines of the vessel. Lester knew he would need to take care in acquiring the boat in order to keep damage to a minimum. She carried a crew of five with eight passengers currently residing onboard. The crew consisted of three ex-Naval officers and two Merchant Marine service employees. Lester paid closer attention to the ex-military men than the Merchant Marines. The El Presdente's Captain had once been a lieutenant in the United States Navy on a guided missile cruiser. The first officer's background was in the Canadian Coast Guard as a mechanic for naval vessel power plants. The last military person was the ship's chef who had spent time in the United States Marines as a cook. Lester folded the edge on the sheet pertaining to the Marine. Although he was only a cook, a Marine is still a Marine. The remaining two crew members spent time on pleasure ships as deck hands for other companies.

Lester studied the ship's course. He needed to pick the best sight for the attack. Lester decided he would engage two speedboats and eight men for the job. The El Presidente would travel past the small island nation of Saint Kitts where two of his mercenaries would acquire one of the boats used by the Saint Kitts shore police and then make contact with the rest of the party. At that point the major task would be initiated. Lester activated the paging system his hired hands used for upcoming job alerts. The mercenaries always responded promptly to calls; after all, the men had become millionaires themselves while working for Lester Crow. Three of Lester's employees arrived within the hour. Lester distributed to each man a copy of the materials that were held in the manila envelope. He instructed two of the men to leave immediately, then briefed the others concerning the time and the meeting place that would be used prior to the job.

The two men entered a room attached to Blackwell's office, which they referred to as the War Room. Blackwell's men usually went there to discuss all the past, present and future jobs worked by the crew. The War Room contained enough weapons and military equipment to start and win World War III. Although the men carried personal side arms, a job required more firepower. The two selected a collage of weapons consisting of a Tommy gun and a Remington automatic twelve-gage police-model riot gun. The Remington was a devastating weapon. Unlike most shotguns, this weapon held twelve rounds that could be depleted as fast as the gunman could pull the trigger. Also selected to finish the collage was a forty-millimeter grenade launcher accompanied by ten teargas grenades, two high explosive rounds and three scatter shells. The scatter shells projected buckshot similar to a shotgun. Finally the men included a high-powered Winchester bolt-action sniper rifle as well as several hand-thrown smoke grenades.

The two left the War Room and stocked the gunboat, a Boston Whaler. The Whaler was outfitted with a more powerful engine for speed and a 7.62-mm M-60 machine-mounted upfront. In the pilothouse a scanner informed the driver of any Coast Guard or police activity. When the two were settled, the pilot fired up the engine, and they ventured out of the lagoon and onto the open sea. The men set out to complete their assignment just as the rest of the crew arrived for the briefing. After the briefing Lester and the others prepared for their end of the job.

The mercenaries located their prey docked on a small island controlled by the Saint Kitts government. Through a pair of binoculars, the mercenaries noted that the patrol craft was deserted. The mercenary in charge of the operation instructed his subordinate to go seize the dormant patrol boat. The man donned SCUBA gear and plopped into the warm Caribbean water.

Halfway to the target the pilot's voice transmitted from the microphone in the mercenary's ear.

"The crew just returned to the patrol boat. Go to plan B." The pilot instructed. There were three men to contend with.

The diver altered his course in order to emerge at a small sand beach about sixty yards from the patrol boat. The mercenary checked his weapons and started through the jungle's foliage towards the patrol boat.

"I'll take the first one out with the rifle; after you hear the shot, you take the other two," a voice cracked in his ear.

The mercenary placed his Thompson in his left hand, removing the pin from one of the smoke grenades and keeping the activation lever secure in the palm of his hand. He waited for the Winchester' report. Moments later the crack of the sniper echoed throughout the bay and the jungle and one of the patrol boat's personnel fell on the deck of the vessel. The officer was dead a split second after the 30-caliber projectile pierced his skull. The mercenary in the jungle lobbed the smoke grenade into the front of the patrol boat near the mounted machinegun.

The smoke screened the area of the boat significantly, reducing visibility for the remaining crew. The crew's reactions were more efficient than the mercenaries had expected. Surrounded by thick gray smoke, one crewmember manned the machinegun, and the weapon spit its devastating rounds in the direction of the mercenaries' vessel. Luckily for the pilot aboard, the rounds missed their target, slicing the air just to the left of the craft. The crew then received gunfire from the jungle they just exited.

While the man in the jungle boarded the patrol boat, he depressed the trigger of the Thompson. Twenty 45-caliber shells peppered the officer as he attempted to use the pilothouse's radio to request help. The message was never transmitted. The Thompson's rounds pierced the man's skin from the top of his back down to the lowest part of his spine, and the officer fell to the deck.

After weighting and dumping the bodies, the mercenary took control of the patrol boat and brought the engine to life. The men opened the throttle all the way and shot back to the safety of the Crow lagoon.

Both boats sat idling in the lagoon. Several yards ahead of the boats stood a large boathouse with a door that rose to display a large opening. The man onboard the patrol boat entered first. Inside, a waterway led deep into the base of the mountain to a large docking. Blackwell Crow's most recently acquired vessels rocked gently next to the wooden pier where busy workers operating heavy machinery changed the appearance of the captured ships.

The two prepared for the next task. They clothed themselves in the uniforms the diver had taken from the bodies of the Saint Kitts Shore agents and informed Lester Crow of their success in capturing the shore patrol boat. Then they boarded the new Saint Kitts boat and set out to complete the rest of the mission. Prior to leaving the subterranean dock, a third solder joined the crew. In his arms he cradled a semi-automatic, 40-mm grenade launcher. This weapon discharged six deadly shells as fast as the trigger could be manipulated. The launcher currently housed teargas and smoke grenades, and the shells were situated so that they would deploy intermittently. A 9-mm sub-machinegun hung at the man's side by a nylon strap secured to his shoulder.

The patrol boat navigated the waterway to the open sea between the mountains surrounding the Crow lagoon. The pilot of the boat opened the throttle and guided the boat away from the calm waters of the lagoon to the ocean's white-capped waves. Twenty minutes later, the men arrived at the prearranged rendez-vous. A cigar boat sat patiently idling, and standing in the craft were Lester and the remaining two mercenaries.

Chapter Four

Eddie stepped out of the elevator and slipped his key into the lock in his door. When he entered his dark condo, a red flashing light on his phone greeted him, informing him that he had new messages. He pressed a button on the phone, and a pleasant female voice said, "Mr. Gilbert, this is Meredith from National Car Rental. I've got good news and some not-so-good news concerning the Mitsubishi Spyder you rented for next week. The good news is that I'm looking at it right now. The not-so-good news is that due to last night's eight inches of snow, the car will not be delivered until tomorrow."

"That's not a big deal; I'm not leaving until tomorrow anyway," Eddie thought to himself.

Meredith continued, "...and our company, unfortunately, does not have a branch anywhere in the Florida Keys. You'll have to drop the car off in Miami. Give me a call at 630-555-8362 some time today to make arrangements. Thanks, have a great day. Once again, my name is Meredith."

Eddie wondered what happened to the other guy he was dealing with. He figured they utilized the best sounding women in the office to tend to the company's shortcomings. With that information in mind, Eddie jumped onto the Internet to investigate options for traveling from Miami to Key West.

Eddie was never much of an Internet junkie. His opinion regarding computers was that they should be used as tools, not as forms of entertainment. As a matter of fact, Eddie had only recently broken down and gotten an email account for himself. He still preferred old-fashioned contraptions and institutions such as the telephone and the postal service for communication.

After about ten minutes online, Eddie narrowed his options down to two: a boat or a plane. The boating company described itself as "a navel bus company," provided reasonable prices, and scheduled daily service to all areas throughout the Florida Keys. However, when Eddie saw the advertisement for the airline that featured a photograph of an open-air biplane carrying a handsome, rugged passenger against vivid blue skies high above the ocean, he made his decision after about two seconds of consideration. Eddie jotted down the toll free telephone number for The Keys' Gate Aviation Service where Captain Marvin Frank was listed as the proprietor. Eddie shut down the computer, picked up his cordless, and dialed the required digits. Twelve rings later, somebody finally picked up the phone.

A man with a Jamaican accent answered.

"This is de Aviation Service, how can I be helpin' ya today?"

Momentarily taken aback by the accent, Eddie responded, "I have a package that needs to be transported from Miami to Key West. The package will contain ten pounds of marijuana."

"Sorry Mon, I only transport eleven pounds or more. Now, what can I really be doin' ya for, mon?"

Eddie laughed and asked the man if he was Mr. Frank.

"You can be sure I am, mon, but I usually go by Capitaan Frank."

Eddie explained his situation to the captain.

Captain Frank told Eddie about what services were available, offering him his choice of aircraft: either a good, old-fashioned, open-cockpit biplane, or a more contemporary four-seated Cessna. He picked the biplane, of course, then informed Captain Frank of the preferred travel date and booked the flight. Captain Frank related the required information to Eddie and ended the conversation suggesting that Eddie should employ UPS for the ten pounds of dope. Eddie deactivated the cordless and walked over to the sliding doors leading to the condo's balcony.

Eddie looked out the glass doors of his balcony that separated him from the hostile winter conditions outside. In the distance loomed the Chicago skyline, and just before him on his balcony, summertime items waited for their next tour of duty under a white, fluffy blanket of snow. The black top of a Smoky Joe, two tiki torches, and four lawn chairs stood defiantly to remind people of the pleasures associated with other seasons. Eddie figured his day would include a trip to the fitness center, a quick round of his place with a broom and a bottle of cleaning solution, packing, and more tying up of assorted loose ends before his long vacation.

After Eddie returned home from the fitness center, he turned on the TV for background noise. The screen displayed Thomas Magnum cruising on a Hawaiian roadway in Robin Master's Ferrari. Then, Eddie found his cordless phone under a pile of newspapers and called Meredith at National Car Rental. She told him the car would be delivered the next day at nine in the morning and relayed the information concerning National's branch in Miami. Eddie asked about a ride to Marvin's aviation company, and Meredith agreed to arrange for transportation to the airstrip free of charge. That was the least the company could do, considering the inconvenience their customer suffered due to the change in plans.

With the cordless deactivated, Eddie threw his laundry into the washer and started sweeping and mopping the condo's hardwood and ceramic floors. Then he sparked up the fireplace and pulled his luggage bags out of storage. Eddie used the larger bag for clothing and shoes; the smaller he filled with toiletries, books, compact disks, and financial materials. He thought about the gun issue, and in the end, he added the weapons to the inventory. A stainless steel Smith and Wesson .357 revolver and a 30/30 Winchester with lever action, just like a cowboys used, ended up in a lockable gun case. Deep within the large bag he buried a one hundred-round box of rifle ammunition and sixty rounds for the pistol.

Island Bound

Eddie sat down on the couch and worked the remote like only a man can, drifting off to sleep while the voices on the television chattered incomprehensibly. Within minutes, he entered the world of dreams, knowing he would be in Memphis in less than twenty-four hours.

Chapter Five

The Antiguan harbor stirred with life as tourists from the cruise boats lined the streets. The crew of the El Presidente prepared to receive passengers, and the captain paused from his duties in the pilothouse momentarily to scan the horizon. Clear skies and a pleasant seventy degrees would provide the crew and passengers an enjoyable cruise.

"I think we're just about ready, Cap," one of the boat hands shouted.

"Great. Mr. Dirk and his family should be onboard soon."

The captain was a veteran of the United States Navy. After ROTC and college, he acted the next four years of his life as an officer on a guided missile cruiser. Over the past year, he spent his time working on the El Presidente for Darrell Dirk.

The two boat hands cast aside the tie lines, and the boat began its journey towards the Bahamas. Darrell Dirk and his family sat on the deck enjoying the sea breeze. As the boat glided into the open sea, he and his wife, Jessica, sipped daiquiris while their children, Molly and Rosalyn, leaned over the sides of the boat, scouting for dolphins playing beneath the waves of the Caribbean. Cal Bernhardt, ex-Marine turned chef, provided the family with refreshments throughout the day.

*

"That's it. That's the one." Lester instructed his group to ready for the action.

"Everyone is in position, Lester."

He lowered a set of binoculars. "I want the patrol boat to contact the El Presidente in five minutes; we'll be in position by then."

Lester's mercenary radioed the crew of the stolen patrol boat to initiate contact. He had already given the men their instructions. Lester fired up the speedboat's engine and approached the pleasure craft. In the distance he could see the patrol boat speeding towards the El Presidente.

*

"What's going on here, Captain?" Darrell Dirk inquired of his top officer.

The captain squinted into the sun.

"Looks like the Saint Kitts shore patrol wants to pay us a visit," he responded.

The captain instructed his crew to prepare for an inspection, then explained to Mr. Dirk, "Don't worry, boss. This isn't anything out of the ordinary."

Island Bound

The captain had experienced this situation before. Saint Kitts shore patrol often inspected luxury ships traveling through the country's waters. The economy in Saint Kitts was rather depressed, and safety inspections added money to the country's coffers. The shore patrol boarded ships and noted various safety violations. Saint Kitts charged fines for the violations, and the shore patrol collected them on the spot.

The dark blue patrol ship glided within twenty feet of the El Presidente, and the voice of a man speaking Spanish boomed from a bullhorn. The captain translated for Mr. Dirk. The man instructed the party aboard the vessel to prepare to be boarded for a safety inspection. The Dirk family continued to enjoy their meal while the ship's crew prepared to meet the shore patrol officers.

Two tan-clad men climbed up the short ladder suspended from the side of the yacht brandishing sub-machineguns and side arms. The captain became concerned. Safety checks may have been routine, but he had never seen the patrolmen so heavily armed. The men instructed the captain to herd his crew and passengers to the front of the vessel. The captain complied and moved to the rear of the boat, shooting a concerned glance at Cal as he passed the galley.

Cal retreated deeper into the galley and took a position behind the cabinets. The captain asked the Dirks to go to the front of the boat. Although the captain was hiding it well, Mr. Dirk noticed the concern on the captain's face. Several minutes later, four crewmen, the owner, his wife, and two children were standing in the fading sunlight on the front deck.

"Is this everyone?" The shore patrolman asked in English.

"Yes sir, it is," the captain replied.

The captain hoped his feeling of concern was just a suspicious overreaction, but he grew more nervous when the soldiers lowered their firearms in the direction of the family and crew.

"I'm sorry to say that this is not going to be your best day," the soldier stated with a wicked grin. "I'll need the women and the children to board the powerboat that will be pulling up soon."

The soldier then instructed his subordinate to handcuff the crew and Mr. Dirk. From the doorway leading to the bowels of the ship, Cal emerged. He leveled a shotgun in the direction of the soldier barking out the orders.

"I don't think that's going to work out, comrade," Cal shouted from the shadows of the ship's passageway.

Several loud pops reported from the side of the ship. Gunfire erupted as the ship's deck filled with thick gray smoke. Cal pulled the trigger of the shotgun one time before falling to the deck. 9-mm rounds entered his abdomen and chest, freeing his spirit from his body. Cal's shotgun blast sent the intruder over the side of ship, creating a splash as the man sank deep into the Caribbean. The first officer of the yacht jumped over the side, hoping to escape the same destiny as Cal. As the first officer's head emerged from the saltwater, he felt the impact of the speedboat knocking into his skull. The first officer joined the intruder floating beneath the yacht.

The confusion cleared the deck. In the silence, Mrs. Dirk huddled with her remaining daughter. The two were crying and choking from the effects of the tear gas and the horror unfolding before them. The rest of the crew, Darrell Dirk his oldest daughter, Rosalyn, were lying lifeless as blood seeped from their bullet wounds. The remaining mercenary on deck crouched as he applied a gas mask to his face, and another masked intruder came on deck.

"Secure those two below deck. Where is Carl?"

"He took a shot gun shell in the chest, Boss. He fell overboard. He's shark bait."

Lester ordered his remaining mercenary to sink the patrol boat and join him in the pilothouse. The driver of the speedboat was on his way back to the lagoon before the Saint Kitts patrol boat started to take on water.

The henchman grabbed the mother and daughter and forced the two below decks. Jessica was attempting to comfort her young daughter, whose cries had now become hysterical. The man led them to one of the staterooms.

"Stay in here and keep your mouths shut. You may live through this yet," he instructed.

At four years of age, Molly's mind was filled with confusion and fear. The stateroom that had once served as a bedroom for the two Dirk daughters now became a prison. The room was filled with the girls' belongings, and a brown Vermont teddy bear sat placidly on one of the bunks. Molly reached out for this comforting item, which she had received a few weeks earlier from Santa Claus.

The evil intruder wrenched the teddy out of Molly's grasp.

"What the hell is this? A teddy for the little brat?"

"Please," Jessica Dirk whimpered. "give it back to her." The man had told them to keep their mouths shut, and she feared that if the man took the bear away from Molly, she would begin to scream.

The man threw it back at Molly and stormed out of the room. Jessica cradled her daughter on her lap, hoping that she didn't comprehend what had taken place. They could hear a chair being forced against the door outside.

"Put on some warmer clothes," Jessica told Molly as she attempted to open the stateroom door. It wouldn't budge. She scanned the small room and her attention fell on a window facing the sea. Opening it, she helped Molly to stick her head and shoulders out of the window. However, when she saw that her four-year-old daughter could just barely squeeze through the opening, she realized escape was impossible. She could never get through the window herself, and if she sent Molly out into the vast, surrounding ocean alone, she would surely drown. Sinking onto one of the beds, Jessica trembled as she wondered what the evil men had in store for her and her daughter.

Island Bound

The henchman returned to the pilothouse as Lester had instructed. Lester was now outfitted in white pants, deck shoes, and a blue and green golf shirt. Sunglasses and a baseball cap completed his costume.

"Are they secure below?"

"Yes sir, I have the door forced shut from the outside. The window is too small for them to escape."

"Excellent, I like the looks of the mother. We'll deal with them when we return."

Lester ordered the man to don his civilian disguise while the yacht slowly changed directions and headed out to the open sea. The rest of the job went off without a hitch. Two hours later El Presidente and her new crew docked snugly in the hidden Crow shipyard.

"Nice job, guys. Dad's gonna be happy," Lester praised his men as he sparked up a Cuban.

Chapter Six

As soon as the rental car arrived, Eddie threw his belongings in the trunk and took off for Memphis. He stopped half an hour later to pick up a road atlas, buy a cup of coffee, and use the restroom, and then he settled in for a long drive. He turned on the Mitsubishi's radio and tried not to let himself get irritated by the Chicago traffic.

After about three hours on the road, Eddie was closing in on a familiar town, Champaign, Illinois. The town was home to the Illinois Fire Service Institute, one of the many training grounds in the state for firefighters. What seemed like a million years ago, Eddie had attended the fire academy at the institute. As Eddie neared the institute, he saw the familiar plume of light smoke in the distance and glanced at the training field to see a line of recruits standing out in the cold in front of a small, single story brick building. Light smoke was puffing from the metal plate covers on the building's windows, reminding Eddie of the time he was faced with the very same challenge.

*

It was a crisp and cool October day, typical for the fall season in the Midwest. A group of students sat in the small classroom. They were mostly young males, but sometimes, older men and women of all ages took part in the program as well. The room was filled with various types of training aides used for the development of new firefighters. The instructor standing at the head of the class was explaining the day's training activity. He was a retired Chicago firefighter, an officer actually, who retired at age fifty and accepted a teaching position with the institute to occupy his time. His task was to insure that by the end of the six-week program, the recruits would understand all the basics of firefighting. At that time, Eddie was halfway through his training.

"Today is smoke appreciation day," the instructor began. "The purpose of this drill is to prepare firefighters for the possibility of being in a fire without the benefit of an air mask."

"I thought it was against the rules to enter without protection," someone protested.

"Of course it is, but you never know if your equipment is going to fail."

Eddie stared out the window as the instructor explained the training. Orange and red leaves tumbled across the training grounds scattered about by the October winds, and thick, fluffy white clouds filled the blue Midwestern skies. Gray smoke drifted into the air and across the expressway. Several of the instructor's aides were carrying hay and pallets into the small brick building that was producing the smoke. An old red fire engine idled near the building, and a hose line rigid with water pressure stretched from the side of the apparatus. Two men in full gear with air masks dangling from their necks stood one behind the other, holding a nozzle attached to the end of the hose. These men made up the ever-present safety crew. The hose line would be employed to suppress the training fire if any sparks went astray.

Although Eddie had been dreaming up ideas for his Halloween costume when the instructor ordered the students to gear up and head out to the training field, he was still aware of the requirements for the drill; he had been forewarned by his comrades back home.

The trainees lined up in a single file line, and Eddie listened to the chatter of the people around while he awaited his turn. The drill called for the fledgling firefighters to crawl on the ground while grasping a hose line that stretched from one end of the structure to the other. The hose twisted and turned around various obstacles. During the drill, the trainees would not wear their usual air masks, but inside the building, instructors wearing full protective gear waited at intervals to prevent any injuries or complications.

The firefighter in front of Eddie dropped to his hands and knees and crawled into the building. Eddie could hear the trainees coughing and choking and the instructors shouting words of encouragement and guidance.

The trainer at the door motioned for Eddie to get moving. He dropped to his hands and knees and winced; they were tender after three weeks of physical training. Eddie crawled forward into the building with the hose firmly in his grip, clasping it between his legs. The heavy smoke hit him in the face and forced him to squeeze his chin against his chest. He let go of the hose with his right hand in order to pull his flame retardant hood over his mouth and nose as tears spilled from his eyes, clouding his vision. Although his mouth and nose were now covered, breathing was still difficult. Ducking his head and closing his eyes, Eddie propelled himself along the path as quickly as his strained arms and legs could carry him. He figured he was halfway through the building when he ran into a heavy object.

"Keep moving, kid. Knock it out of the way," a muffled voice ordered.

The hose running under the obstacle provided a space between the floor and its lower edge, so Eddie wedged his gloved fingers into the crack and tipped the item out of his way. Later, Eddie would learn that the item was a simply a large wooden box placed in his path for added confusion. Eddie scurried a few more feet when the hose ascended over a ledge. He crawled over what seemed to be some sort of a barrel, taking a moment to feel the floor on the other side of the barrier for stability.

"Nice job kid, you're almost to the end," the same muffled voice spoke up.

Ten feet later the hose and the firefighter exited the building where the crisp and clean air rewarded him. Eddie stood and coughed.

"Are you all right?" an instructor inquired. "Take a load off and grab a Gatorade." Then the instructor entered the building to guide another of Eddie's peers through.

Eddie took a seat by the rest of the trainees that had already completed the drill. Although most of the students were in relatively good shape, even a short revolution left an individual feeling drained.

*

Eddie smiled at the recollection. Training for firefighting could at times be taxing, but he had collected many fond memories at the institute. One of the things Eddie liked best about the fire department was the way it tended to extend the men's immediate families. Firefighters have their traditional families: mothers, brothers, wives, sisters, and so on. In addition, the relationship that developed among the workers in a fire department bore the same closeness of a nuclear family. Whether or not the men liked each other as individuals, they had to learn to live and work together smoothly. After all, an average firefighter spends one third of his life alongside his co-workers, eating meals with them and sleeping in the same quarters.

Four hours later Eddie found himself just outside Memphis. On the horizon a steel-framed expansion bridge rose from the flat farmland and forests, and soon the peak of a bright triangular object could be distinguished. Eddie recognized the shape, knowing that it was a concert hall constructed to resemble a pyramid. The bridge allowed motorists to cross the Mississippi river, and just below and to the right of it Eddie saw a place known as Mud Island, a tribute to the Mississippi river and its history.

With Memphis rising before him, Eddie turned the radio up full blast and added a little pressure to the gas pedal. The vacation had officially begun. Eddie would be staying at the Peabody Hotel. Even though he took the trip to Memphis to indulge his nostalgic sentiments for the city, he felt no desire to reminisce in one of the seedy hotels he used to stay in with his buddies. A sign on the highway indicated that the exit for Beale Street lay only ten miles ahead. "Ah, Beale Street," he thought to himself fondly. "New Orleans has Bourbon Street, Key West has Duval Street, and Memphis has Beale Street."

Eddie noticed red and blue lights flashing behind him in the rearview mirror and checked his speedometer. It registered ninety-four miles an hour. He cursed himself for being so complacent as he steered the Mitsubishi to the right side of the road. In the driver-side mirror he caught the reflection of an officer in blue and gold. Eddie rolled the vehicle's window down.

"Driver's license and proof of insurance, please," the officer croaked. His voice displayed a southern twang.

"I wasn't speeding, was I?" Eddie asked with surprise in his voice.

"Yes sir, I've got you going ninety-six in a sixty-five zone. What would you like to post as bond?" The officer took Eddie's license and registration.

"I don't suppose you guys give breaks to firefighters down here?" Eddie asked as innocently as he could.

The officer stood silently for a moment. A small grin emerged from the side of his mouth.

"You got any proof of your position?"

Eddie allowed the officer to examine his badge and identification.

"You on vacation?" The officer turned his head and spat a load of brown tobacco juice on the ground.

Eddie briefly described his plans to the officer. In the end, the officer asked Eddie to slow it down a little and enjoy his vacation. Eddie thanked the officer for the professional courtesy and continued on his way. The Mitsubishi traveled over the extension bridge and into the city limits of Memphis, and after a short drive inside the downtown, Eddie pulled into the driveway of the Peabody Hotel where a valet attendant approached the car.

Memphis was still too far north for the weather to be warm, and Eddie discovered he would need to travel deeper into the South to truly escape winter. Retrieving two bags form the back of the car, he signed the valet slip and handed the attendant a five-dollar bill.

The lobby of the Peabody was impressive. A comfortable but classy feeling enveloped Eddie as he strolled through the gracious doors.

"How may I help you sir?" a young woman working the front desk inquired. Eddie liked the smooth tone of the girl's voice. He noticed her dark brown, gently curling hair and her emerald eyes and wondered if he might bump into her again after her shift ended.

"I have a room reserved - my name is Eddie Gilbert."

The girl located the room and motioned for a bellboy, explaining that he would lead him to his room. Eddie wanted to ask the girl out for the night, of course, but he was too shy for such upfront tactics. He concluded she was too young anyway. The bellhop led Eddie to his room and received a decent tip for carrying the bags.

Eddie settled into the room and decided it was just about time to grab a meal. Since he was going to be going solo, he figured he would head out, have a good meal and a couple of cocktails, then return to the room for a good night's sleep. He was still tired from his last shift at the fire department, and he wanted to get an early start the next day.

Eddie quickly showered and changed into a fresh set of duds. Before leaving the room he called the front desk to arrange for a cab. The walk to his intended target of Beale Street was not long, but considering the temperature Eddie preferred to ride in a heated taxi.

A yellow cab was waiting at the hotel's front door, and after inquiring with the valet to make sure it was his, Eddie settled into the backseat. Attempting to make conversation with the cabbie, he asked what the action on Beale Street would be like that evening.

"Beale Street!" the driver grunted, an obvious chain-smoker. "Not too much tonight. It's gettin' late and it's a weeknight."

Eddie asked the driver to drop him off at the closest point of the strip, and the two men shared small talk while the cab traversed the city streets. The cab driver told Eddie that he had been born and raised in Memphis, and in fact had never really been out of the city.

Eddie exited the cab and ventured out into the cool evening. The cabby was right, there was absolutely no action. After stepping into a couple establishments for cocktails, Eddie settled into a place bearing the name "Big Harry's" because it was comfortable, but more importantly, boasted a wide array of recipes on the menu. Meals in Memphis had always been difficult for Eddie because the mainstay of the residents was Bar-B-Q. Eddie shied away from meat, and accommodating menus were tough to come by.

As Eddie waited for the waitress to take his order, he chuckled at the memory of his experience in another restaurant on Beale Street. He and his friends went to get some chow after a long day at the Beale Street festival. They were hungry and ready to have a good dinner.

"O.K., guys, let me tell you what you *can't* order tonight," a friendly, young waitress began. "We don't have salads, burgers, the little pizzas, or french fries."

"How about the chili?" one of the friends asked.

"We don't have that either."

"So basically what you're tellin' us is that our dinner choices are," he consulted the menu to see what was left, "the 'Hungry Steer Beef Fest' and the 'Pulled Porkwiches'?" Eddie, in disbelief, attempted to determine if there were any vegetarian options.

"Yup. That's about it. You could also get the corndog appetizer or a side of fresh pork rinds." She then asked to take their orders.

Eddie explained his predicament to the waitress and asked if it would be possible to get a grilled cheese sandwich. The waitress wasn't sure but promised to ask the cook, telling Eddie it might be difficult because the restaurant was so packed. Eddie took a look around after she left, noticing there were only two other groups in the place.

The waitress returned to the table brandishing a tray of alcoholic beverages.

"Hey, good news!" she stated with unusual excitement. "You're gonna get that grilled cheese sandwich."

The waitress must have butchered the pig herself. Forty minutes passed before she returned with three orders of Hungry Steer Beef Fest and a second round of drinks.

Island Bound

"Hey sweetie, I'll be back in a flash with your sandwich," she assured Ed as the others dug into the hunks of flesh swimming in red sauce on their plates.

The waitress eventually emerged from the kitchen carrying a red plastic basket lined with wax paper. She placed it in front of Eddie for his indulgence, and Eddie stared sadly at a forlorn hamburger bun shivering naked on the wax paper. At first, Eddie wondered if the waitress hadn't been able to find any cheese and had assumed he would settle for just a grilled bun. Upon further inspection, however, he found the cheese. Its plastic consistency had hardly been altered even after a quarter hour under a heat lamp. Eddie took a bite and laughed. The sandwich was still cold.

"Don't eat that too fast," Jim cautioned. "You need to save room for dessert."

"What's dessert going to be?" Eddie laughed. "A sugar cube?"

The bill arrived and Eddie learned that his grilled cheese cost him six bucks.

Hoping that the first night of his vacation would yield better food, Eddie took a place at the bar and ordered a Martini concocted with vodka and raspberry booze, a Caesar salad, and a side of macaroni and cheese. The bartender sat a chilled cocktail glass in front of Eddie as she rigorously shook the beverage. The cool, fruity liquid filled the glass. Eddie sipped his drink and inspected his surroundings. A young couple sat at the end of the bar smoking cigarettes and conversing quietly. Across the room, a second couple was playing pool, and a guy sat alone at a corner table, talking into a cellular phone.

The bartender placed Eddie's meal in front of him.

"What's your name?" he asked flirtatiously.

The bartender's name turned out to be Tracy. They chatted for a few moments because she didn't seem to be very busy, and Eddie learned that she had been working at Big Harry's for the past year while attending the local community college. Eddie was instantly attracted to the girl. Medium length brown hair, green eyes, and a great figure, along with neat, colorful clothing lent her an air of intelligence and charm. Tracy informed Eddie that the place would be shutting down at midnight. That was only one hour away.

Eddie ordered a Dewar's on the rocks and continued his assessment of the restaurant. The bar's style reminded him of some of the bars back home in Chicago. Brick walls and high ceilings provided openness but still felt cozy. Memorabilia of saloon history, sports, and the city's downtown decorated the bar, giving customers something to stare at as they perched on the barstools. A door at the back of the main room led out to an empty beer garden, and a combination of blues and bluegrass music filled the air.

Eddie finished his meal and ordered another Scotch, not wanting to return to the hotel quite yet. He felt a chilly gust of air as the door of the establishment swung open, and he saw two men enter the building. One approached the bar while the other remained at the front door. They attracted Eddie's attention because, with garish tattoos and long, greasy hair, they stood out from the other guests. The man who lingered by the door shot a glance to the corner of the room, and Eddie turned around just in time to see the man with the cell phone move to the back of the building near the restrooms. One of the men stepped up to the bar and called the bartender for service. Tracy greeted the new customer with a friendly smile, overlooking the man's improper attire.

From where he was seated, Eddie couldn't make out what the man said, but he sat close enough to see the man open his coat to reveal an automatic pistol.

"Is this some sort of a joke?" Tracy inquired.

Eddie saw the man's lips moving, and he ascertained from the stern expression on the man's face that what he had said was no joke.

Eddie attempted to stand up and make his way to the door, but as he did so, the other man posted near the door drew a short rifle from his jacket. A pistol grip replaced the butt of the rifle, and the barrel had been sawed off. Eddie regarded the thick scar marring the right side of the man's face and concluded that a dangerous man stood before him.

"Where do you think you're going, tough guy?" he spat.

"I guess I'm not going anywhere." Eddie returned to his stool.

Meanwhile, the guy who had been sitting at the corner table, clutching an old revolver in place of the cell phone, herded the rest of the patrons to the middle of the bar. The man confronting Tracy must have been the guy in charge, because he ordered the cellular phone guy to get the employees out of the kitchen. A moment later the man emerged from the kitchen area with a bus boy and the cook.

"Listen folks, no one needs to get hurt, so I don't want no hero shit. Place your cash and your wallets on the top of the bar," the chief bandit ordered.

As Tracy nervously fumbled with the register, the startled customers relinquished their cash and wallets. The leader ordered the man with the short rifle to watch the door and instructed the cell phone guy to empty the wallets of credit cards and cash. The leader considerately allowed personal items to be left behind.

"There's a badge in one of them!" the cell phone guy exclaimed.

"Let me see that." The leader snatched the wallet impatiently out of his underling's hand. After a brief examination, he addressed the cowering captives. "All right, whose badge?"

Eddie raised his hand. "That would be me, Boss. But I'm no cop. I'm just a firefighter."

"I ain't your boss, asshole." The leader strode to Eddie's stool and looked him over. Eddie wondered if the man intended to shoot him, but in the end, the man said, "Just keep your nose clean. I'll be watching you."

"Hey man, I want to get this over with as much as you do," Eddie said. He couldn't resist adding, "I'll even count the cash for you if that would help you guys get on your way."

"Don't be a wise guy. You'll live longer," the leader threatened.

As the criminals stashed the wallets and cash in the bag, the front door opened, and a Memphis police officer entered to investigate the silent alarm that Tracy had set off while she was at the register. The tense air in the bar exploded as a gun fired and the police officer fell back into the wall and the smell of gunpowder filled the room. A woman screamed uncontrollably, but the room was otherwise silent as the rest of the captives stared dumbly at the officer spilling blood on the floor.

"I thought I told you to watch the front door," the leader hissed. "Are there any more out there?"

"There doesn't appear to be. Oh, wait here comes another one." The man nervously informed his boss.

The leader instructed his junior partner to pull the officer over to the pool table and prop him up. A dark red stain covered the left shoulder of his uniform. The rifleman yanked the officer's side arm from its holster and shoved the weapon into his own belt.

Eddie could see the reflection of red and blue lights on his glass of scotch. He inconspicuously turned his eyes to the window and saw patrol cars outside.

"How the hell did this happen? Did you hit an alarm, bitch?" The leader directed the question at Tracy who, too nervous to answer, remained silent. The leader ordered the cell phone guy to check the back doorway, instructing him to come back if it was all clear. If not, he should secure the door somehow. While the cell phone guy checked the back, the leader looked out the front of the bar.

"There's cops around back. I locked the door and shoved the freezer in front of it," the bandit reported.

A police officer outside spoke into an electric bullhorn, informing the thieves that the place was surrounded. The voice ordered the men to surrender.

"Surrendering isn't an option. I've got nine hostages in here, including one of your cops and a fireman. Don't push it. I have no problem wasting precious lives," the leader screamed through the partially opened door.

The chief shut the door just as the phone started ringing. The leader told Tracy to answer it. A man on the other side of the connection introduced himself as a police officer, and Tracy informed the leader that the officer asked to speak to the guy in charge.

The conversation lasted about three minutes, and then the leader slammed the receiver back on its cradle. He looked at his prisoners and told them a car would be arriving soon. This car would be used for the bandits' escape, and to ensure their safety, they would take a hostage along with them. The customers and employees of the bar stared silently at him, each one hoping that someone else would be chosen as the hostage.

Minutes ticked by. The criminals posted themselves on bar stools, holding their guns ready for any sudden movements among the huddling of captives. The only sound in the bar came from the pool table, where the stricken police officer gasped periodically.

Tracy's compassion for human life overcame her fear and confusion. "That cop's not looking too good," she said quietly to the leader. "He should get some medical help."

The leader thought for a moment and decided that the officer was going to stay put. However, he looked at Eddie and asked if he had any medical experience. If anyone in the room did, it would be the fireman. Eddie told the leader that he was a paramedic as well as a firefighter.

The criminals allowed Eddie and Tracy to cross the room in order to tend the officer's wound, but the two remained under the watchful eye of the cell phone guy. Eddie asked Tracy to grab some clean bar towels, hot water, and a first aid kit if the bar had one. Tracy nodded and hurried to collect the items. Eddie began to remove the officer's uniform top and bulletproof vest as the phone rang once more.

This time the leader answered the phone, and the caller turned out to be someone wanting to order a pizza. The leader actually took the order and added that the pizza would arrive within the hour. Laughing, the man hung up the phone. The phone rang again. This time it was the police.

The crook's attention wavered as Tracy moved around the bar grabbing the items Eddie had asked for. The crook figured he ought to focus his attention on the girl rather than on the injured officer and Eddie.

Eddie noticed the guard's lack of supervision and used the opportunity to inspect the officer's ankles. Most of the officers Eddie knew carried a second firearm, quite often stashing it in an ankle holster. Eddie hit the jackpot - a small, automatic pistol was attached to the officer's right ankle. The criminals also overlooked the pepper spray on the officer's gun belt. He quickly grabbed the pistol and slipped it into his trousers. Knowing the ploy was dangerous, Eddie reasoned that if the criminals planned to slaughter everyone in the bar, he preferred to go down fighting.

Eddie returned to caring for the wound as Tracy approached with the kit, water, and bar towels. The bullet just missed the protective barrier of the vest, but the officer would have no problem surviving with the proper medical care. Blood poured from the wound as Eddie inspected the injury. There was no exit hole, so he assumed the projectile was still lodged in the officer's shoulder.

The kit was well stocked, but Eddie still felt a twang of disappointment when he saw that the only pain killer in the kit was a bottle of aspirin. He asked Tracy to drench a towel and clean up the blood as best as she could. The officer was breathing fine, although his pulse was a little rapid, and his skin took on a pale tone as the blood rushed out of his face. Eddie and Tracy laid the officer back and raised his legs. Using some peroxide and gauze sponges from the kit to clean the wound one more time, Eddie placed a thick bandage over the opening. The blood stopped flowing. At that point, the only thing to be done was monitor the officer's condition and hope for the best.

With that done, Eddie tried to think of a way out of the jam. He couldn't use the small pistol to shoot all three men but felt compelled to do something. Praying things would play out and everything would be O.K., Eddie decided he could only sit tight and wait for the best opportunity.

The leader hung up the phone and faced his captives.

"We're gonna be gettin' outta here soon. We'll be taking the bartender with us and the rest of you will be staying here."

"Don't take her!" Eddie cried. He hated to think what the criminals would do to the young, attractive girl. Impulsively, he offered, "Take me instead. I won't cause any problems." Everyone in the bar turned to Eddie in astonishment.

Recovering from his surprise, the leader replied, "No thanks, although your gesture is touching. I imagine we could have more fun with the bartender."

Eddie now felt he had no choice. He had to act soon. In a fetal position on the floor, Tracy buried her head in her hands and began to sob. Eddie felt nauseous as he envisioned her body floating in the river weeks later.

The bandits began to calm down, figuring they were going to get away with the loot and the girl. The leader instructed the cell phone guy to check the office in back for anything valuable and ordered the rifleman to lock the door and grab a few bottles of booze for the road. The rifleman checked the lock and walked towards the back of the bar area, stopping for a moment to ask the leader what his preferred poison was. The two men were only standing a few feet apart, and the third bandit was still in the back office. Eddie figured if something was going to be done, it had to be done then. He took a deep breath and slowly reached into his pants for the small pistol.

Eddie felt sweat dripping from his forehead. His hands were clammy and his mouth dry. At a distance of twenty feet, he hoped he wouldn't miss - it would be the only chance. His whole life flashed before his eyes as he pointed the automatic at the leader of the pack and pulled the trigger twice. The rounds smashed into the leader's right knee and the man collapsed to the floor. Eddie adjusted his aim and screamed at the rifleman, "Hands up, I want you to keep them where I can see them!"

The rifleman cautiously raised his hands to face level, pleading, "Don't shoot, man, just don't shoot."

Eddie directed him to disarm and slide his guns across the floor. Eddie knew he had to hurry, because cell phone guy could bust through the kitchen doors at any second. He kept one eye on the kitchen and his gun pointed at the rifleman as he walked over to pick up the guns.

"O.K. man, you should thank God that I didn't take you out. But I want you to keep in mind that I have absolutely no problem doing that if you try anything funny. You got that?" The man nodded, his eyes wide. "Now, what I want you to do is get flat on the floor, face down."

The man did as Eddie said, and Eddie put one foot on the back of his neck as he aimed at the kitchen doors, waiting for the cell phone guy to return. Everyone in the bar was deathly silent except for the leader, who whimpered and rolled on the floor in agony. Some of the customers had taken cover under their tables while others froze, their eyes darting from the kitchen doors to Eddie and back again. Several breathless moments passed as Eddie, adrenaline pumping, balanced gingerly with one foot against the rifleman's neck, pinning him to the floor.

Finally, his heart returned to a more natural rhythm, and he began to think it was ridiculous to continue waiting for the cell phone guy, who probably had escaped when he heard the shots. Without breaking his watch of the kitchen, he called to Tracy.

"How you doin' back there, Tracy? You O.K.?"

After a few seconds, Tracy's timid voice answered, "I'm fine. I'm O.K."

"Could you come over here, please?"

Eddie felt her standing at his side, so he gave her one of the guns he had taken from the rifleman and instructed her to point it at the man's head. Before he went to check out the kitchen, Eddie leaned down to the rifleman's ear and said, "Listen to me, because I've got something very important to tell you. Your job right now is to remain as still as you possibly can. You do so much as wiggle your pinkie finger, and you're a dead man. You got that?"

The man answered that he understood. Eddie, still keeping his eyes and gun directed at the kitchen, explained to Tracy how to remove the safety and pull the trigger. He didn't expect her to have any problems, because he could hear muffled crying from the man with his face against the floor.

Eddie had never been trained in how to do what he was about to do, but he'd seen enough gangster movies to take a guess about how to secure the kitchen. Stopping momentarily to retrieve the leader's gun from where it had slid under a barstool, he approached the doors from the side and looked through their windows. Smoke rose from a steak on the grill as it burned, and a pot on the stove boiled over. The dishwasher doggedly continued its cycle, oblivious to the scene in the front. There were no signs of the man or his cell phone.

Carefully, Eddie pushed open one of the doors, then stood with his back to the wall while he went over every detail of the room. He didn't find the man, but he did notice an open window on the side wall. More confidently now, Eddie went over the kitchen and determined there was no hiding place large enough to conceal a full-grown man. Deciding the cell phone guy must have escaped, he went back out to the bar to relieve Tracy of her post. He smirked in disgust when he saw the rifleman - a dark puddle of urine stained the floor around his legs.

As the excitement faded, an army of police investigators entered the bar to collect statements. Several paramedics tended to the injured leader, and the wounded officer gave Eddie a thumbs up as the paramedics wheeled him out to an ambulance. The patrons and staff came through without a scratch. After the police collected the statements and contact numbers of the witnesses, they released everyone from the scene.

Eddie returned to the Peabody playing the scene over and over in his mind. He was exhausted but proud. After a shower and a couple drinks from the mini-bar, he stretched out on the bed. If he wanted an adventurous vacation, he was certainly off to a good start.

Chapter Seven

A white Camaro shot down the expressway in the direction of Key West. Katie, the driver, was of the opinion that some anal-retentive control freak had masterminded the whole concept of speed limits and traffic regulations, so she chose not to pay them any mind. She preferred to write a check for any fines this mode of thinking might incur rather than submit to the rules of the highway. This belief system also won her the role of official driver on every excursion with her girlfriends. Jennifer, on the other hand, rode shotgun knowing that the other girls would never let her take the wheel. Everybody agreed that she suffered from some driver's learning disability that caused her to sideswipe other vehicles and take out mailboxes. Two other girls, Melissa and Marcie, sat in the tiny backseat, giggling, chattering, rolling joints, smoking them, and making fun of people in other cars as the Camaro whizzed past.

The four girls were planning to spend one or two days in Key West to kick the holiday off. Jennifer didn't know what was waiting for her after Key West; the girls wanted to surprise her because she always complained that her life was too predictable. Melissa had seen an article in a travel magazine that featured a private island resort about one hundred miles south of Cuba. Katie, as maid-of-honor, had brought up the idea that the three of them should take Jennifer on one last hurrah before the first of their ranks settled down with a husband, so as soon as Melissa saw the article she dialed Katie's cell phone.

"Listen to this," she said enthusiastically when Katie picked up. "One hundred miles south of Cuba, a private resort island rests peacefully on the Caribbean. Visitors in search of an exclusive get-away should find the island satisfying; the proprietors allow only one group of guests at a time to delight in its virgin landscape..."

"Hm," Katie interrupted. "That sounds nice, but 'virgin landscape' makes me a little nervous. Are you sure we wouldn't have to stay in a hut or a tent or something? And what about bugs? And diarrhea?"

"No, no!" Melissa assured her. "The article says what the house is like." She skimmed to the section in the article that discussed accommodations. "Let's see...main house sleeps eight people; there are four bedrooms, five full bathrooms, a kitchen...recreation room. 'Guests will find a pool table, dartboard, and a very large-screened television joined by a top-of-the-line surround sound system.' Doesn't exactly sound like a hut to me." Melissa read further on and said, "Oh, and there's a lot of stuff to do there, too. 'Outdoor amenities include a heated swimming pool, hot tub, two tennis courts, a putting green, and a secluded white sand beach.'"

Katie liked the part about the secluded beach. "Cool," she said. "But wait; do we have to share the house with anybody? You said it sleeps eight, right?"

"See, that's the beauty of the whole thing. We're going to be the only people on the whole island. I mean, the innkeeper will be there because they have to have somebody to keep it maintained and everything. But he lives way over on the other side of the island. We'll probably never even see him."

After a few more phone calls, Melissa reserved the house for two weeks.

"Hey, Jen, don't be hoggin' that thing, pass that bad boy back here," Marcie screamed. Having moved to Florida only one year before, she was a new addition to the group of friends. Her father was a wealthy Boston land developer. The most remarkable period in Marcie's life happened while she was in college at the University of South Florida. Her father spoke to a few people and succeeded in landing her a job as a ball girl for the Boston Red Sox. She spent three seasons there until she got sick of it and went back to school, and she still hadn't graduated because she skipped three semesters. She was in no hurry to initiate an adult lifestyle. Her father's wallet provided her with everything her heart desired: funds for shopping, tuition, and a two-bedroom two-bath high rise condo in the heart of Tampa.

"Don't worry Marcie, there's plenty to go around." Melissa reassured her partner in the cramped back seat.

Melissa was born and raised in the Tampa area. Her father and mother, two of Tampa's most respected surgeons, sent her to study law at the University of South Florida where she met Marcie in a political science class. Except for Marcie, all the girls grew up together.

Jennifer had her head crouched far below the dash of the car, hiding from prying eyes as she took a hit. When she emerged from the hunched position, she passed a small, white, smoking object back to Marcie.

"Wow, that is some good stuff," Jennifer commented as she reclined the passenger's seat slightly.

"Hey, watch my knees, bitch. It's crowded enough back here," Melissa complained.

Jennifer's only response was laughter - she had long ago grown accustomed to Melissa's abrasiveness. With the top down, Jennifer could feel the heat of the Florida sunshine baking her skin. Shortly after the last of the joint was thrown to the wind, all the girls except Katie, who refused to smoke while driving, were exploding with laughter. The drive from Miami to Key West consisted of several long bridges constructed to connect the Keys to the mainland. At the end of the road sat Key West. In the not too distance past, the only transportation to the island was by boat or by plane.

Halfway over one of the longer bridges, Melissa asked Katie to pull into the parking lot of a small restaurant at the end of the bridge. Several months ago, Melissa and a boyfriend stopped to use the facilities at the very same establishment and found what turned out to be the best conch burgers the Keys had to offer.

The parking lot was surrounded by thick, green foliage. A cobblestone path led the girls down to a small waterside restaurant. The building looked like a large gazebo; the floors of the cafe were constructed of light hardwood, stained from years of use. Country music spread throughout the seating area and stretched out over the rocks below where several groups of people enjoyed their meals. A thatched roof covered the bar and kitchen area, and three ceiling fans stirred the moist sea breeze. A sweet and salty breeze drifted in from the sea where the surf crashed into jagged dark rocks. After the girls had selected a table, a middle-aged man approached sporting a soiled apron that hardly covered his keg-size beer belly.

"So, what are you girls looking for today?" The portly man inquired.

"Four conch burgers with the battered fries and four Long Island ice teas." Melissa did all the ordering.

"And four watermelon shots, please," Marcie added.

Three patrons sitting nearby slammed shot glasses to the table as Jennifer thanked the waitress who brought their drinks. The trio of men sat around one of the tables laughing boisterously and sucking down clams from a big paper bucket sitting in the middle of their table. One of the guys made eye contact with Katie and winked. When Katie returned the gesture, the man stood up and closed the short distance between the two tables.

"Hi, my name is Bob Clipper, but everyone calls me Bobby," he said with a Casanova grin. As he shook Katie's hand, his other hand flicked cigarette ashes on to the old wooden floor.

After a brief conversation, the two groups decided it would be a good idea to join forces. Bob Clipper and his friends turned out to be Air Force men on leave. All three were stationed in Texas as military police where they guarded a launch sight for a nuclear missile. When they found out they had the same two-week leave, they decided to head for Key West. They looked like triplets; all three were in their mid-twenties, sporting short, buzz cut hair and well-exercised bodies, trimmed mustaches, and cut-off military-issue pants accompanied by gaudy Hawaiian shirts. Bobby introduced his friends.

"This guy is Timmy Roeka, and this is Ricky Bender."

After drinking, eating, and laughing the afternoon away, the two groups planned to hook up in Key West.

"We're gonna hang here for a little while, but we'll see you all tomorrow," Bobby announced after some discussion with his buddies.

"The Iguana Cafe at ten o'clock tomorrow night, right Bob?" Katie confirmed the plans.

The girls returned to the Camaro. As they were pulling out of the parking lot, a man in a gray convertible BMW went speeding by, causing Katie to slam on the breaks. She just missed the speeding vehicle as it swerved to avoid the collision. Katie stuck her head out the window, shook her fist at the car, and said, "Slow down, asshole!"

Taking out her aggression on the Camaro's gas pedal, Katie screeched the car out of the parking lot. She was a little tipsy and should not have been driving.

After another hour, the girls finally reached their destination. The group booked an entire bed and breakfast located a couple of blocks off Duval Street. A light breeze caused the wooden sign above the home's porch to sway gently, announcing to visitors their arrival at Calico Corners, a Key Western bed and breakfast. The proprietors' names appeared on the bottom of the sign: Frank and Karen Calico. The sign complimented the house's handsome exterior.

Ten years ago, the Calicos noticed the house for sale during a visit to the island. Since they were planning to retire early, they purchased the property. The Calicos took six months to settle their affairs and have the home remodeled for use as a bed and breakfast. Running an inn had been something the two had considered for quite some time. Mr. Calico had enjoyed a successful career managing his own real estate brokerage, and Mrs. Calico spent her years as a district manager in a high-end retail store known for its specialty kitchen equipment.

The home was a large Victorian, three stories tall, boasting five bedrooms and six bathrooms after the renovation. A brick fireplace sat in the home's large parlor while a formal dining room was sandwiched between the parlor and a professional-style kitchen that could allure any chef. The couple had the exterior painted light cream with hunter green trim. Unusual for modern day Key West, the home sat on one full acre of land. A brick driveway was laid next to the home, stretching past the house and into the yard, ending at a two-stall garage. The backyard provided guests with an outdoor swimming pool, hot tub, a field for pitching horseshoes, and a large wooden deck. Tropical foliage lent comforting shade during the really hot days, and a screened porch wrapped around two sides of the structure. A modest coach house nested between the palms and acted as a home for the innkeepers.

Katie parked the Camaro in front of the home, and the four young ladies collected their gear, heading for the front door. Jennifer and Marcie, still feeling the effects of the day's earlier activities, collapsed into two of the porches' patio chairs while Katie and Melissa entered the home in search of their host and hostess. The two found Mrs. Calico working in the kitchen where the scent of cinnamon and coconut filled the air. A blender was spinning away on one of the counters, and inside it, Katie spied a white, creamy concoction. Mr. Calico was in the back of the home pouring kerosene into torches placed around the deck and pools.

"You must be the young ladies we're expecting." Mrs. Calico welcomed the guests as she removed a fresh tray of cinnamon rolls from one of the kitchen's ovens. "I'm making some piña coladas, if you're interested."

J.D. Gordon

Katie thanked the woman but told her they'd like to get settled in first. Mrs. Calico called her husband to help with the suitcases while she gave the girls a quick tour of the home, directing each girl to her room. Afterwards, they relaxed by the pool, indulging on those creamy coconut cocktails.

Island Bound

Chapter Eight

Prior to leaving the Peabody, Eddie phoned his buddy Frank in Tampa to advise him of his plan. It was still early, and the phone rang six or seven times before a groggy voice answered. After a few minutes in which Eddie struggled to keep Frank awake, the two made plans for Frank to meet Eddie at his hotel just before setting out on the boat. From the very beginning, when Eddie first got the idea to vacation on the Caribbean, Frank had unabashedly urged Eddie to include him in his plans.

It had been a while since the last time Eddie saw Frank. They grew up on the same block in Chicago and had always been close friends, but after graduating high school, the two went their separate ways; Frank headed to Florida to pursue a career in law enforcement while Eddie stayed behind in Illinois to go to college. Frank spent two years working security at Disney World before landing a job with the Tampa Bay police department.

Eddie liked the prospect of bringing Frank along on the boating excursion, but he was apprehensive about taking him out to the open sea far from grocery stores, fast food restaurants, and bakeries. He hoped that the boat could carry enough food to keep Frank's stomach satisfied. During those summer road trips Eddie took with his buddies while growing up, half of Frank's baggage always consisted of Ho-Hos, snack chips, cookies, and all sorts of other fat-filled, sugary, or salty treats.

Likewise, Eddie was quite the big eater during his years of development in high school. Naturally, an eating contest was inspired. For the big event they ordered two family-sized stuffed pizzas and laid them out on Frank's kitchen table beside two half gallons of ice cream and two bags of Chips Ahoy chewy chocolate chip cookies. An hour later, all the food was gone and the over-stuffed duo sat down to rest as their stomachs digested the feast. The contest appeared to be a tie. However, after a couple of minutes, Eddie developed stomach pains and nausea. His stomach rejected its unreasonable quantity of food, and Eddie ran to the bathroom to vomit. When he emerged from the washroom, he found his adversary bragging on the phone. "I won - Eddie couldn't hold it down."

Over the years, Eddie's appetite steadied, but Frank's grew larger. As Eddie recalled the contest on his way to Miami, he wondered if it was the only time in Frank's life that he had gotten enough to eat.

As the highway stretched before him to the horizon, Eddie's mind went over the events of the previous evening. He couldn't believe that he had shot a man in the knees. Even though he knew that he had quite possibly saved Tracy's life, he still found a contradiction between his use of a handgun and his code of ethics as a fireman and paramedic.

His thoughts drifted back to Chicago, and he almost wished he could be back there just for an hour or so to check-up on the guys.

*

Back in Chicago, two paramedics worked in the back of the ambulance while a firefighter in the front guided it rapidly to the hospital. Just thirty minutes ago, the Salt Creek firefighters were sipping coffee and preparing for the day ahead of them. Suddenly, the alert tones rang, dispatching the rescue workers to assist an elderly man possibly having a heart attack.

"That's Bob Warner," Donny informed Eddie's usual partner, Hank, who had been back on duty only two days since his vacation in Wisconsin. "Eddie and I just took him in a couple of days ago."

"Isn't he the World War II paratrooper?"

Donny confirmed Hank's question.

Hank was driving the box today. He backed the ambulance into the home's driveway, and one of the rear wheels spun on the icy black top. The two medics exited the ambulance, grabbing the emergency equipment needed to manage a possible heart attack. Donny carried the heart monitor/defibrillator as well as the drug box, and Hank was clutching a red airway bag and a portable cellular phone. The home's front door opened as Hank approached.

"He can't breathe," a wild-eyed woman said, meeting them at the door and following them anxiously to the bedroom. "Hurry, please!"

The paramedics entered the bedroom where Mr. Bob Warner lay on his back in the center of the bed. His eyes were wide open, and he was clutching his chest. With every breath, Bob produced popping and crackling sounds from his mouth, and his skin looked pasty and white. The two paramedics immediately fell to work.

"Don't worry, Bob. We're gonna take good care of you." Donny said softly, actually displaying a little compassion for once.

The emergency crew treated Bob aggressively, placing intravenous lines in his arms and an oxygen mask over his mouth and nose. One of them watched the heart monitor in order to report the heart rhythm. A small clip attached to another smaller monitor clasped Bob's index finger, measuring the oxygen in his blood.

The paramedics administered several different medications to aide the old soldier, and then put him on the stretcher to be quickly transferred to the waiting ambulance. Donny and Hank jumped into the box and continued to care for Bob. The ambulance was halfway to the hospital when Bob's condition deteriorated. He looked up into Hank's eyes briefly as he prepared the intubation supplies. The monitor produced a high-pitched, electronic alarm, and Hank's glance at the heart monitor revealed a solid, flat line running across the small screen. Bob had stopped breathing as well.

The duo continued to treat Bob, hoping to revive the kind old man. Ten minutes after transferring Bob's care to emergency room staff, the doctor had no choice but to suspend the life saving efforts. Bob was dead.

*

After several hours of driving, Eddie cruised beyond the Florida state line. In just two day's time, the weather surrounding Eddie transformed from icy cold breezes to pleasant gulf winds. The sky was blue, marked occasionally with fluffy, white clouds. The sun was setting in the distance, and Eddie's back was stiff from the long ride. Passing under a road sign that informed him the exit for Tropic Grove was coming up soon, Eddie activated the right turn signal and left the highway. Cattails and marshes sided a two-lane road traveling towards the town of Tropic Grove.

A traveler could blink and practically miss the town's center. A few small brick buildings lined the town's main street: a modest grocery, a hardware store, post office, city hall building, a bar, and a diner in front of which sat an antique police cruiser. At the end of the line, a motel appeared. A sign in front of the motel read "The Tropic Motel" in red block lettering. The letter M in motel was lit up, but the rest of the bulbs had burned out and were never replaced. Eddie pulled into the motel's drive, figuring the lodge would have a vacant room. Twenty rooms forming an L stood around the parking lot and a small swimming pool. Across from the swimming pool, Eddie saw the door of the office flanked on each side by vending and ice machines.

Eddie parked and entered the office. A lanky teenager with blemished skin and braces greeted him in the office and guided him through his check-in. After signing the appropriate papers, Eddie was on his way to his room with the key in hand. The room was plain and consisted of a television, a desk, a bed, and a washroom with a stand-up shower adjoining the main room. Eddie thought about checking out the bar scene in town, but after the previous night, he decided against it. Instead, he meandered down to the local diner.

Eddie could find nothing extraordinary on the menu, so he just ordered a plate of spaghetti and a beer. The waitress delivered rock hard Kaiser rolls and runny spaghetti. After paying the bill, he returned to the motel, checking out the pool on the way. The pool was clean, and the water was warm enough for swimming.

Eddie changed into his swimsuit and walked back out to the concrete swimming hole where a little diving board and a faded blue slide stood silently at the deep end. Eddie couldn't help himself; he just had to try the slide. He floated around the pool after swimming some laps until the lanky teenager appeared and informed him that the pool was closed.

Eddie returned to the room, showered, and crashed for the night. The next morning found him back on the road. Before leaving the motel's lot, Eddie threw on a sweatshirt and dropped the Mitsubishi's cloth top. In just a few hours he traversed the Everglades, and to his pleasure, signs for Miami began to pop up frequently.

Once in Miami Eddie presented himself and the car at the prearranged car rental office. As the girl from Illinois promised, the southern branch provided Eddie with transportation to Marvin Frank's Aviation Company.

Marvin's company was located on a small airfield just west of Miami. The drive wasn't the most pleasant trip in Eddie's lifetime because the cab driver didn't have a handle on the English language. He also chain-smoked, and the taxi's air conditioning was on the fritz. Regardless of the difficulties the driver did manage to drop Eddie at the doorstep of Marvin Frank's Transportation Company.

The day turned out to be a hot one, even for Miami. The mercury touched the ninety-six degree mark, and Eddie noticed waves of heat bouncing off the aluminum roof of an old dilapidated hanger. A sun-faded tin sign identifying Marvin's business was tacked above the large front door. As the taxi drove away, Eddie took his bags and entered the old hanger. Two planes called the structure home; one was a modern day Cessna twin-engine aircraft, the other was an old, old biplane.

Pulling at his lip, Eddie took a long, hard look at the latter. It wasn't too late, he reasoned, to find another way to get to Key West. The plane's wings curved disconcertingly on the ends, and the engine revealed by a fly-encrusted wire mesh looked no more powerful than the engine of a lawn mower. Walking around to examine the other side, Eddie was surprised to discover a pair of sausage-like legs protruding from beneath the plane's belly.

"Hey mechanic guy, excuse me!" Eddie yelled over the din of a drill mixed with reggae music.

Startled, the sausage legs wiggled, and after a loud bang and a string of obscenities, a man emerged. "You scared the hell outta me, mon!" the man stated as he rubbed a small bump swelling on his head.

"Sorry - at least you didn't break the skin. I'm Eddie Gilbert, I'm looking for Mr. Frank."

"Jus' call me Marvin, mon. Toss your bags into de compartment on de udda side. I jus' be doin' a liddle tinkrin'. We be on de way soon."

Eddie's concern increased when he noticed large puddles of oil and twisted pieces of metallic debris beneath the plane. "Are you finished tinkering?" he asked. "I don't mind waiting for you to finish up here - I'm not in a hurry."

The man just laughed and smacked Eddie on the back. "Don' ya worry 'bout it, mon. We be jus' fine." He hopped in the pilot's seat and threw a helmet and a parachute to Eddie, who saw nothing to do but follow suit. In moments, they were buzzing in the direction of Key West.

Several cabs waited for fares in front of the airport, and Eddie made his way through a herd of tourists sporting sunglasses and fresh pink sunburns, then settled into a cab and asked the driver to take him to his hotel, La Conchia. Situated on the highest point of the island in the heart of Key West and its Duval Street establishments, the hotel boasted a rooftop bar and swimming pool that had attracted guests for almost eighty years.

After carrying his bags to his room, Eddie marched down to the end of Duval. A band was playing, and tourists were mulling around waiting for the sun to set. Eddie ordered several drinks and munched on conch fritters while the sun slowly dipped beneath the horizon. Normally Eddie wouldn't want to digest sea slugs, but he figured "when in Rome..." The drinks were nice and strong, and Eddie's head floated during his walk back to the hotel. He would sleep well. Eddie returned to his room and sparked up a cigarette he bummed off of some girl on the street. After changing clothes, he settled down on one of the room's double beds. Eddie came upon an old Bogart film as he flipped through the channels. Eddie drifted to sleep as Bogart and E.G. Robinson plotted against each other.

Chapter Nine

It was late the next morning by the time Eddie opened his eyes. One of the hotel's employees decided to bang on Eddie's room's door.

"Housekeeping." Bang, bang. "I said *housekeeping!*" The voice bellowed even louder.

Eddie pushed the covers away and started to sit up in bed. The room was dark and cold; the air conditioning had been pumping away all night at maximum power. The door of the room opened, allowing the mid-morning sunshine to spread across Eddie's eyes. He blinked drowsily and turned his head away from the doorway.

"I'm sorry to intrude, sir, but you need to place the "Do Not Disturb" sign on the door if you don't want service in the morning." A young Latin girl held one of the plastic signs in her hand, presenting it to Eddie.

The girl went about her chores as if Eddie weren't present. Although the girl looked to be no older than sixteen or seventeen, she vigorously tended to her duties. Eddie figured her for one of those no-nonsense types.

Eddie glanced at his watch and walked into the washroom.

"Don't be in there too long. I'm almost finished out here!" The housekeeper ordered.

"Never mind me, I'm only payin' for this place," Eddie muttered under his breath. He should have protested, but the truth was the young housekeeper scared him a little. After splashing his face with water and brushing his teeth, Eddie swiped his armpits with deodorant, and then the housekeeper and guest traded places. Hurriedly throwing on a pair of khaki shorts and a Cubs jersey, Eddie hoped he could get dressed before the housekeeper emerged from the bathroom. He was just putting on his sandals when the girl reappeared, loaded her cleaning supplies back onto her cart, and set out for the next room without a word.

The first order of business for the day was settling the acquisition of his watercraft. With a small map the hotel provided, Eddie took off for the yacht broker's office. According to the map the office looked to be on the other side of the island, so he decided to rent a motor scooter, a fancy red one with what the dealer called a "larger-size" engine. The sight of a grown man on a scooter was goofy, but Eddie didn't care. It was fun, and he was on vacation. Eddie pulled the small bike out on to Duval Street. After about a block, a traffic light turned red, causing Eddie to pause just before an intersection. While Eddie waited for the green light, he started to wonder if he had taken a wrong turn out of the parking lot. He puzzled at the street signs and was busy looking in his pockets for the paper with the address of the boat rental when he heard a breathy voice call out, "Any particular shade of green you're lookin' for, you big, bad biker guy?"

Island Bound

He looked up to see a group of pretty girls loaded with shopping bags. Two sacks escaped the grips of a brown haired, well-tanned young lady, and Eddie smiled and tipped his ball cap in the girls' direction. A horn blared behind him, and Eddie twisted the bike's throttle to its limit. The little engine made a cartoon buzz and propelled the vehicle to a heart-stopping rate of twenty-five miles an hour.

Eddie made a couple of wrong turns on his way to the yacht shop and ended up on a maze of back roads that certainly didn't compare to the island's main streets. Rusty trailers and old neglected wood frame houses lined paved paths. Finally, Ed and the red scooter happened upon one of the island's fire stations: a good place to ask for directions. Eddie turned a small silver key on the scooter's dash. As the scooter stopped its sputtering, Ed imagined that the trio of hamsters undoubtedly churning the pistons of the motor knocked off for a couple of beers.

Two guys in blue shorts and white tee shirts sat on folding director's chairs in front of the brick building. Ed set the kickstand and dismounted the bike.

"Well, well...What do we have here, a Chicago Cubs fan?" One of the guys greeted the visitor without standing up. The other drained a can of iced tea, then conscientiously examined his fingernails.

"Cubs rule!" Eddie said, walking towards them. "I was heading to this yacht place, but it seems that I decided to get lost instead." Eddie thrust the detail-lacking hotel map towards the two men.

"Everybody stops at firehouses for directions; I wonder if that service is included in the job description," the man remarked in a friendly enough manner.

Eddie introduced himself as a firefighter from the Chicago area, and the three talked shop for an hour before Eddie finally received his directions. As it turned out, Eddie had made it within four blocks of the yacht shop.

"Thanks for the directions, don't work to hard today" Eddie said as he mounted his scooter.

"Gotta save some work for tomorrow's shift."

Sure enough, four blocks later sand and wooden piers replaced the asphalt of the road. Vessels large and small rolled with the motion of the sea. A bar carrying the name of The Schooner Wharf Saloon acted as a welcome center for the dock area. When Eddie saw the name of the bar, he realized just how badly he allowed himself to become misdirected; he had visited the Schooner Bar every past vacation to Key West, and it was located only six blocks from his hotel.

Eddie walked into the saloon to grab a cold one before heading for the broker's office.

The bartender placed the brew on the counter in front of Eddie, white foam emerging from the bottle's opening. Just then, Eddie felt the weight of a hand patting his right shoulder.

"Barkeep, you better add another beer and two shots of to-kill-ya on to that order," a husky voice erupted.

Eddie turned on his stool to see the beaming face of a tall, older man. The man's face was deeply tanned, and blue eyes spied out from beneath a wide-brimmed, tan boonie hat. A smiling mouth full of white teeth completed the face. The lanky body was covered in blue jean cut-offs and a crisp white tee-shirt.

"Young Gilbert, well I'll be damned. It really is a small world."

"Not so small, good people hang in good places. What the hell are you doin' here Paul?"

The old tanned man turned out to be Paul Hazelstone, a Salt Creek firefighter who retired three years after Ed began his career. The two men spent that time on the same shift. One year Paul suddenly retired and moved south with his wife. Since that time the old fireman only existed in stories told around the kitchen table by others who still remembered him.

Paul went on to explain his presence in the saloon so far south of Salt Creek. After retiring, he and his wife slowly moved south, eventually ending up in the Naples area of Florida. This week, his wife and her friends were on a large cruise ship sailing the Pacific waters around the Hawaiian Islands. Paul was using the time to catch up on a little fishing and occasionally a little trouble-making. The two shared drinks and stories throughout the afternoon as Eddie related his experience in Memphis.

"No shit, you've had quite a trip already." Paul was beginning to slur his words.

"So have you backed over any trees lately?" Eddie was referring to a driver's training drill the two had participated in. Paul had almost completed his turn through a driving course, and the last leg was backing a fire engine down a forty-foot row of cones placed near a curb. The distance between the cones and the curb was just barely wide enough to fit the emergency vehicle. Everything was looking good for the old firefighter until the very last moment when the diesel began veering off course and up onto the curb. Several of Paul's co-workers screamed and waved to grab his attention, and the instructor blew his whistle, but after years of exposure to sirens and power tools, Paul developed difficulty hearing. The back bumper of the engine rolled solidly over a ten-foot maple tree. Paul and the engine dragged the up-rooted sprout twenty-feet before he noticed and stopped the rig. The diesel shut down, everyone stopped screaming, and the whistle went quiet. Paul jumped from the driver's seat to the ground and examined the scene behind the large red vehicle. "I guess I failed the test, huh, Ronnie?" was Paul's only response.

The two men laughed together for a few moments before Paul composed himself enough to answer Eddie's question. "No, Edward, I stay away from trucks. I'm driving that little boat over yonder." Paul motioned to a nearby dock where a modest-sized fishing boat bobbed on the waves.

"So how is the retired lifestyle?" Ed asked his old friend.

Paul rocked back on his bar stool and drew a great breath into his lungs.

"Well, Edward, it's good. Very good, if one can be financially stable," Paul answered after exhaling. "Take your time Ed. There is a lot ahead of a young man like yourself. I couldn't count the amount of times I've heard people say that they are just buying time until retirement, waiting for their twilight years before they begin to truly live for themselves. The working is done, the kids are all grown up...It's a nice time, but the one drawback is looking in the mirror and seeing an old man staring back. You realize the change in the balance of your life; the years in your future no longer outnumber the years in your past." Paul continued sharing his wisdom. "So slow down my friend, enjoy all the years of your life, and take some time to build yourself a nice family."

The sun was setting in the west when Paul announced his departure. Eddie realized he had missed his appointment with the yacht broker, so he accompanied his friend on the short walk to the fishing boat where they said farewell with a hearty handshake and a pat on the back. Eddie was worried about Paul's safety while out on the water after nightfall and thought it would be a good idea to invite Paul to hang out for the night.

"No, young Gilbert, but thanks. Don't fret over me. It takes more than dark skies and open water to scare me. After all, even my fishing rod is older than you. It was nice to talk about the old times. Tell the guys I said," he paused a moment, "Ah, don't tell the guys anything." The boat slowly floated around the other docked vessels. Paul turned around in the boat and lifted his arm to offer a final wave good-bye. His outstretched arm surrounded by the deep orange glow of the setting sun would be Eddie's final memory of his old friend.

Eddie hiked down to the broker's office at the end of the dock. The front door was locked, and the lights were out, so he ran back to the schooner bar and borrowed a pen and a coaster from the bartender, scribbling a note for the boat broker to let him know why he missed his appointment. As he turned to leave the bar, he noticed the girl who laughed at him and his scooter earlier in the day sitting around one of the tables with three other girls. Eddie caught her eye, and she waved shyly. The blonde girl beside her pushed her out of her chair, gesticulating at Eddie and mouthing something unintelligible.

Realizing that after Katie's forceful encouragement there was nothing to do but talk to the guy, Marcie gathered as much composure as she could, crossed the bar, and, unable to think of anything more clever, said, "You're that guy on the scooter."

"You're that girl on the corner. You dropped your bags." Eddie extended his hand to her and said, "My name is Ed."

Marcie introduced herself and grabbed his arm. Dragging him back to the other girls, she let loose a rapid string of chatter to hide her shyness. "We have a table over here in the corner. One of my friends is getting married, so we took her on a bachelorette vacation. See her over there with the brownish hair? Can you believe how crowded it is in here? It wasn't this crowded half an hour ago. I hate having to stand at the bar when they run out of chairs. Some people like it, because if you're standing up, other people can see your whole outfit, but I'd rather just sit. We got lucky because we've got a huge table - you should just sit with us."

Ed smiled benevolently.

"This is Jennifer," Marcie continued when they arrived at the table, pointing to each girl in turn. "That girl there is Katie. Watch yourself around her - she's our wild one. Last, but definitely not the least, is Melissa."

Katie interjected drunkenly, "And who are you? Do you have a name, other than Scooter Boy, which is what we've been calling you…"

"I'm Ed," he answered, already guessing that Katie would not be his favorite of the bunch.

Typical vacation conversation erupted, and Eddie told them about what happened in Memphis. Tugging a lock of hair, Katie drawled, "I saw a movie just like that one time."

Obviously irritated by her friend's lack of social graces, Marcie elbowed her in the ribs and hissed, "Shut up, Katie. That's rude."

"It's alright," Eddie said, overhearing. "It does sound like a movie." He didn't care to convince the girls it really happened, but his indifference won them over.

"Are you telling me that you actually shot a guy in the knees?" Melissa said in astonishment. "What are you, an undercover cop?"

"No, I'm an undercover fireman," Eddie quipped.

After they'd conversed for a few hours, Katie looked at her watch and announced, "I think we're going to have to take off pretty soon. We met some Air Force dudes on the way down here, and the plan was to meet them at the Iguana Cafe around ten o'clock."

"You're welcome to come, if you don't have anything better to do," Marcie added.

"We'll see. Thanks for the invite, but I've got plans of my own," Eddie lied, not wanting to spend the evening with Katie and the Air Force dudes. Marcie looked disappointed, so he added, "Listen, if we don't hook up tonight, give me a buzz in the morning. I'm staying at the La Concha, room 412." He handed Marcie a napkin with the number of the hotel written on it.

The four girls left Eddie behind at the bar and set out to keep their appointment. Duval Street was crowded, but the girls darted skillfully through the pedestrian traffic. When they arrived at The Iguana Cafe, they found the three airmen bellied up to the cafe's street-side bar. Bobby Clipper slammed a shot glass on to the bar's top as the girls approached. Ricky seemed to be half in the bag already and Timmy enthusiastically munched jalapeno poppers as if they were carrot sticks.

Island Bound

Fourteen shots, twelve beers, six cocktails, and one hour later, the group decided it was time to say good-bye to the Iguana Cafe. The Iguana's bartender suggested the group check out the Hog's Breath Saloon where a blues band was scheduled to be playing late into the night. The band was all set up and ready to play when the group arrived. The Hog's Breath was just as crowded as any other establishment on the island, but they were still lucky enough to find a table.

The night was spent dancing, drinking and socializing. The hour was late and Timmy had passed out in his chair when Katie mentioned it was probably time to start heading back to the Calico.

"Are you guys going to head out with us tomorrow? Where are you staying?" Katie asked the airmen.

"Actually, we haven't registered anywhere yet," Ricky Bender slurred.

"I guess there's plenty of room at our place," Katie winked. She was developing a crush on Bobby Clipper.

Jennifer and Marcie supported each other during the walk back to the Calico's Inn while Bobby and Ricky both had to half-carry, half-drag Timmy. Katie led the way while Melissa followed behind, singing show tunes as loud as she could.

The inn was dark when the group finally made it back, but Mr. Calico had left the lights around the swimming pool on. Katie fired up the stereo system and got to work on the blended drinks while the rest of the group either jumped into the pool or settled down into one of the patio's lounge chairs.

After two and a half hours, two bottles of rum lay empty on the counter, half-eaten snack foods littered the kitchen and porch, and dirty dishes filled the sink. The group finally decided to end the night. Katie quickly assigned rooms to the rest of the group - Katie and Bobby conveniently ending up in their own private room. Timmy, after getting sick twice from his over-indulgence with the jalapeno poppers, spent the night on an inflatable raft floating around on the pool.

Chapter Ten

Morning arrived way too soon for the girls and their newfound friends. Jennifer was asleep on the couch in the living room when Mrs. Calico activated her electric coffee grinder. The sound was irritating, but the aroma that soon followed coaxed her into the kitchen in search of a mug of the freshly brewed, hot beverage.

"Seems you girls had quite a night last night. Who's that boy floating around in the pool?" Mrs. Calico inquired of her first waking guest. She handed Jennifer a mug of steaming coffee.

Jennifer related the night's incidents to Mrs. Calico as she prepared the morning's breakfast: fresh baked biscuits, scrambled eggs, sausage, chocolate chip pancakes, home style potatoes, orange juice, milk, and of course, the recently prepared coffee. One by one, the group joined each other in the kitchen, although Tim continued to float around in the pool. Introductions of the new guests were made as needed.

"May I use the telephone, Mrs. Calico?" Marcie asked. Mrs. Calico directed Marcie to the front room where she could have some privacy.

"Marcie's gonna call Scooter Boy," Katie sniggered as soon as Marcie left the room; she loved to tease the other girls about their amorous pursuits. "Eat this, I'm full," she directed Bobby as she handed him a half-eaten biscuit. She rose from the table and helped herself to a cup of coffee. "We're heading out today," she announced between audible sips. "We appreciate the hospitality you've offered us. We really made mess of the place last night, and I'm sorry you had to clean up."

"That's all part of the job dear. Don't worry about it," Mrs. Calico said indulgently. "So you're heading down to that Spike Island place? Sounds really nice. What time are you leaving?"

"We'll pack up shortly after breakfast. We should be out of here by two o'clock," Katie judged, never hesitant to speak for the whole group.

The airmen's rental car actually turned out to be a "borrowed" Air force Hum Vee utility vehicle painted in desert camouflage. Bobby had a friend working as a mechanic in his base's motor pool, and he owed Bobby a favor. Almost a year ago, the mechanic had gotten drunk and started a bar fight, but fast-talking Bobby Clipper had been able to convince the police who arrived to break up the fight that they should let the mechanic go home to sleep it off instead of carting him off to the slammer. Finally, when Bobby and his buddies planned to spend their leave in Key West, he figured it would be the perfect opportunity to cash in his IOU.

The oversized military vehicle had plenty of space for all seven passengers and their luggage. Bobby piloted the large vehicle, and Katie, who had

Island Bound

presumptuously jumped into the passenger's seat, assumed the role of navigator. Between the two of them the group only got lost twice on the way to the dock area. Bobby parked the utility vehicle in a spot next to the dock's yacht club.

"I sure hope no one tows Uncle Sam's vehicle while we're gone." Bobby commented as he assisted Katie safely to the ground.

The rest of the group started unloading the luggage as Katie presented herself to the receptionist of the yacht club. The keeper of Spike Island instructed the girls to meet him in the lounge of the club. The receptionist directed Katie to a large lounge area where the island keeper relaxed, reading a newspaper, smoking a pipe, and sipping on a cup of coffee.

"Mr. York, I presume?" Katie asked as she strode towards him.

"Rod York, just call me Rod. I like to keep things pretty casual." Rod folded the paper up, tapped the pipe's ashes into an ashtray, then finished off his coffee. "Just keeping up on current affairs. Are we all ready to head out?"

Katie called to her friends. Mr. York noticed three additions to the party and looked inquiringly at Katie. When she explained the situation to the keeper, he didn't appear to be too concerned.

Rod discussed some of the resort's features, then led the young people out to the boat. "Everyone get comfy; we've got about a three-hour ride ahead of us." Mr. York said as he settled his passengers for the trip.

Bobby and Katie claimed the front sun deck for themselves while the remaining passengers shared the swivel chairs located in the space at the back of the boat. Mr. York got some tunes going and set out refreshments: mostly fruit, veggies, dips and assorted breads. Liquid refreshments included soda, water, juices and a fresh batch of hearty rum punch. As the boat eased out of the dock area, everybody began to relax, enjoying the wind, sun, and sea. Jennifer, who still had no idea where they were going, pestered Melissa for hints regarding their destination.

Melissa, savoring her curiosity, rose from her lounge chair to fetch a drink from the buffet. She stubbornly announced, "I'm not going to answer any more questions about this place. The only thing I'll tell you is that you're just going to die when you see it."

Chapter Eleven

    Late morning sun broke into Blackwell Crow's office as he prepared himself a cool glass of ice water and set off for his morning business. Normally, Blackwell would not visit the cavernous docks, but today was a different story; he couldn't wait to inspect his newest possession, the El Presidente. Usually any shipping acquired by Lester and his band was painted to conceal its true identity, after which the Crows would sell the ships on the black market. However, Blackwell wouldn't dream of selling his newest acquisition, and he threatened to shoot anyone who dared to come near it with a can of that cheap paint. He intended to keep the yacht, even though he would probably never have the chance to enjoy the ship on the open sea. The El Presidente was a true collector's piece, and Blackwell felt himself to be the ultimate portrayal of success and manliness when he sat at its helm.

    Blackwell scanned the dock area searching for his son. The docks had been busy all month, and at first he had difficulty finding Lester, who should have stood out despite the number of workers, if only for the exquisite cut of his suit. Finally, Blackwell sighted his son among a group of dockworkers standing near the cells. Lester had just slammed a heavy steel gate shut, and he had a devilish grin on his face. Imitating a woman's voice, he joked with the men, "Don't! Don't, please!" and broke out into a scornful laugh. The dockyards included three prison cells where the Crows kept captured women and children. The pirates executed males as a matter of course; they could be hard to control. Women, on the other hand, and children, could sometimes fetch a pretty penny if the right buyers could be found. Before he transferred the goods, however, Blackwell would reward his men by letting them have their fun with the prisoners.

    "Where did these two come from, Lester?" Blackwell pointed into the occupied cell.

    "They were on your new yacht - the only survivors."

    Blackwell peered more closely into the cell. "The women is attractive enough," he said. He turned to Lester with a pleased expression, as if he had just had a wonderful idea. "You know who I think would like her? Do you remember Mr. Tomo?"

    Lester nodded conversationally, taking a cigarette from his jacket.

    "Not two days ago he expressed an interest in a mother-daughter team, and I said, 'Han, do you know what you're asking? I just do this as a side thing.'" Blackwell shrugged as Lester chuckled. "I told him I would see what I could do and left it at that. Then, what do you know? They fall right into my lap."

    "Yeah, well I'd watch it, if I were you. Pretty soon, you're gonna have a bunch of weirdoes standing outside your office, thinking you're the delivery service for fat ladies, grandmas, who knows what," Lester remarked. Father and son chuckled as they walked back to Blackwell's office.

Jessica and Molly Dirk huddled together in the back of the cell. Mrs. Dirk leaned her back onto the rough brick wall and rubbed a bruise covering her eye. The dark room held a bed, a foul toilet, and a sink. The interior of the cell was quite cool, causing the prisoners to shiver. Jessica wrapped a scratchy old wool blanket around her daughter, who still stubbornly clutched the teddy bear. Jessica strained to hear the voices outside the cell, but the noise of assorted power tools at work doused any chance to collect information. Jessica held her daughter tightly, sobbing and praying for a way out.

"Lester, finish up what you're doing and join me for lunch. Our chef is preparing a fine meal for our enjoyment." Blackwell extended an invitation. "We need to discuss your next job."

Blackwell gazed at the classic yacht one more time before leaving the cave while Lester spent the next twenty minutes directing the dockhands. Before following his father to his office, Lester walked past the prison cells to check out the captives one more time.

"Don't you two look adorable all huddled together and freezing," Lester smirked, tossing a plastic bottle of warm spring water at the Dirks.

Lester entered his father's office. On the verandah, a pot-bellied chef busied himself setting steaming trays on the table. Staring out to sea, Blackwell sat at the table sipping dark rum on ice out of a short glass. Lester joined his father under the shade of the verandah's lattice ceiling. A glint of sunshine reflected off of one of the old British artillery pieces, and dark skies rumbled about in the horizon threatening a storm. The air was moist, cool, and carried with it a fresh, sweet scent. A tray of grilled meats laid smoking in the middle of the table. Beside it, a white cloth covered a basket of fresh baked bread while another pot held steaming rice and black beans.

Blackwell addressed the chef, "Jerrard, bring us another round and then take a hike. No interruptions this afternoon. My son and I have business to tend to."

Never one to waste his words, Blackwell began, "I should be receiving information on Ms. Klien's whereabouts shortly. I want you to forget what I told you in Tampa. Now, just do what you have to do. Keep her alive, though. She's no good dead."

"Look, what's the point?" Lester questioned as he helped himself to another serving of the meat. "Aren't you the one who taught me to always calculate the risk involved in a job? The way I see it, no amount of money is worth kidnapping Bruce Klein's daughter."

"Its not just the money, its the principal!" Blackwell interrupted. "Due to her father's efforts, the Coast Guard confiscated three out of our last four shipments. That's four million dollars that arrogant American bastard has stolen from me! I want that money back, and I want the pleasure of teaching him a lesson after we've received it." Blackwell's face flushed as he slammed his fist to the table, and his glass slipped to the floor. "Dammit, the ice to rum ratio was just coming together."

Lester went to the bar and poured his father another glass of the dark rum as well as another beer for himself. Picking a chunk of meat from his teeth, he set the drinks on the table and said, "Try not to drop this one, old man." He sat down again and remarked, "I would like to know how Klein knew about the shipments."

Blackwell handed his son a soft leather case. A pair of binoculars rested inside.

"Look to the right of that large palm hanging over the lagoon, on the white sand beach."

Lester examined the area with the glasses. A small sandy beach met the calm waters of the lagoon. The small beach was unprotected from the hot equatorial sun, and at the beach's center a nude man lay exposed to the heat of the mid-afternoon. The unfortunate's arms and legs were lashed viciously to four wooden spikes sunk deep into the ground. Lester couldn't tell if the man was still alive or not.

"I take it we had a spy among us." Lester replaced the glasses in their case. "You are truly evil - death by baking. You should have basted the sucker with mineral oil." The taut muscles of Lester's face tightened in anger as he pondered the audacity of the traitor.

"What do you mean, 'should have?' I did. As a matter of fact, I've assigned personnel to continue basting him throughout the rest of the day. If he is living still tonight, the same people will spend the night hosing him down with cold water. If he makes it through the night, the next step will be pouring maple syrup on him. I hope he makes it. It will be interesting to see what the island's insects could do to a man's body." Blackwell continued with excitement, "He shall serve as an example to any other person who may want to jump ship."

The two Crows finished their meal off with large cinnamon rolls topped with a brown sugar and cream cheese frosting, then retired to the cool air in the elder's office. The men each enjoyed a cup of strong Brazilian coffee while puffing away on Blackwell's Cuban cigars. Ceiling fans hovered above, stirring the cigar smoke about the room.

Blackwell tossed one of the manila envelopes into Lester's lap. Setting the coffee down, Lester fingered through the documents contained within. As usual, the envelope contained information to aid Lester with his assignment.

"Spike Island…Never heard of that one. Looks good - tourists practically alone on the island," Lester mumbled out loud, really just speaking to himself.

"Almost everything is there: the layout of the island, the communication and transportation available. The last pages pertain to the targets expected to be present."

"Who are these guys?" Lester asked. He held a few photographs for Blackwell to see.

"They're some military men on leave. Our man snapped their pictures because they met Klein's party on the way to Key West," Blackwell said. "They might show up later on, but I wouldn't bet on it. That last guy, though, he's not with the military men."

"Who's he?"

"That is Edward Gilbert of Salt Creek, Illinois. He's another acquaintance of the girls."

Lester scoffed at the picture and said, "This guy couldn't hurt a fly."

Blackwell pursed his lips wisely and finished off the rum. "I wouldn't be so sure. Our man overheard him telling Ms. Klein's party about some bar that was held-up in Memphis. Apparently, Mr. Gilbert managed to overcome three armed men."

Glancing at the picture again in disbelief, Lester cried, "This guy? Are you nuts? He probably just made up that story to impress the ladies. It's the oldest trick in the book."

"Ah, but his story checks out," Blackwell contradicted. "It's not so unbelievable. Think about it: Joe Shmoe takes a vacation, rents a fancy sports car, gets a little tan, pretty soon he starts thinking he's James Bond. It's the hero types you've got to watch out for."

Lester shot an incredulous look at his father.

"I'm not saying he could wreck the whole job," Blackwell argued, "but he could sure as hell mess things up royally and take a few men down with him."

Lester sat back in his chair, weighing his father's words. He decided to humor the old man and said, "Look, if he's so dangerous, why don't we just take him out? I'm sure that Mr. Gilbert could have a little boating accident or fall out a window."

"Exactly," Blackwell said, locking Lester's eyes in a significant gaze.

Chapter Twelve

A loud knock on the door aroused Eddie from a deep sleep. Eddie thought he recognized the heavy-handed knock.

"Come back later. I'm sleeping," Eddie called before turning over and pulling a pillow over his head. The knocking continued, so he heaved a sigh, crawled out of bed, and prepared to give the housekeeper a piece of his mind.

Instead of the housekeeper, Eddie found Frank on the other side of the door.

"What's wrong with you, man? I drive all the way from Tampa to see you, and when I get here, you tell me to go away," Frank joked as he pushed past Eddie and made himself at home in the hotel room.

"Frankenstein Bablouski," Eddie said, closing the door. "How ya been?"

Frank hadn't changed much since the last time Eddie saw him, except that he might have grown still larger than he was before - Eddie figured he must have started pumping iron after joining the police force. He towered over Eddie and must have weighed in at well over two hundred fifty pounds. The guy was solid as the third little piggy's house. Frank kept his hair fashioned in a short Mohawk, which pushed the limits of the Tampa police department's dress code policy. He wore an unbuttoned, short sleeved cotton shirt with a tropical scene on its back depicting a bottle of Banana Boat sun lotion and a group of scantily clad women playing beach volley ball. The shirttails hung over a pair of faded denim cut offs, and further down, his huge feet were stuffed into a pair of well-worn boat shoes.

Frank and Eddie got caught up while Eddie prepared for the new day in the washroom. From the bedroom, Eddie heard the sounds of Frank helping himself to the mini bar and switching on the television. When Eddie had finished his personal morning duties, he exited the washroom and took a space at the small round table by the window. He soon became involved in the news program Frank had settled on.

"What's all this?" Eddie asked Frank as the screen flashed photographs of several different yachts.

"It's a story about the Dirk family that just came up missing," Frank answered as he craned his neck to glance at Eddie. "Have you heard of Darrell Dirk? He's one of the richest guys in Florida. He took his family out on the Caribbean in his boat about a week ago, and they never came back."

A reporter on the television commented that it was the third pleasure boat to go missing that year and that the authorities suspected foul play in all three incidents.

"That's just what I wanted to hear the day we set out on a boating trip," Eddie said.

Just then, the telephone rang. Eddie was happy to hear Marcie's voice.

"Hello, Ed?" she said. "I'm sorry we didn't get a chance to stop by your hotel. We're going to the island today."

"That's too bad. I'd have liked to see you and your friends again."

"Well listen, you're welcome to stop by Spike Island, since you're going to be out in your boat anyway. It might be nice to stop and get your feet on land," Marcie suggested.

"You're right. Why don't you tell me where it is, and I'll see if I can't navigate my way over there."

He found a pen and wrote down the details of the island's location. Ed liked the idea of hunting for the tiny island, as well as the prospect of seeing Marcie again. He was flattered that she had taken the time to call him before her departure.

As soon as Eddie hung up the phone, Frank switched off the television, full of curiosity. "Who was that? Was it a girl? Where'd you meet her? Does she have any friends? Are they pretty?"

Eddie fielded Frank's questions as he started packing, and by ten thirty, they were ready to go. Telephoning the boat rental office, Eddie apologized for missing his appointment and rescheduled for later that afternoon. He knew Frank would insist on stopping for something to eat on the way to the docks.

As they crossed the lobby, Frank spied tables of breakfast food laid out for the hotel guests and loaded a bag with donuts and cookies. "C'mon, man," Eddie protested. "You're not supposed to take stuff with you. Look, we're going straight to a restaurant. You're going to spoil your breakfast."

"Eddie, I assure you that I will eat every crumb of these donuts within the next hour, so why should it matter if I eat it here or on the street?" Afraid that Frank would insist on wasting time in the lobby if he pushed the issue, he instead stood guard while Frank selected an array of pastries.

A trail of donut and cookie crumbs followed the two the entire way to the restaurant. Eddie asked if he could have a fritter, but Frank said, "No way, you had your chance back in the lounge." He tended to be very possessive of his food.

"You got a whole bag full of stuff there. Are you gonna eat all that? What do have in there?"

"Let's see. Three fritters, a chocolate cream-filled croissant, a blueberry muffin, one lemon poppy seed, a rice crispy bar, and something they were calling white chocolate chip, key lime, and coconut cookies. I've got three of those. Oh, and one of those little cartons of skim milk. I'm trying to watch my fat intake." Frank rummaged through his doggy bag.

"How selfish of me. I didn't realize that you just barely had enough for yourself," Eddie said with some annoyance.

They came to a breakfast place and decided to check it out. It looked like a truck stop gone tropical. Typical menu choices such as pancakes, waffles, eggs, bacon, and so on arrived on plates garnished with canned pineapple, plastic statues of hula dancers stood in the hallway leading to the bathrooms. Eddie ordered a malted Belgian waffle stuffed with coconut and a large glass of milk, and despite the half dozen pastries he had consumed as an appetizer, Frank managed to swallow a three-egg Cajun omelet, a plate of silver dollar pancakes, and an order of hash browns.

They hadn't walked ten minutes before Frank informed his buddy, "I've got to find a john big time."

A quick scan of the area yielded a set of washrooms across from a hotel's outdoor swimming pool. Frank found the door to be unlocked.

"I'm going to be a little while," Frank warned.

Eddie leaned against the wall of the restroom, gazing in the direction of the swimming pool. Although a very large 'No Trespassing' sign was staring him in the face, Eddie decided to stick his foot into the glimmering water. The water was cool and smooth and felt nice after walking in the hot sun with all that heavy luggage. Just a foot wouldn't do. Figuring he could leave his shirt on the side and let the sun dry his shorts on the way to the boat, Eddie decided to jump in.

The water was perfect. The pool was rather long, and Eddie wondered if he could swim its entire length without coming up for air. He clamped his mouth shut, submerged his head, and pushed off the side. The momentum provided by the kick off was beginning to fade, so Eddie stroked with his arms and kicked with his legs. When he reached the far wall of the pool, he figured his lungs still contained enough air to make a return trip. He twisted his body and once again pushed off the pool wall with his legs. Enjoying the challenge, Eddie was almost across a second time when he felt the urgent need to take a breath. He emerged, popping his head out of the water like a turtle checking its location.

Gasping for breath and rubbing chlorine from his eyes, Eddie heard a sarcastic voice ask, "You havin' fun out here?"

"Hotel security," another voice bellowed.

Eddie was standing in the shallow end of the pool. He raised his hand to block the sun from his eyes and apologized to the guards, "Sorry guys, I was waiting for my buddy while he was in the washroom." Eddie pointed towards the hotel's poolside washrooms. "The water just looked so inviting."

"Yeah well, if you're not a registered guest, you're not invited to use the pool. Even if you were a guest, you shouldn't be swimming in it. It was just treated with chlorine, and it's not healthy to be in there," the guard commented.

"Once again, I'm sorry. As soon as my buddy is out of the john we'll be on our way." Eddie climbed out of the pool and picked up the bundle containing his dry shirt and wallet.

"The police will be here shortly. You guys aren't going anywhere until then. You're going to need some identification." The guard seemed to have some sort of attitude problem. His partner stood in the background puffing away on a

Island Bound

cigarette. The two rent-a-cops were well tanned, in their forties, and wore blue golf shirts tucked into white cotton pants accompanied by a black belt strapped around their husky middles. Black athletic shoes covered their feet, and the word "Security" was stenciled to the men's chests in bold white letters.

After about ten minutes, a young police officer arrived. Unlike the rent-a-cops, the Key West police officer looked to be in excellent physical condition. As the three officers conversed about the situation, Eddie watched and waited for Frank, who was still in the washroom.

"Are you sure your buddy's in the head? What the hell is he doing in there?" the vocal guard asked. His partner hadn't said one word throughout the entire incident.

"That's standard for him. Stay clear of that washroom for a little while," Eddie responded. The police officer grinned knowingly and asked Eddie for some identification.

"The hotel wants all violators to be punished to the fullest extent of the law," the second guard piped up.

Finally, Frank emerged from the washroom, a comfortable expression spread across his face.

"What the hell is going on here Ed? I leave you alone for a few minutes and when I come back, you're soaking wet and chatting with three police officers." He took a second look at the rent-a-cops and amended, "well, one police officer and two security guards."

"You guys are both in big trouble. Those washrooms are the hotel's private property," the first guard threatened Frank.

"Oh, gimme a break," Eddie said. "Frank, show the officer your badge." Frank displayed his Tampa Bay Police Department badge and identification to his fellow Florida officer.

"You guys are cops?" The officer chuckled.

"I am," Frank responded. "I work for Tampa P.D., and my buddy here is a firefighter from the Chicago area."

"Chicago huh? I'm originally from Chicago. I actually used to be a cop in Glen Ellyn before I moved down here." The three Illinois natives began to converse about their home state while the guards waited uncomfortably in the sun, shutting themselves out of the conversation.

"You guys ever hear of a place called Burritoville? That's not the real name. That's just what everyone calls it. The real name is El something-or-other. It was in Summit. Best damn burritos I ever had!" The officer rubbed his stomach as if he had just enjoyed eating the Mexican treat.

"Damn skippy! El Farol is the name. Those things are the size of footballs! That's a must whenever I get back home. I usually order mine double-wrapped and double stuffed." Frank's excitement level began to rise with the memory.

"Best time to visit is in the middle of the night. It's always packed," Eddie added.

The chief guard interrupted the three men and asked the officer to get back to the business at hand.

"Oh yeah, sorry. You guys can go. Enjoy the rest of your trip. My name is Todd, by the way." The mid-westerners exchanged handshakes.

"Here's my card. If you get up north, feel free to stop by the firehouse." Eddie and Frank bid the officer farewell, leaving the officer to deal with the now disgruntled guards.

They arrived at the office with a couple of minutes to spare. Unfortunately, they found the office's door still locked up. Eddie figured they were a little early, and noticing an old tree stump sticking out of a small patch of dirt next to the office, he took a seat and waited. Frank planted himself on the doorstep in front of the office's glass door.

Ed's shorts were dry by the time the leasing agent arrived. She told them the owner, T.R., had a rough night and was running late. She suggested that they start the paperwork while they waited for T.R. to show up and give them the dime tour of the boat. After that, Ed and Frank could be on their way.

"Well, let's get started. This should only take about an hour." Marlene set an inch-high stack of papers on her desk. Eddie filled out a variety of legal documents including insurance papers, waivers, Coast Guard forms, inventory documents, and so on. T.R showed up as Eddie was signing the dotted line on the last sheet of paper.

"You ready for your tour of the Nordic Tug?" he asked Eddie.

"T.R., this is my buddy Frank. He's gonna be hangin' with me for a little while." Eddie offered an introduction. "You mind helping us drag our stuff over?"

The pile of luggage was still sitting outside in front of the office. The load was much easier to manage with three people carrying it rather than two. They stashed the gear in the tug's pilothouse for the duration of the tour, then the three men used the next couple of hours to cover all the principals of the tug's anatomy.

The tug went by the name of The Bourbon Trader, and its port of call was painted on the back of the boat in large black letters. The tug was forty-two feet long and had accommodations to sleep six people in relative comfort. The fresh water system was designed to store just over two hundred gallons. Two heads, complete with standing showers, the galley, a wet bar, and the laundry all drew from the same supply. The pilothouse and rear deck area were designed for almost completely unobstructed views anywhere around the craft and were equipped with all the modern electronic bells and whistles. The skipper had access to all sorts of informative devices, which included radar, sonar, directional equipment including global positioning, and an array of communication devices.

A large diesel provided the tug with power, and the boat could travel at speeds of over fifteen knots, cruising over a thousand nautical miles before needing to be refueled. The same diesel also provided the means to support a generator, which powered all of the tug's electrical systems and was also responsible for recharging the batteries.

As far as creature comforts, the tug was equipped with extraordinary sound and visual entertainment systems. The wet bar was stocked to the hilt - even the best barkeeps would be impressed while the galley included any and all utensils needed to provide passengers with fresh, made-to-order gourmet meals. The interior was comfortably decorated, and fine finished wood provided accents to the decor.

The hull of the craft was painted a deep forest green, and the surfaces above the hull came in a light cream color. The same deep green of the hull accentuated the tug's lines. In the front of the vessel, just under the windows of the pilothouse, T.R. led Frank and Eddie to an uncovered sundeck. The deck in back, just off the rear parlor, functioned as a covered patio area outfitted with a small propane grill, refrigerator, and dry bar. A swim step jutted out over the water in the rear of the vessel. On the roof of the rear parlor, T.R. pointed out a four-person, gasoline-powered jet boat that could be used as a run about or a life boat if need be. The raft could be removed by employing a ramp and pulley system which stretched down to the water over the rear of the vessel, allowing it to gently slip into the water. An electric pulley system drug the raft back up the ramp after use. Eddie thought the whole system looked jerry rigged and a little out of place.

"This is pretty damn nice…it's even got that new boat smell," Frank admired.

"It's only about six months old, but even our older boats keep the new smell. We try to take tip-top care of all of them," T.R. responded to the big man's comments. "Well, that's about it. Have a blast, but be careful."

"By the way, what does T.R. stand for?" Eddie asked.

"Don't laugh. My parents were hippies - my real name is Transistor Radio. They were listening to one when I was conceived. At least, that's how the story goes."

Although Ed and Frank decided to wait until the next morning before heading out to explore the open seas of the Caribbean, they thought they might as well spend the night on the boat. It took the rest of the afternoon to get settled in, and the sun was setting by the time everything was organized and stowed away.

"What's up with all the fire power?" Frank asked when he noticed the rifle and pistol that Eddie had included in the luggage.

"It's for pirates, of course!" Eddie answered.

"Pirates?"

"Sure. You know, Blackbeard, Billy the Kid…"

"Billy the Kid's a cowboy, not a pirate," Frank corrected.

"He could show up, too. You never know what might happen," Eddie joked as he hit the lights and settled down to sleep.

Chapter Thirteen

The bartender working at the yacht club in Key West lifted the hand piece of the bar's phone shortly after Jennifer's party left for Spike island. The bartender may have served drinks at the yacht club, but his real employer was sitting in a luxurious office several hundred miles away. Blackwell had been anticipating the bartender's call for a couple of days now - he had paid the employee well to keep the Crows up on the possibilities of future business. Today the information included the time Bruce Klien's daughter left the island and the fact that the company included three extras as well. The added company didn't concern the crime lord. His son and his mercenaries should have no problem dealing with the extra baggage.

Lester, meanwhile, was sitting comfortably in a plush Central American plantation owned and run by Dominiek Carzell, a high-powered, high-financed kingpin and racketeer. The two families often joined forces in their black market activities when the stakes were high enough. The two men were bantering the day's business while enjoying ice cold Coronas. The Latin crime boss offered his guest local grown jalapeno peppers stuffed with spiced meats and cheeses and fried until golden brown.

"So Lester, it has been a number of years since I have seen your father. How are things for him these days?" Carzell inquired. Blackwell generally tended to the family business personally up until the time that Lester matured enough to take over all of the families field operations. Lester updated Carzell about his father's latest escapades.

"I have an addition to our typical day's business. I have several heads of cattle that need shipment to any port of your choosing in the States." Carzell was referring to a group of Mexican citizens that had paid their life's savings in order to be safely smuggled into the US.

Lester and the shady entrepreneur settled on a price for the cargo. Lester told Carzell that he and his men had another stop to make in Brazil, but assured him the vessel should have room to spare for the illegal immigrants.

The telephone sitting next to Carzell rang out, and after a brief conversation, he hung up the phone.

"The duties at the pier have been completed," he told Lester. "My men will be transferring the live stock into one of your containers. Your crew should be ready to go by the time we go down to the dock. Do you think the Mexicans will survive the transport?"

"If they already paid your price, then what's the difference?" Lester replied, irritated by Carzell's uncharacteristic concern. Of course, most of the illegal immigrants would not survive. A handful of them might pull through, depending upon how the crew loaded the cargo, but Lester never troubled himself over such concerns. The Mexicans would be stowed in standard modular storage units that could be found anywhere in the legitimate business of cargo transportation. The units were constructed to be stackable, allowing their use on ocean-going vessels, air cargo crafts, railroad transporters and even in trucking operations. Although the cartons protected the Crow shipments because they would not be subject to the same customs inspections as were containers designed to carry living creatures, their unfortunate drawback was that the livestock inside them often perished from lack of oxygen.

After the meeting was adjourned, Lester and his crew boarded the cargo vessel and prepared for departure. The cargo vessel was disguised as a legitimate ship belonging to a company called The Gulf Coast Storage and Transportation Company, which the Crows ran as a front for their underground activities.

Once on the open sea, the ship pointed in the direction of a similar plantation located on one of the northernmost shores of Brazil. The trip would take a good portion of the day to complete. As the crew took in the fresh sea air, forty-two Mexican refugees contended with the heat and stale air of the cargo container stacked in the hold below. The container shared the ship's hold with six other similar units.

A couple of hours of daylight remained when the freighter docked at the pier of a banana and pineapple farm. This operation was much smaller than Carzell's, but still the Crows found the business to be just as profitable. When they docked, Lester's crew loaded banana crates stuffed with illicit substances into one final empty container.

Lester sauntered up to the plantation's main building to settle up the financial end of the operation while the crew arranged the container in the hold. Suddenly, gunfire erupted in the distance.

Hector, one of the most prominent of the Crow's force of mercenaries, barked orders to the crew. "You two go check on the boss. The rest of you finish shutting this crate up while I go to the pilothouse and fire this pig up. We don't need any trouble today."

Hector's position under Lester could be compared to that of a Lieutenant. The men respected him for his cool-headedness, and he called the shots when his boss wasn't present. That day, the freighter's crew consisted of thirteen men, not including Lester. Two of them grabbed the mini M-16 sub-machineguns that they had stashed in the hold of the ship and ran towards the main building while the other men picked up the pace of their work with mechanical proficiency. In the pilothouse, Hector heard the intensity of the distant gunfire increase as the plantation's guards started to return fire. "Goddam snitch," Hector said to himself, wondering who had informed the Brazilian authorities of the day's black market transaction.

The main building was in sight when the two mercenaries ran into Lester. He and the plantation manager had been in the middle of discussing the next job when they heard the unexpected gunfire. The meeting ended abruptly as the manager rose from his chair and stashed the account book along with a second sheaf of documents in a hidden safe. Lester took his payment and concealed it in his briefcase, then hurried down the path back to the boat.

Meanwhile, at the gates of the plantation, guards returned the fire of a large group of black-clad Brazilian drug enforcement officers. The Brazilian authorities took heavy loses because the plantation was well fortified. Protected behind heavy stone walls, the plantation guards were all armed to the teeth.

When Lester and the two mercenaries reached the cargo ship, its decks were swarmed with activity as men dressed in the company's blue jump suits hastened to prepare for a rapid departure. Smoke billowed from the cargo ship's stacks signifying that Hector had started the ship's engines. The crew cut the tie line securing the ship to the dock, not taking the time to untie them, and the ship pulled away from the pier the moment Lester set foot on the deck.

"Let's get this thing out to open water," Lester shouted as he proceeded to the ship's pilothouse to confer with Hector.

"We'll be fine once we're out of Brazilian waters," Lester assured Hector after he congratulated him on his handling of the situation.

After a few moments of silent concentration as the two men worked to coax the ship to its highest speed, Hector remarked, "We're not in the clear yet, Boss." Motioning for Lester to look out the window, he pointed out six Brazilian patrol boats speeding across the water in an attempt to intercept the cargo ship. Lester noticed dual fifty caliber machinegun turrets in the front of each boat and decided that it was time to abandon ship. The freighter's crew would have a good chance of repelling any boarders, but the ship itself would be no match for the high-powered Brazilian weaponry. If the men remained with the freighter, they would almost certainly find themselves with the cargo and the ship at the bottom of the sea.

Lester issued the order to abandon the ship, summoning all personnel to the cargo hold where a cigarette-style speedboat waited to aid in their escape. The speedboat was hidden beneath a false floor near a set of large doors. Lester took a head count. It was difficult to find good help, and he wanted to make sure the entire crew would be able to make the escape. The boat emerged from its hiding place beneath the floor of the cargo hold and all the men boarded it. The ship's rear cargo doors opened, allowing the speedboat to slip into the water and seawater to rush into the hold, sinking the ship in less than two hours. Although it was regrettable to lose the cargo, it wouldn't do to let the Brazilian officials discover it, either. As the escape craft jetted through the doors' opening, screams of terror rose from the refugees who tried futilely to penetrate the steel reinforcements of the containers.

The speedboat bounced into the salt water, and Lester drove it to its top speed. The approaching Brazilians opened fire, shooting thousands of rounds at the getaway boat. Although most of the fifty caliber slugs harmlessly slapped the water around the boat, it was inevitable that the speedboat would eventually take a hit. One of the Brazilians aimed at the speedboat's fuel tank, hoping that the ignited gasoline would cause an explosion. He made his target, but the boat didn't blow up. Instead, the shot punctured the tank, draining the boat of its fuel. Fast.

Lester turned around to see where they were hit and caught a glimpse of the cargo ship, her hull dipping gracefully into the sea. None of the Brazilian officials would be foolish enough to board the ship and inspect her cargo at that point. He heaved a sigh of relief when he determined the ship, deep below the surface in its watery grave, would never reveal the secret operations of Crow Enterprises.

Four patrol boats continued the pursuit. Although the gap between them and Lester's craft grew greater and greater, they knew their get away craft could run out of fuel at any moment.

Lester's mind raced as he tried to think of a plan. He needed to find a safe harbor soon, but he couldn't possibly return to the Brazilian shore. Lester spotted a large island in the distance and hoped the speedboat would make it to the far side before the last of its fuel spilled into the ocean. With luck, the crew would have a few moments out of sight of the Brazilians in order to beach the speedboat and disappear beneath the thick jungle canopy.

The speedboat's engine sputtered, coughed, then died as Lester drove on to a small sandy beach. For the moment they were in the clear but it wouldn't take long for the Brazilians to catch up to them. After leading his men to a favorable position in the island's thick jungle, Lester quickly studied the sea chart he grabbed before dismounting the speedboat. He wasn't exactly sure about which island they were on, and to plan an effective escape, he would need to know if the island was inhabited or not. The island wasn't even referenced on the chart.

"Looks like we're going to have to fight it out boys." Lester began to bark out his orders. He plotted to ambush his pursuers and steal one of the patrol crafts.

After about ten minutes, four patrol boats arrived. Lester wasn't sure if the Brazilians were going to wait for reinforcements or not - hopefully they wouldn't. It seemed Lester was out of luck until several men dropped from the boats and into the water. There were sixteen of them. The Brazilians briefly stopped to study the abandoned boat lying on the small beach. Then, one by one, the Brazilians entered the thick jungle foliage.

Lester had his men spread out into a V-patterned ambush and instructed them to hold their fire until he himself opened up. The smugglers possessed a wide range of firepower: everything from sub-machineguns to shotguns. Some of the smugglers were armed with assault rifles, and two of Lester's killers were armed

Island Bound

with forty-millimeter grenade launchers. All the barrels were trained on target, awaiting Lester's order to open fire.

Lester lined his sights on the Brazilian group's point man and pulled the trigger to initiate the fight. The point man fell to the ground after the 30-caliber shell ripped through his chest. The area around the ambush sight quickly took on an eerie appearance as heavy gun smoke suffused the air with a strong sulfuric smell. The Brazilians were not completely taken by surprise; their training and quick instincts allowed most of the posse to hit the ground and return fire before taking hits themselves.

The fighters were evenly matched. Lester's first assumption had been that the officials belonged to the Brazilian drug enforcement agency. However, when he saw their expertise and determination, he concluded that their uniforms concealed what they really were. Although the Brazilian group outnumbered Lester's men and rivaled them in skill, Lester's crew did have a slight advantage; their arsenal equipped them with the firepower of a small army. The grenadiers poured a steady rain of the deadly grenades on to the Brazilian's position, and as high-powered explosions alternated with fragmentation rounds, the Brazilian ranks faltered and eventually broke apart. A short time later, Lester's mercenaries mopped up the remaining members of the law enforcement team. Of the smuggler's forces, only two of the original thirteen mercenaries had been mortally wounded. Each of the Brazilians had fought to his death - regrettably for Lester who would have liked the opportunity to find out who had sent them to the plantation.

Lester reassembled his team and headed back to the small beach area, wary of the sudden silence in the air. At least two, and possibly more by now, patrol boats were on their trail, and he expected to find some men guarding the abandoned speedboat.

After returning to the small sandy beach, Lester and his crew discovered that the Brazilians seemed to have made a major mistake. The speedboat was still lying in the middle of the beach, and all four patrol crafts gently rocked in the waves, anchored only a few feet away from the shore. The boats appeared to be unguarded. Lester motioned for three of his men armed with mini M-16's to investigate. One of the mercenaries remained on the sandy beach while the other two waded out into the calm water approaching the patrol boats from the front. The men first boarded the closest of the four boats and found it deserted. Then, the man holding back on the beach moved out into the surf and climbed aboard the next boat by using the craft's rear loading ladder. Stepping on the rear deck of the ship, he spied a lone man squatting in the boat's pilothouse, frantically trying to raise someone on the boat's two-way radio. The mercenary stealthily approached him, put the barrel of his mini assault rifle to the back of the man's head and pulled the trigger.

The last two boats were searched and found to be empty, so Lester ordered his crew into two of them and sank the other two.

The captured patrol boats and their passengers jetted to the relatively safe open spaces of international waters, Hector patiently surveying the sea behind them all the way with a pair of binoculars. After they left Brazilian territory, he reported to Lester that he still saw no sign of any further pursuit in the sea or the sky.

"We're still not safe, though," Lester pointed out. "We'll be spotted soon if we stay in these boats. Armed patrol boats aren't permitted in neutral waters." Motioning for the second boat to draw up alongside his own, Lester told all his men to look for another boat. They would have to rely on their eyes, because the patrol boats were not equipped with any radar.

Lester piloted the boat in the direction of home, the other boat staying close by. The crew silently kept vigil over the surrounding waters in an attempt to locate alternate transportation or to warn of approaching authority crews. As Lester scanned the horizon, his mind churned over the events of the day. A close call for capture as well as losing a large and immensely profitable drug shipment was a tough one for any dedicated criminal to bear. True, he had already received payment for transporting the cargo, and Carzell wouldn't trouble himself over the fate of the illegal aliens who now lay drowned at the bottom of the sea - he had probably forgotten them the moment the ship set out. There was the matter of the lost container from the second plantation, but Lester could probably explain the situation to the manager and negotiate a happy settlement. What really bothered him was the question of who was responsible for the predicament in which Lester now found himself. When he located the scoundrel, there would be hell to pay.

Cresting over the northern horizon, one of the crew members caught a glimpse of another watercraft. The vessel was still too distant to be clearly identified, but the rotation of the ship's radar device on its control tower was relatively noticeable. The smugglers had only covered half the distance needed to reach the safe port of Blackwell's subterranean docks, the best route leading the patrol boats close to the US controlled Virgin Islands. The Caribbean mobsters in their captured Brazilian patrol boats were now, for a short time, in US territory.

Lester was concerned that the radar mast would turn out to belong to a US Coast Guard vessel. The Coast Guard had knowledge of the Crow's business activities, but as yet had never had the opportunity to capture any of the racket's upper hierarchy. Any of the Crow subordinates that US authorities successfully apprehended refused to cooperate in any way, shape, or form, even if the G men offered money or light sentencing. The Crows paid the mercenaries well for their unbending commitment, and if one of their lawyers couldn't get the hireling out of trouble, the Crows would arrange a good, old-fashioned jail break in order to free the team member. If that failed, the Crows would arrange for their comrade to be as comfortable as possible while visiting the big house.

Lester stood up and addressed the men in the other boat. "I want you to position your craft as far away as possible, still keeping in sight. I want enough space between us that an aircraft carrier could sail through with room to spare. If there's trouble, take off. Otherwise, follow my lead." If the ship did belong to the coast guard, this position would allow for at least one of the patrol boats to escape capture.

The boat turned out to be an enormous privately owned pleasure craft. In addition to solving the problem of the armed Brazilian boats in US waters, Lester figured some of the loot they had lost earlier in the day could be regained by commandeering the large pleasure boat.

Lester moved his craft into into a standard flanking position, and the other boat did the same. Lester found this type of action more satisfying than the usual pre-planned jobs, and he grinned at the prospect of overcoming the unknown.

As the vessel approached, Lester sized up the situation. Deep shaded glass wrapped around the vessel's three levels, and outdoor decks formed tiers to the front and rear of the ship. On the roof of the yacht, a small helicopter crouched like an insect.

The big yacht began decreasing speed as the two crafts approached; the captain of the yacht probably assumed that the patrol boats were legitimate, even if he wondered what they were doing so close to the Virgin Islands. Likewise, Lester questioned the presence of the other boat in US waters - a flag flapping in the breeze just beneath the boat's radar equipment identified the yacht as German.

Lester ordered all four of the patrol boats' large caliber machineguns to target in on the pleasure craft. Finding an electronic bullhorn in the pilothouse, Lester hailed the yacht in English, instructing the Germans to prepare for boarding. After asking first in Portuguese if any of the boat's passengers could understand him, he switched to English, remembering to imitate an accent. Hector, enjoying his employer's self-confidence, nevertheless crossed his fingers and hoped that the boat's captain wouldn't stop to consider why nine men in camouflage fatigues driving Brazilian patrol boats in US waters wanted access to his vessel. The pleasure craft dwarfed the two patrol boats, and it would be impossible to board the ship if her crew resisted.

The captain of the pleasure craft fell for the hoax and even provided a boarding ladder for the smugglers to use. Lester and his men scrambled up to the deck, leaving one man behind in each patrol boat with instructions to station themselves behind the dual fifty-caliber machineguns.

"How many are in your crew, and where is the owner?" Lester demanded of the captain. The boarding party faced the yacht's crew members, lowering their weapons threateningly.

"The owner is in the parlor on the top level entertaining, and my crew consists of twenty two." The blond haired, blue-eyed man appearing to be in his fifties answered. His English carried a heavy German accent.

"Well, who is he? Who is being entertained? Give it all up - make it easy on yourself," Lester warned.

"His name is not important. He is entertaining clients. What is this questioning for? Get on with your safety check, then get off my ship." The German captain was getting a little irritated.

Lester chuckled - "Sorry sauerkraut, but this isn't a safety inspection." He allowed his voice to return to its accustomed fluency in English. "It's a high jack. Collect your crew and passengers and have them assemble on deck." He nudged the captain in the belly with his gun and cautioned, "No funny stuff. I've already killed several people today, and a few more will make no difference to me."

After the crew was assembled, Lester ordered his hirelings to pat them down for any weapons or communication devices. Of the twenty-two crew members, only fifteen stood before Lester's men. The captain stated that those absent were the yacht's food and beverage attendants. They were on duty in the parlor where the owner was entertaining.

"I warn you, you don't know who you're dealing with," the German warned his captors as they frisked him.

The shake-down produced an unexpected result - almost every crew member carried a weapon. The situation did catch Lester a little off guard, and he momentarily questioned why it had been so easy to take the boat. He evaluated the captain's warning and wondered what kind of man the owner might be. In the end, the challenge of capturing this mysterious, powerful, owner overcame his sense of caution.

Two mercenaries acted as lookouts while the others went to work securing the ankles, hands and lips of the German crew members with duct tape. The captain, however, kept aside under Lester's guard - Lester needed him as an informant and bargaining chip when it came time to subdue the rest of the yacht's crew and company.

With the yacht's crew secured, Lester grabbed the captain and headed for the parlor on the top floor, assigning the two lookouts to stay behind, telling them, "take care of the captives before I return." Lester exchanged his automatic rifle for the Thompson one lookout carried. He preferred the old Thompson sub-machinegun for inside jobs because the circular magazine of the antique gangster gun carried one hundred rounds of 45-caliber ammunition. Lester was confident in and respected any weapon with such a large supply of man-stopping, heavily leaded slugs.

Lester and his mercenaries took the captain into an empty room and held him against the wall. Careful not to inflict visible injuries, Lester slammed him in the stomach with his shoulder while two other men held his arms from the side. "Tell me about the parlor where the owner is, how do we get to the parlor?" he said as the captain crumpled and wheezed. It didn't take long to get the information.

Noticeably unaccustomed to physical persuasion, the captain whispered between gasping breaths, "an elevator and two stairwells provide access to the deck. The elevator opens up in the middle of the parlor, and there is a stairway located at each end."

Lester sent Hector with two other men to the front set of stairs where they would secure the front balcony of the top floor's parlor. They quickly found the winding spiral staircase that, according to the captain, should open onto the outdoor deck. However, when they reached the top, they found a doorway. Hector put his ear to the door and heard the clatter of dishes and running water. "That lying bastard," Hector muttered before carefully turning the doorknob and quietly peering inside. The door opened onto a small galley, and he saw two very attractive women in black, short-skirted maid's outfits busily preparing cocktails. One woman had her back to the door, but Hector could see the other's face.

Hector swung the door wide and beckoned the woman to come out onto the staircase. Slightly irritated, but never suspecting that the ship had been hi-jacked, the waitress left her work and curiously came to the door, saying something in German. Hector coaxed her a little further out the door, and within half a second one of the other mercenaries clamped a hand over her mouth and drug her down the stairs to bind her. The second woman turned at the sudden movement in the doorway and found Hector's gun pointed directly at her. Like a lamb, she allowed the mercenaries to wrap duct tape around her mouth, wrists, and ankles.

When Lester, the captain, and the remaining smugglers arrived, the galley was secure. After congratulating the men on their neat work, Lester left one man behind. "Watch these two, but try to keep them alive if you can," he told the mercenary. In his mind, Lester kept a tally of where his men were posted. Two men perished back on the island, there were two men in the patrol boats, two taking care of the rest of the yacht's crew, and one behind the stairwell. That left six men, not including Lester himself. Lester assigned Hector and two other men to secure the front balcony while he and the remainder of their party posted themselves in the galley to sum up the situation.

Lester peeked through the service room's door, attaining a visual reconnoiter of the main room. The room was charged with tobacco smoke; several people were either inhaling cigarettes, chewing on hand-rolled cigars, or puffing on pipes. Dark green carpet decorated the room, and the ceiling was constructed in glass in the style of an atrium. Lester could see the blades of the small helicopter branching out over the roof. The parlor's shaded wrap-around windows stretched from floor to ceiling, showcasing a view that stretched for miles around the boat.

There were two men for every woman in the room, and altogether, they numbered approximately forty. With only seven people to control such a large party, the pirates would have their work cut out for them. Lester wasn't worried, though, because most of the people in the room clustered in manageable groups around the central bar or around three gaming tables near the balcony. Since the crewmen had all carried weapons, Lester took careful note of the service employees. One lone man in a tuxedo served up a variety of cocktails at the bar while another waitress clad in the black outfit carried a tray brimming with assorted finger foods. On the other side of the room, a single dealer operated each gaming table.

"A little Vegas style party. This may turn out to be very profitable," Lester whispered to one of his henchmen standing behind him. After the first inspection intended to size-up the situation, Lester took a closer look and noticed several of the men gambling were outfitted in some kind of military uniform. The rest of the men sported suits that appeared to be of the highest quality. A majority of the women were scantily clad - prostitutes most likely. Lester studied the men wearing the military styled clothing. He wanted an idea of the kind of men his team would be up against. Some of the uniformed men blandished sidearms holstered at their hips. If any other weapons existed in the crowd, they were concealed. With shock, Lester realized just who these men were.

The uniformed men wore red armbands, and two flags rested on either side of the centralized bar. One represented the standard for the modern combined German government, and the other flag was all red with a black swastika in its middle. The armbands wrapped around the uniformed men's arms carried the same design. They were Nazis.

Lester moved away from the door, momentarily wondering if he had somehow traveled backwards in time to Hitler's administration. He had always thought that Nazis in recent times were just troubled, racist teenagers with shaved heads. He never expected that their party could have any kind of military organization or power.

"They must be from Brazil," one of the mercenaries behind him thought out loud. "A lot of the war criminals from WWII fled to South America - maybe they started an underground movement."

Lester decided that this was no time for speculating on the social or economic power of an organization that had, for all practical purposes, gone defunct almost fifty years ago. With almost the entire crew executed by now, there could be no turning back. Besides, Lester would take a special pleasure in ending the life of any person sick enough to wrap one of those symbols of ultimate evil around his arm. His mind formulated a strategy. Once again rising to the challenge of overcoming any unknown obstacle, Lester glanced in the direction of the German boat captain. A smug and defiant look decorated his face, as if he expected Lester to start quivering in fear as soon as he discovered who owned the boat.

Lester quietly relayed instructions to his teammates, contacting Hector with a satellite comlinks. Just prior to initiating the action, Lester slammed the butt of his Thompson into the face of the German captain because his smug look and attitude pissed him off immensely. He just couldn't help himself. In his mind he was the only one allowed to feel superior to everyone else.

After asking several times if his boss was joking, then, with concern, inquiring if he felt feverish, Hector informed Lester that his crew was ready and in position to attack the Nazis. Lester started the intrusion off simply by walking into the room and firing a single shot into the glass ceiling. The weapon providing the first round was from one of the German 9-mm automatic pistols that he had confiscated earlier. In their drunkenness, very few of the parlor's occupants even noticed the crack of the pistol. Lester exhausted the pistol's supply of ammunition, and soon, a roomful of startled faces fixed their eyes on him.

Hector's crew entered through the front doors leading in from the outdoor patio, and Lester's men burst through the door of the service room, both teams spreading apart to cover the entire room.

Two of the uniformed men in the group attempted to draw their side arms and took rounds to the chest before their hands even touched the handles of their pistols. Puddles of their freshly spilled blood stained the carpet around them.

"All right, who's in charge around here?" Lester demanded.

A large man stood up and identified himself as the group's main man, and Lester ordered Hector to separate the men and the women into two groups. The men were to join the yacht's crew in the back of the boat while the women would be secured in a room below. Lester told Hector to make sure that he stayed out of trouble while he herded the confused and terrified women below. Then, he assigned another man to find and collect any personal weapons that anyone else may be carrying, keeping an eye out for trouble and, of course, collecting any valuables as well. Lester and two men stayed behind with the German claiming to be the group's leader.

Even Lester found the top Nazi to actually be a little intimidating. He was tall, and a slick shaved head lent a husky, formidable quality to the man's dominant features. Lester had the captain dragged into the room and asked the him if the large man was his superior. The captain confirmed the big man's authority, so Lester's mercenaries secured the top Nazi and the captain in front of the central bar. Taking a seat on a barstool that he set about ten feet in front of his captives, Lester pointed the barrel of the Thompson directly at the bald man's gut, and once again, the trusted duct tape was used to bind both men to the chairs.

"Well, well. Now what should I do with you guys?" Lester was really just thinking out loud. He didn't want an answer.

"If you are an intelligent man, you'll let us go. You don't not know what you've gotten yourself mixed up in. If it's money you want, that could easily be arranged," The large German commented.

"Of course it's all about money, asshole. Ultimately everything is about money. I should just kill you guys and get you out of my hair. Give me one reason why I shouldn't do that," Lester ordered, slapping the bald German's head with his open palm. Hector entered the room, updating the situation to his boss.

"The female prisoners are secure and stashed below deck. The men are bound and gagged. I've got them on deck in the back like you asked, sir. All of our members are accounted for and uninjured. You give the word, and we'll be ready to roll."

"That's great, Hector. Sink the patrol boats and let's start steaming home. I'll make a decision about the prisoners shortly. Hey, grab that Nazi flag and burn it."

Lester returned his attention to the big man once again. "Well, have you got an answer for me yet, Adolph?"

"I'm not going to beg for my life. If you kill us, I can guarantee that our brothers will track you down and torture you and your families to death. We are expected to arrive in South America within two days, and if we don't make it, our comrades will investigate our disappearance. They will surely discover the source of our demise - Lester."

The old German laughed at Lester's surprise that he knew his name. He continued, "There will not be a safe place on the globe for anyone involved in Crow Enterprises. Our party is preparing to rise once again from the ashes of the Second World War, and we will take our place as the ruler of all the world's political systems and economies." The bald man sounded as if he was giving a recruitment speech to millions of admirers.

"Would you listen to this guy?" Lester asked the room of frightened people. "You are one fucked up motherfucker. I think your comment about families and friends being hunted down and tortured to death has brought me to my decision. Don't get me wrong, Cabbage Head. I'm all for death and destruction as much as the next guy, but only when it comes to business. The pointless destruction of millions of people - I don't think I'm up for all that." Lester actually had it in his mind that he was typically a pretty good guy. Smuggling drugs, selling women into prostitution, stealing yachts for resale and just drowning the passengers was O.K. as long as it was all done in the name of money. Lester didn't go for all that political stuff. Anyhow, Lester liked himself too much to think he was bad guy.

The motion of the large ship slipping through sea could once again be noticed by the mercenaries as Lester gave Hector his orders. The women would be kept under lock and key below decks while all weapons and valuables were inventoried and cataloged. He posted guards on the upper decks and decided the male passengers would be tossed overboard. One unlucky mercenary received instructions to clean up the mess that the bodies of the slain Nazi's would produce on deck. As soon as he had given his instructions, the barrel of the Thompson jumped as Lester pumped fifty rounds into each of the Nazis.

The return sail proved to be restful for the younger Crow. Although the day's original shipment had been lost, the capture of the pleasure boat and the female captives should easily make up for the lost revenue. Lester contacted his father over the satellite communication link, using secret codes to bring his father up to speed on his day's activities. He could only give the most general information over the link - the specifics needed to be relayed on a face-to-face basis.

Chapter Fourteen

When Ed woke up the next morning, he felt as if a construction worker wielding a jackhammer was going to town on his skull. His tongue felt like it was swollen and fuzzy. After popping a couple of aspirins into his mouth and swallowing them with difficulty, he brushed his teeth. "You're getting too old for this kind of shit, Ed. Every time is the last time," he told the man in the mirror staring back at him with bloodshot eyes.

Ed slowly stepped into the stand up shower, and after a few minutes of hot water and soap, the night's effects seemed to slip away. Ed toweled himself off, slipped on an old pair of cutoff army pants and a white tee shirt displaying the logo of Chicago's Rock Bottom Brewery, then unlocked the stateroom's door and headed out to see if Frank was moving around yet.

During the late night's booze binge, which rack was whose became a hot topic of discussion because the master cabin was designed to accommodate a queen sized bunk rather than just the small double in the second stateroom. Frank argued that he should get the master cabin because the only way to squeeze his bulky frame into the small bunk was to either sleep in a fetal position or hang his feet over the edge. Eddie, on the other hand, reasoned that he was picking up the tab, after all, and should get the first choice of cabins.

The two debated the issue drunkenly for some time until at one point in the night, Eddie excused himself to hit the head. He told Frank that he would be right back, but he never returned. After deceiving his friend, Eddie did actually feel a slight pang guilt, but he knew that subversion was going to be the only successful tactic for securing the large room for himself. He didn't lie entirely, though. He actually did need to hit the head - he just locked himself into the bigger cabin before hitting the master room's private washroom.

In the morning, Eddie found his friend still sitting in the tug's rear parlor, out like a light, sitting with his chin on his chest. His right hand still clutched a warm and flat half-empty bottle of beer. Eddie was anxious to kick off the day, but he let his friend sleep while he brewed up a batch of extra strong Joe. He slipped two Pop Tarts into a toaster sitting next to the sink on the counter of the ship's galley. As Eddie's favorite childhood pastries browned, he watched slow drips of Java dropping from the maker's filter and into the awaiting glass pot below.

"What are you cooking?" Frank yelled from the parlor as soon as he smelled the Pop Tarts. "Make me some, I feel like shit." His hunger overcoming his grogginess, Frank stumbled into the galley to supervise the breakfast preparations.

Eddie and Frank chose the tug's open rear deck to enjoy their breakfast of Pop Tarts and steaming, fresh-brewed coffee. It was nine o'clock in the morning, and the docks and pier were already bustling with activities. Crafts of all shapes and sizes meandered back and forth between the rows of anchored boats bobbing up and down to the rhythm of the harbor's brown waters. The amount of industrial and commercial shipping traffic present stirred up the harbor's mud and muck and gave the typical clear Caribbean water a dark appearance.

"Where did you pick up the Pop Tarts?" Frank asked between bites of his second package of the toasted pastries.

"They were in the galley. This baby came fully stocked." When Eddie arranged to rent the boat nearly a month before, T.R. had sent him a detailed list of various goods including everything from canned vegetables to top-shelf liquors. The only thing Eddie needed to do was put a check mark beside the items he desired. The company stocked the items on the boat before he took possession of the craft. Ed's selections included breakfast and snack items, frozen pizzas, pastas, soft drinks and most importantly, beer and booze. The inventory was capable of sustaining Eddie and a guest for at least a couple of weeks, although Frank's tremendous appetite could possibly put a strain on the rations.

Within the hour, Eddie and Frank were standing in front of the tug's controls. Eddie fired up the engines and backed away from their mooring point, then cautiously merged the tug into the dock's late morning traffic. He was a little concerned about his piloting abilities; it had been a few months since he had last stood at the controls of a water-borne vessel. The trip out to open water went a little slower than desired, and at times, fellow boaters had to wait patiently while the tug-like craft drifted towards its destination. Once out on the shipping lanes, Eddie felt more confident in his abilities, so he opened up the tug's throttle and headed out to sea.

After about two hours sailing, Eddie weighed anchor about one hundred yards away from a small island. The Bourbon Trader shared the water with a couple other pleasure boats, and Ed and Frank both waved at the occupants aboard the other vessels as they peacefully slipped past them. After anchoring the tug in thirty feet of water, Ed grabbed the sea chart and a pair of binoculars and joined his friend sitting at the rear of the craft in the open sun. The day's weather was warm and pleasant, and a swift breeze kept the humidity at a very comfortable level. Scattered fluffy white clouds floated overhead, dotting the afternoon sky. Dressed in shorts and sandals, Ed and Frank basked in the sun under a thick layer of Banana Boat tanning oil.

The clump of soil and greenery on the island nearby looked deserted, but closer inspection with the binoculars revealed a mast standing erect on the far side of the small island. A white sandy beach ran up and down the entire exposed side along the clear, calm sea. Training the binoculars' focus on the waters separating the tug and the beaches on the small islands, Ed could make out a virtual aquarium of sea life darting about just below the surface. Ed handed the binoculars to Frank and consulted the sea chart.

"I'd like to find a place to dock tonight," Eddie said as he scanned the chart for a harbor with an interesting name. "I'm not quite ready to spend the night on the open water."

"Where did that girl say she and her friends were staying?" Frank asked. With the binoculars still pressed to his eyes as he continued to inspect the island's landscape, he added, "Hey, let's swim out to that beach over there. I think I see a small cave."

"Oh shit, I can't remember the name. If I heard it, maybe I could recognize it. I don't remember the name sounding like the norm for the Caribbean, like Saint this or that. I'd be up for swimming in. The current doesn't seem too bad. You check out the chart, and I'll go grab the fins and stuff. Hey, maybe we'll find buried treasure." Eddie did a bad imitation of old pirate speech. He handed the chart over and left the rear deck, returning in a short time with two sets of fins, a couple of masks, snorkels, and lung-inflated bouncy compensators. Similar to their larger cousins used by SCUBA divers while exploring the world beneath the waves, the BC's were bright orange in color for safety purposes.

Frank and Eddie geared themselves up in the snorkeling equipment and dove from the side of the boat. Warm, soft seawater enveloped the snorkelers as their bodies plunged through the waves. During the short swim to the small island's beach, the mask provided Eddie with a chance to admire small clumps of marine vegetation that sprouted from the sea floor in haphazard patterns across the rippling sandy bottom. Scattered groups of small fish hovered above the plant life, searching for their next meal.

At the halfway point the water became shallow enough to stand. A short walk later both men found themselves standing on the small beach where the waves gently splashed against their flippered feet.

The two traversed the terrain exploring the surface of the small island, but the cave Frank thought he had spied from the tug never materialized. They did, however, come upon a man and woman sitting on another white sand beach with a traditional style red and white picnic blanket spread beneath them. The two shared the blanket with a wicker basket, several bottles of wine, a cooler, and a few assorted trays of food. Fortunately for all parties involved, as far as apparel was concerned, everyone was decent. The double-masted ship that Ed had noticed earlier was anchored about twenty yards off shore, and a small rowboat was beached in the sand nearby.

"Oh man, I'm sorry. We didn't mean to intrude," Eddie mentioned to the couple. The male counterpart sitting on the blanket struck a familiar cord in Eddie's memory, but Eddie couldn't place the face with a name or any type of actual identity.

"Oh please, you're not intruding yet. Maybe in half an hour we'll tell you to get lost, but for now, the more the merrier. Would you like to join us for a glass of wine or a bottle of beer?"

The beachcomber began to stand up from his position on the blanket. As he walked towards Ed and Frank he lifted his right arm, an offer of a handshake. The man stood about five-foot, ten inches tall, and his relatively thin body frame still boasted a soft, slightly puffed mid section, most likely the result of comfortable living. The sailboat bobbing in the background, Eddie noticed, was an old, handsomely refurbished schooner. Eddie was familiar with a schooner's sail arrangement because he had encountered a number of the old-styled ships while working the summers off of Navy Pier back in Chicago. The sailboat was constructed out of wood polished to a glossy shine, and beneath the rear mast's sails, just next to the boat's large, round steering wheel, a brass bell hung proudly. All items on the deck were shipshape and stowed in such a manner that even old Captain Bligh would be satisfied.

The couple's relaxed appearance contrasted sharply with the refinement of their boat. The man wore a raggedy old pair of beat up, cutoff, blue jean shorts and a comfortable-looking pair of Birkenstock sandals. His companion, an attractive woman with blonde hair and blue eyes, must have taken a dip in the water a short time before. Her hair, still wet, fell down her tan back in ringlets. Small, colorful bracelets adorned her right wrist and left ankle, adding a quirky flavor to her otherwise simple attire, a knee length, white linen shirt and bikini top.

"I'm Hans Klemmer, and this is Charlene," the man said. The woman beside him smiled and lifted her hand to Eddie and then to Frank as each one introduced himself. After they settled themselves on the blanket, Hans continued, "You have three choices of wine: an Australian Riesling, a late harvest Muscat from Oregon, or a port put out by a small winery in Aspen - it's fortified with brandy. I've got a variety of microbrews there, in the cooler, too, if you prefer beer." He turned to Charlene and asked, "Is there any more of that rum punch left?"

"Oh yes, there's plenty. We've barely tasted it," Charlene said as she searched in the basket for a couple of extra glasses.

All the while, Eddie's mind was racing in an attempt to discover why this Klemmer fellow seemed so familiar.

Eddie accepted a glass of the Muscat Hans had been chilling in the bottom of the cooler, and Frank chose the rum punch without hesitation when he saw hunks of fresh fruits floating about in the sweet liquid.

"Did you mix this up yourself?" Frank asked, his face registering obvious enjoyment.

"It's just a little something I like to throw together for picnics," Hans explained. "You should be careful with it, though. That stuff is a lot stronger than it seems."

Hans peered into the basket, saying, "After a swim, it's always good to eat something. What would you like? We've got sandwiches of toasted foccaccia bread wrapped around tomatoes, roasted red peppers, and pepper jack cheese with garlic-infused mayonnaise, pasta salad of fusilli noodles mixed with roasted zucchini, eggplant, green onions, and a very nice accent of soft mozzarella cheese…Well, let me set them out for you, and you can take your pick." Pulling dish after dish from the basket, he laid them out on the blanket for Eddie and Frank to inspect. In addition to the sandwiches and pasta salad, the basket produced a bowl that held a concoction of diced mangos, kiwi, bananas, strawberries and pineapple, a mound of flaky biscuits covered with a cloth towel designed to match the picnic blanket, and a ramkin of lightly whipped butter chilling on top of a wide bowl filled with small, crystal clear cubes of ice.

"Remember to save room for dessert, boys," Charlene said, winking as she lifted the lid from a platter to reveal a light textured, buttery cake flavored with coconut and key lime juice. "Hans even prepared a delicious whipped cream topping - it's flavored with dark rum and fresh vanilla beans. You shouldn't miss it."

"Don't worry, ma'am," Frank assured her as he scooped nearly half of the pasta salad onto the plate Charlene gave him. "I never run out of room."

Eddie sipped from the glass of wine that Hans had presented to him, finding the liquid perfectly chilled. The late harvested grapes gave the beverage a smooth, sweet texture and tone. Taking a look at the pleased expression on Hans's face as he watched Frank attack the food, a light bulb popped into Eddie's noggin.

"You wouldn't happen to be Hans Klemmer of Portland Oregon, the proprietor of Portland's Grand Hotel?"

"That would be correct," Han's said, glancing at Charlene and laughing lightly. "Well, I guess the secret has been exposed."

"I met you three years ago at a store on Michigan Avenue in Chicago. You were there for a book signing promoting a cookbook you had just released." Eddie slapped his knee as it all came together in his mind. "You signed my copy. I stood in line for two hours just to get an autograph."

"That's me. I remember being in Chicago because, as the saying goes, that's my kind of town. That was my second cookbook, and it was very appropriately titled for today's situation, I believe."

"Absolutely - *The Yachting Cookbook of the Pacific North West*. I even brought it along with me on my vacation - it's back in the boat."

Hans laughed in disbelief. "You don't say!"

Charlene, reclining now, added, "Chicago is a lovely city. Do you remember that pizzeria, Hans?"

"How could I forget? Best pizza I've ever had. I've forgotten the name." Turning back to Eddie, he asked, "Do you know of a pizza place on one of those

Island Bound

lake-named streets. Maybe Ohio and Wabash, or maybe Ontario. I'm not sure. This place we went to had a great atmosphere, and the food was excellent."

"That probably would've been Uno's or Saint Angelo's," Eddie suggested. Hans recognized the first name, and the conversation for the rest of the afternoon was set. Besides discussing Chicago's best and worst restaurants, the firehouse chef and the professionally trained culinary expert exchanged recipes and cooking techniques. Frank nibbled contentedly throughout the afternoon while Charlene basked lazily in the sun, joining into the conversation when she felt like it.

Noticing that the sun had begun to dip close to the horizon, Eddie asked the chef if he could recommend a friendly harbor to head out to for the night.

"Saint Pete's isn't too far, and I'm a member at a yacht club there," Hans answered as he reached his hand into the pocket of his cutoffs and pulled out his wallet. "Let me give you a guest pass." Offering a gold card made of perforated paper to Eddie, he continued, "It's about a two-hour trip, and the actual name of the island is Saint Petronelle. Keep your eye open for the Saint Petronelle Harbor House and Yacht Club - that's the name of one of the local clubs. It's on the southwest side of the island. It's a private club, so you'll need that card when you get there. As my guest, you should get all the privileges of an active member. They may contact me to verify that I gave you the card myself, but that shouldn't be a problem. Here's my business card, too. If you ever get to Portland, stop by. We would love to have you."

Eddie thanked his new acquaintance and presented Hans with a similar offer to visit the firehouse if he ever found himself in Chicago again. Then, Ed and Frank headed to the far side of the island. The tug floated peacefully moored in the same place where Eddie had anchored it earlier in the day, but now the swim seemed more difficult than it had been earlier in the day since their bellies were now weighted down with the food and drink their generous host had provided.

After a quick shower of fresh water and a change of clothes, Eddie set out to locate Saint Pete's on the sea chart. The engine bucked up like a champion racehorse, and Eddie opened up her throttle. Three hours later under clear, dark skies, Eddie found himself maneuvering the tug through the docks and piers owned and operated by the Saint Petronelle Harbor House. Signs appeared periodically directing the Skippers of the pleasure crafts to the appropriate areas, and Eddie pulled the tug into one of the several empty slips set aside to accommodate newly arriving visitors.

After docking Ed and Frank cleaned themselves up and changed into clothing a little more presentable than cut off army pants. From the looks of it, the yacht club appeared to be a classy joint, and they didn't want to look out of place among the other guests. Eddie wore his typical khaki shorts, leather sandals and a white, button down collared shirt. Imagining that shirt tails hanging over his shorts would look sloppy, Eddie even tucked his shirt in and wrapped a brown leather belt around his waist. Replacing two gold hoops dangling from his left ear with genuine diamond studs, Eddie surveyed himself in the mirror. He almost strapped a watch onto his wrist, but figured that keeping track of time was just too much ask of someone on a six week vacation. The shirt was by Ralph Lauren, the pants from Banana Republic, and Eddie figured that if that wasn't good enough, then to hell with them.

Stars filled the night sky and the round moon shone clear and bright, providing Ed and Frank with enough light to safely tie the tug. The rhythm of a steel band playing in the distance drifted in the warm breeze as the two amateur sailors finished securing the tug and stepped onto the whitewashed wooden planks of the visitors' pier. Two men dressed in tan pants and white short-sleeved shirts approached the newcomers, their gold badges and shoulder patches identifying them as harbor masters - a fancy title that really meant security guard. One carried a flashlight, the other a portable radio and a clipboard. Eddie noted that each of them were armed with pistols holstered to their sides with black support straps.

"Gentlemen, welcome to Harbor House. May I see your pass?" the senior harbor master inquired of the two temporary patrons. Eddie reached into his front pocket, fishing for the card, then handed it to the harbor master for him to inspect. The senior officer studied the card for a moment, ripped it in half along the perforations, and returned the lower portion to Eddie.

"So you're guests of Mr. Klemmer. He just left earlier today - too bad you missed him. Anyhow, the gold card allows full access to the entire club for a period of forty-eight hours. If you would, please check in at the reception area at the end of this pier, and the courtesy staff will be happy to get to settled in. Just keep your half of the pass with you while occupying any common areas." Tipping their hats, the harbor masters took their leave, one of them saying, "Please enjoy yourselves."

"These security guys are a hell of a lot friendlier than those creeps back in Key West," Frank commented as he watched them walk purposefully along the pier to greet another party.

Ed and Frank found the reception office within five minutes, noticing a remarkable number of luxury ships along the way. Vessels of all shapes and sizes shared the club's harbor, and some of the larger ships had crews on board either lounging around or performing general maintenance tasks while they waited for the master of the house to return.

The reception area was housed in a large, white, three-story stucco building at the end of the marina, its peaked roof constructed of red Spanish tiles. All pathways from the harbor's piers led to the building's entrance where several club employees clad in crisp tan uniforms courteously greeted members and visitors. Bellhops secured the parties' luggage, ensuring its prompt delivery to the appropriate accommodations while doormen and valets assisted individuals throughout the entire reception procedure. Recreation and activities directors also posted themselves efficiently at intervals before the doors with clipboards like the one the harbor master carried. Their job, as Eddie and Frank soon learned, was to set up activities such as golf, horseback riding, SCUBA diving, and snorkeling. Less adventurous activities included dance lessons, shuffleboard, and yoga classes. Nearby, an abundant tropical flower garden, dwarfing any other found in public resorts, lent its aroma and color to guests as they waited. Stretching between the white walls of the stucco building, the vivid garden, and the strong blue of the sea, a patio of red ceramic tile completed the exquisite prism of color.

After traversing the army of well-intended service employees, Ed and Frank found themselves standing in an expansive room, all one level apart from the slightly elevated dining area at its far side. High above, ceiling fans stirred the air collecting in the ambient spaces thirty feet overhead while three circular, two-leveled fountains constructed out of a light, smooth, native stone spurted water as high as twenty feet. Fresh plants and flowers encompassed each fountain, and the spray of the fountains' cool, clear waters provided the entire reception area with a fresh, clean scent. The floor of the room matched the patio outside the building.

Directly to the left of the two visitors, they caught sight of a long, hotel-styled front desk with a lightly shaded marble top supported by white, hand-carved wooden columns. Behind the desk, two men and two women with skin the color of hazelnuts typed on computers, smiled at guests, and commandeered the bellhops.

"Wow," Frank whispered in awe to Eddie. "That chef hooked us up."

"May I be of service to you gentlemen?" said one of the young girls stationed behind the reception desk.

"Um, yea, actually," Eddie said as he stepped up to the girl's corral somewhat sheepishly. "We have this guest card, and the men on the dock said we should check in." Eddie handed her his half of the gold card that he had received from Hans earlier in the day.

"Mr. Klemmer has issued you a gold guest card. If I may ask you to sit down in the registration office, we'll get you settled and on your way," the young woman explained with a slight British accent. She ushered the two men into a comfortable office located just off the main room where a pair of large, soft chairs upholstered in tones of cream linen sat in front of a large desk crafted out of a light shaded wood. A middle-aged man dressed in a double-breasted, olive colored suit entered the office.

"My name is Jonathan Darwell. I am in charge of guest services, and I ask for just a few minutes of your time to acquaint you to the club and its amenities," Mr. Darwell began with a well-practiced air of sincerity.

Over the next ten minutes, Eddie and Frank endured Mr. Darwell's briefing, at the same time salivating over Mr. Darwell's description of the services provided by the club and wishing he would get on with it so they could go and explore the grounds for themselves. The exclusive resort offered almost any service or activity, plus a few that Eddie and Frank never dreamed of doing. Mr. Darwell told them that they would stay in Hans Klemmer's two-bedroom cottage home, but regretted to inform them that they would only have off-water views of the club's expansive professional-styled golf course. The club grounds housed three restaurants, all on the water, and the most popular of the three hosted the tri-weekly, formal attire preferred, dinner and cocktail party. Ed and Frank were fortunate enough to arrive on one of the three nights that the event took place. After reviewing what was available on the island, Mr. Darwell supplied Eddie and Frank with maps and brochures detailing information about the club and the island of Saint Petronelle.

"Please use this club card to provide for any expenses you may acquire during your stay," he said finally. "Can I answer any questions?"

"What kind of expenses? What kind of currency do we need on the island? Do we need passports?" Eddie asked.

"Usually, we find that our guests have no reason or desire to leave the club grounds, but as far as passports are concerned, it's not a bad idea to carry one if you leave the yacht club's grounds. It's not as if you'd be thrown in jail if you're not able to present one to the patrolmen, but it could aid in the bureaucracy if you have your passport readily available," Mr. Darwell explained. "You see, Saint Petronelle was once a British possession up until about ten years ago. Now, it's still considered a protectorate or commonwealth, even though it is self-governed in all respects in a form fashioned after the British standard of political system. The Saint Petronelle government still pays tribute to Great Britain, but in return, we receive goods and services and, more importantly, political support.

'You can use British pounds here, as well as the local currency, the Petronelle dollar, if you wish to pay for anything in cash," Mr. Darwell went on. "Generally, the only charges you need to cover are tips, alcohol, and meals, but you don't even have to worry about that, do you, since you have the gold card?" he finished.

"You mean to tell me that everything we spend goes back to Hans?" Eddie asked for clarification. That much good fortune could not come from one surprise meeting.

"That's correct, Mr. Gilbert," Mr. Darwell answered with confidence.

A valet attendant came to assist the guests to their accommodations. As they left the room, Mr. Darwell called after them, "By the way, the gold visitors card is good for two days only."

Chapter Fifteen

Back in the 1970's, a popular punk band out of the United Kingdom purchased Spike Island and hired an entourage of architects and designers to turn it into their own private retreat. Typical for a lot of entertainers following the fickle trends of their industry, the band's popularity and fanfare dried up after ten years, and once the cash stopped flowing, the musicians could no longer afford the enormous cost of maintaining the property. Their manager employed aggressive sales techniques and succeeded in attracting a group of well-heeled investors in Caribbean real estate. After the island's landscaping and buildings received a facelift, the proprietors opened the island up for the enjoyment of the world's rich and famous.

A long wooden pier stretched out into the crystalline water lining the northern coast of Spike Island, and as the resort's fishing boat approached, Rod pressed a button on the control panel, issuing two loud blasts from the air horn. Katie and Bobby Clipper, who had been resting on the sun deck throughout the entire voyage enjoying a little reefer, didn't expect the ear-splitting signal. Their bodies popped about a foot in the air.

The signal alerted Rod's family of the boat's arrival, and his wife, Carolyn, made her way out to the dock as Rod carefully parked the fishing boat next the pier. The fishing boat was to share the pier's space with several other crafts. A powerboat for water skiing with six seats, a single-masted sail boat, and four two-passenger wave runners were available for use by the island's visitors. At the end of the pier, Rod's children, Tommy and Paulina, waited with great curiosity about the new arrivals.

Once the boat was secured, Rod, his family, and their guests worked on transferring the luggage to one of three golf carts parked nearby. After the luggage was loaded, everyone piled into the remaining carts and followed Rod and his family to the main villa.

Steep, rocky roads lined with thick jungle foliage wound their way to the highest point of the island where the main villa was located. Sounds of tropical wildlife filled the air around the group; insects buzzed, birds chirped, and occasionally a small animal could be heard scampering away, frightened by the golf carts. In various places along the route the jungle gave way to open air, and the visitors caught awesome glimpses of jagged, rocky cliffs rising above the wide-open waters of the sea.

After about ten minutes, the plant life around the path spread apart, revealing an open field occupied by several different buildings, the largest of which was the villa where the girls and their companions would stay. Forming an H-shaped pattern, the ranch-style villa had four wings. The roof's green shingles surrounded glass domes that suggested a bright, roomy interior.

"Well folks. While I'm moving your luggage inside, my wife will give you the dollar tour," Rod announced after stopping his cart in front of the villa's front door. Leaning over to his wife, he quietly said, "Carolyn, don't forget to tell them about Ugh."

The children set out for their own home, a modest cottage located on the far side of the clearing, and Carolyn led the party into the villa. She looked to be in her early forties, was of medium build and height, and her brown eyes beautifully complimented her short, brown hair. In a calf-length sundress that revealed her tan skin, a wide-brimmed straw hat, and a pair of low-cut leather boots, Carolyn looked comfortable and relaxed.

She started off by distributing small paper maps of the island, pointing out some unique features of the island's geography. "The front of the map covers the gravel paths on the island, and I think you'll find it very helpful. It's easy to get lost, because the paths don't go in straight lines. If you'll turn the map to its other side, you'll find a description of the island's indigenous plant and animal life as well."

A portion of the island on the map was blacked out, and a caption warned guests to keep clear of that area. Timmy interrupted Carolyn to ask why.

Carolyn hesitated momentarily, then answered with a laugh, "That area is not officially part of the resort. You see, the purchase contracts made some provision for a native resident of the island, a somewhat eccentric and reclusive character that we affectionately call Ugh."

"Ugh?" Jennifer asked.

"We don't know his real name, if he even has one, but my husband calls him Ugh because that's the only thing he ever says. You'll know him if you see him - he's the guy with messy hair, green shorts, and flip flops who walks around kind of hunched over and says 'ugh' all the time," Carolyn explained.

"Is he dangerous?" Marcie questioned, noticeably unsettled by the fact that she and her friends would be sharing the island with such a strange individual.

"Oh, no. Not at all," Carolyn hurried to assure her. "He's quite shy, and chances are you'll never run into him. I've only seen him once, although Rod says he has had the pleasure of a conversation. He's absolutely harmless. If you do see him, just give him his space."

Thinking it best to move on with her description of the island's less worrisome features, Carolyn told the guests where they could find the pool, water skiing equipment, and fishing rods. "We have a new addition to the resort as well," she said brightly. "About six months ago, the owners built a stable which you'll find marked on your maps. There are six horses, and you're welcome to go for a ride between the hours of eleven and eight."

After giving the guests a tour of the house and outdoor facilities, Carolyn left them to explore by themselves.

Island Bound

With a week of pampering and recreation ahead of them, the bachelorettes and Air Force men settled themselves into the villa. Bobby and Katie shared one of the six bedrooms, as they were becoming pretty close, and the rest of the party set off to claim private rooms for themselves.

When the group reassembled in the villa's spacious living room, they began to discuss what to do with the rest of the evening. As Katie and Melissa debated the pros and cons of swimming in the ocean at night, Timmy walked over to one of the windows and peered out the curtain. "I don't think we're going anywhere. Take a look at this."

The airman parted the curtains to reveal the scene outside, and the group watched in wonder as black clouds encompassed the sky and the wind attacked the trees on the other side of the clearing.

Refusing to let a little rain to interrupt their fun, Marcie turned on the stereo while Katie and Bobby went into the kitchen and set the blender going, inventing new tropical drinks for everyone to taste. All the while heavy drops of water bounced above the ceilings overhead.

The next morning was welcomed by the presence of clear, bright skies and warm breezes. When the guests awoke and made their way to the kitchen, they found Rod standing behind a smoking griddle in a fluffy chef's hat.

"You just wait until you taste my pineapple flapjacks," he bragged. You've never tasted anything so good in your life."

After their breakfast, the group split apart. Bobby and Katie moved lazily to lounge chairs beside the swimming pool, Marcie and Jennifer planned to saddle up two of the horses and check out the rest of the island, and the rest of the party set off with Rod in the speedboat.

Marcie and Jennifer found the stables quickly and went inside to see the horses. The steeds enjoyed a fine existence. The structure was clean, ventilated, and well-maintained, and all the stalls were equipped with fountains that circulated fresh water for the horses. A large glass jar mounted on the far wall contained little red and white peppermint candies, and the girls weren't sure if the hard candies were for human or animal consumption. The looks of anticipation on the horses' muzzles as Jennifer walked over to the jar hinted that they might enjoy a peppermint or two upon occasion.

By the time the girls arrived at the paddock area, the young Tom York already had the mounts saddled up and ready to go, each animal patiently waiting in its respective stall. Jennifer asked who the candies in the jar belonged to.

"You can eat 'um if ya' want, but the horses love 'em - they'll be jealous if you don't share." Tommy casually relayed the information. Stepping over to the jar, he reached in and withdrew six pieces of the sweet candy, one for each of the stable's residents. After unwrapping the first piece, Tommy held the candy in the palm of his hand and offered it to one of the horses, who traded a large wad of spit for the treat. The boy wiped his paw on the front of his denim trousers.

Marcie and Jennifer each offered up a piece of the candy to each of the horse's that would be carrying them about the island. A large black beast named Sinbad would be Marcie's transportation, and Jennifer mounted a beautiful gray horse named Tandy. With maps in hand and canteens sloshing, they set off for their ride. The Spike being such a small island, the girls were surprised how much time it took to follow the stony pathways back down to the beach.

Their path ended as the jungle undergrowth gave way to a beach that stretched at least two hundred yards ahead of the riders. Palm trees spread over the beach, creating odd patterns of shade on the sand. Through the clearing in the trees, Marcie caught a glimpse of the speedboat as it skidded across the salt water, trailing behind it someone harnessed high above in a tri-colored parachute. The girls spurred their steeds into action, and the horses bolted at top speed towards the other end of the large beach. Holding to their saddles for dear life, they endured the splash of salt water as the hooves of the animals churned the hard sand near the water's edge. As the girls tugged on the reins to slow the steeds, the parasail drifted, lost altitude, and eventually splashed down in the warm waters surrounding Spike Island.

"That was a blast. I've never had the chance to parasail before," Timmy commented as he bobbed up and down in the water, the brightly colored chute billowing in the water. Mr. York carefully pulled the rider and chute on board, and ten minutes later, Timmy was resting comfortably on the sun pad in the front of the boat with an ice-cold Corona. Melissa strapped her harness and got ready to take her turn.

Mr. York gunned the boat, the chute filled with the moist Caribbean air, and Melissa momentarily felt her stomach drop as her body lifted into the sky. At one hundred feet the view took her breath away. Gradually, the wind's whistle in Melissa's ears replaced the sound of the speedboat's engine. The height opened the panorama of the entire island and its surrounding sea, its surface littered with neighboring clusters of islands. In the distance Melissa noticed one large island and wondered if it was inhabited.

Back on the ground, the girls reigned in their horses and set off on a different path leading back into the jungle. The path was just wide enough for them to ride side by side, and as they explored the island, they talked about Jennifer's relationship with Dexter, Katie's relationship with Bobby, and men in general.

"I wish we could've run into that Ed guy before we left Key West," Marcie remarked as the horses rounded a curve in the path.

"Had the hots for him, huh Marcie?" Jennifer's commented, causing Marcie to blush and release a small giggle. Jenny continued, "Well don't worry, you never know where Fate is going to lead you."

The sun was setting when the two equestrians finally returned from the stable and found the others sitting about the pool area. Rod wore his signature fluffy white chef's hat as he flipped steaks on the poolside grill, and Carolyn was caring a tray of beverages from the kitchen. Kate and Bobby floated side by side on a raft in the same place they had been when the girls left for their ride, while inside the house, Melissa, Tim, and Rickey were busy playing pool. Marcie commented on the quality of the culinary spread laid out on a picnic table near the pool.

"This is nothing. Wait till tomorrow night - we're doing a bonfire on the beach." Carolyn smiled brightly at her young guest.

Chapter Sixteen

The night of their arrival to the club, Frank suggested that they check out what the resort had to offer in the way of victuals.

"Are you kidding?" was Eddie's response. "You just gobbled everything in the Klemmers' picnic basket a few hours ago. You ate almost an entire cake by yourself. How can you be hungry again?"

"Look," Frank said, appealing to his friend's logic. "It took us about half an hour to swim back to the boat, three hours to get here, and another hour to get through all the hoopla at the front desk. That means that it's been four and a half hours since the time of our last meal. How can you *not* be hungry?"

Eddie put up a good fight because he could just imagine what a restaurant in this ritzy resort must be: most likely a candle-lit dining room with crystal chandeliers and oriental carpets, stuffy women in strapless evening gowns with diamonds in their ears, miniscule portions of weird food set pretentiously in the middle of expansive white plates...After a day in the hot sun, the last thing Eddie wanted to do was worry about which fork to use for his salad. In the end, however, he gave in. Frank's eyes exhibited such a desperate longing.

As the two sauntered into the venue Frank selected from the brochures Mr. Darwell had given them, Eddie fortunately found the situation to be quite different from what he had expected.

The circle-shaped restaurant stood at the end of a long pier that stretched to the length of two football fields. Gas lit lanterns flickered on either side of the doorway, welcoming Eddie and Frank as they entered and a pleasant young hostess greeted them. Eddie pointed a finger in the direction of the bar. "We're going to head up to the bar for a few," he told her.

For the most part, the look was casual, but clean and attractive. The bar where Eddie and Frank found their seats stretched out along the kitchen, providing room in the middle of the restaurant for a small stage. The walls encompassing the room were only about four feet tall, and the ceiling was seven feet above that. That left a large space for bugs and critters to invade if not covered, so fine meshed screens stretched between the walls and the ceiling above to protect the diners from hovering insects. Eddie and his sidekick had no problem fitting in with the crowd, at least as far as attire was concerned.

A Cajun Caribbean band known as the Greenback Alligators was setting up on the stage prepping for the evening's entertainment, and there wasn't a bad seat in the house. The two men had to wait a few minutes to order their drinks, because the place was getting a lot of business that night.

After serving a couple on the other side of the bar, the bartender came to take their order. "What'll it be mates?" he said with a thick Australian accent. He

Island Bound

looked like a surfer type with sun bleached, wavy hair sprouting from his dark tanned scalp.

"I'll go with a phoofy drink, piña colada. Make it with a double shot of one fifty one."

"A double of one fifty one? That's no phoofy drink," the booze slinger said as he gestured in Frank's direction. "How about for you, big fella?"

"Pete's rum on the rocks." Frank chose the locally distilled rum, which turned out to be slightly sweeter than usual with a light caramel color.

Eddie spun around on his bar stool, taking a look around the cafe. The band was about to start filling the room with music. By now most of the tables were occupied, and the wind took on a cool moistness. Looking above, Eddie noticed dark clouds obscuring the moon's light, and he heard rumblings of thunder. A light rain was already falling, and occasionally a bright flash of lightening streaked the sky. As the first chords of music emanated from the center of the room, Eddie's began to tap his foot along with the smooth rhythm.

As Frank ordered his second cocktail, Eddie noticed two women approaching the empty stools to his right. He wasn't the only one who noticed - in fact, the two of them turned every head in the room. With long, flawless legs, brilliant hair, and well-tailored, even glamorous clothes, it seemed as though the women had come to the resort for a fashion shoot or the making of a film. Eddie nodded hello as they claimed the empty stools, and the Australian approached carrying Frank's cocktail.

"Hello, darlings, what can I get for you?" The bartender greeted the women with a toothy grin. They gave their orders quickly, then entered into their own private conversation as the bartender set two frosty martini glasses on the bar top. The bartender then turned his attention to Eddie and Frank.

"Well, mates, what'll be for munchin' tonight?" With a gnawed pencil, the bartender quickly took their orders.

"You folks sound like you're from the American midwest?"

"I'm from Florida now," Frank replied. "He still lives in Chicago." Frank waved his cocktail filled hand in Eddie's direction.

"Chicago, Ay! Spent two years there when I was just a lad of twenty-one. Nice enough town, it is. Had a blast while I was there. Friendly people. Damned too cold in the winter though."

"Chicago's definitely one of the best places I've known," Eddie stated with pride for his hometown.

"What's so great about Chicago?" one of the two women piped up with a native accent. "The way I see it, it's just another cold, dirty, American city." Eddie asked if the girl had ever been there.

"I've never been north of Miami," the girl revealed, as if she was proud of her inexperience outside the South.

"Well, let me enlighten you," Eddie offered, warming up to a friendly argument. "We've got the Sears Tower, the Hancock, more museums than one could shake a stick at, Michigan Avenue, the Great Lakes, some of the best colleges and universities, great pizza, and most of all, we've got the Cubbies."

"Actually Keri, he's right. I've been to Chicago on business a couple times, and I thought it was beautiful," the other girl said, supporting Eddie's points.

The first woman who spoke, Keri, took a cigarette out of her purse and lit it, exhaling smoke as she asked, "What do you do in Chicago?"

Flattered by the attention from the beautiful women, Eddie and Frank introduced themselves and bought them a round of drinks ten minutes later. The women listened attentively as Frank told stories about his adventures on the police force between bites of steak, and Eddie joined in with a colorful description of what it's like to enter a burning building. Although they were a rapt audience, the women avoided mentioning any details about their careers, homes, or families, apart from the comment of the woman furthest from Eddie, Jeri, describing her business trips in Chicago. For instance, when Frank asked Keri what she did for a living, she waved her hand flamboyantly and said, "I'm in retail," and when Eddie asked Jeri where she was from, she just smiled and said, "Where do you think I'm from?" When Eddie guessed blindly, "California," Jeri nodded and answered, "Yes. I'm from California."

After a few hours of conversation, Jeri excused herself, saying that she had to make a phone call. Meanwhile Keri, who remained behind at the table, invited Eddie and Frank to join them the next evening for a night on the town.

"We're going to place known as Pete's Point," Keri said, pointing to a structure on top of a small mountain in the distance. She explained the point's history until Jeri returned from making her phone call.

The point was one of the earliest missions established on the island. In later years as the commerce among the islands picked up, the point became the foundation of a lighthouse. The site had been abandoned a few years ago, but the light still rotated like some memorial to days gone by. Now, tourists and the island's high society had appropriated the point for decadent evenings of food, wine, and gambling. When Eddie and Frank eagerly agreed to take her up on her invitation, she arranged to meet in the bar the next evening. The Australian offered to hold their seats for them, and with that, the two gorgeous creatures disappeared into the night.

*

The night started off at the same bar where the four had met. As promised, the Aussie had four stools ready and waiting for their rendez-vous. Keri and Jeri looked good, as if they had just stepped out of the pages of a department store's summer catalog. Eddie was glad that he had had enough foresight to pack his warm weather Armani suit. A lapel pin affixed to his jacket displayed his membership to an international union of professional firefighters, and beneath the jacket, he wore a crisp white shirt and an Italian silk tie. Naturally - anything less would be uncivilized.

Eddie was surprised to find that before leaving Tampa, Frank had actually taken the trouble to resurrect his suit from its grave of mothballs. In all the years he had known the man, Eddie figured he had only seen his good buddy in a suit two or three times. The suit was a basic three-buttoned jacket, its light-weight wool dark gray in color.

Prior to hitting the casino, the foursome enjoyed a gourmet dinner and tropical drinks on an outdoor patio situated on a rocky cliff that allowed diners to gaze down upon a large bay from a distance of fifteen hundred feet. All four watched the sun slowly fade away while they enjoyed the establishment's cuisine. When the sky had given up its last tones of gold and pink, darkness fell upon the point. Eddie, Frank, and the two women headed off to the casino.

Two hours later, Eddie was looking down at a pile of chips and a king of clubs and whispering, "Come on, come on, baby. Give me the ace, gimme the ace." Keri sat to his right, and on his left, Jeri busied herself lighting one match after another and watching their flames dwindle in the ashtray. One seat further down, Frank managed his cards with an unhappy grimace spread across his mug from cheek to cheek. He was definitely not having a good night at the tables.

"Oh yeah! Baby's gettin a new pair of shoes!" The dealer had just set an ace on top of the king lying in front of Eddie - it was his third black jack. Unfortunately for Frank, lady luck decided to ignore him. The two friends started the evening off by cashing in on two hundred US dollar's worth of the casino's chips, and during the course of the night, Eddie had turned his two c-notes into three thousand dollars. Poor Frank was sitting at the green felt-topped table with thirty bucks lying in front of him. Keri and Jeri watched from behind, enjoying the free cocktails that the casino offered to guests gambling their fortunes and occasionally offering tidbits of advice to the novice gamblers.

"I'm not wasting anymore of my hard earned cash on this place. Let's head back to the club," Frank whined, keeping on until he had his way. Finally, Eddie cashed in his small fortune and all four headed back, hopping into a taxi that patiently waited for a fare.

When the taxi left them off at the front entrance of the resort, Jeri turned to Eddie and asked, "Didn't you say your boat is docked here?"

"Sure," Eddie answered. He had somehow left out mentioning that the tug was a rental, and, to Frank's as well as his own astonishment, had awkwardly created a story about how a sea-faring millionaire had presented him the boat in gratitude after Eddie saved his life in a fire three years ago. Jeri and Keri both exhibited enormous interest in seeing the boat, which, from Eddie's description, could have rivaled the luxury of the Titanic. Upon their insistence, the four of them concluded their night on the tug's deck, increasing their alcohol-induced giddiness.

"Jeri, do you think you'll be able to drive safely?" Keri asked with some concern as the evening drew to a close.

"It's probably not a good idea. Maybe we should take a taxi," Jeri answered, unable to restrain herself from shooting an expectant glance at Eddie and Frank.

Frank coughed, and Eddie said, "You ladies don't need to worry about that. It would probably be a pain for you to come back here in the morning for your car. Why don't you just stay here?" Not wanting them to think he was making an indecent offer, he added, "The condo where we're staying has a pull-out sofa. There's plenty of room."

Keri, rising from her chair and coming to stand close beside Eddie's chair, put her hand on his knee and said seductively, "Why don't we just stay here on your boat? It's - very romantic here, under the stars." Post haste, the four of them agreed to stay on the tug. On the deck, the sea breeze smelled fresh and enticing, the sky was cloudless, and stars twinkled untouchable in the night sky. The temperature was a perfect seventy degrees, and a warm sea breeze drifted about the tug. The time was good.

Chapter Seventeen

Hector piloted the large yacht into the safety of the underground dock area, and Lester left him at the wheel to inspect the craft for valuables. He checked out the captives as well, trying to decide which prisoners could produce profit and which ones should be weighted and chucked overboard. In the end he spared three of the women the agonizing death of drowning - only to prepare them for an agonizing life of slavery. The rest were shackled and made to walk the plank. In order to prevent any possible chance discovery, Lester ordered his men to litter the Nazi men's bloody bodies in one big watery grave. The sharks would feast that night, preventing any bodies from floating away and winding up on some distant shore. Hector expertly parked the large boat in one of the docks stalls while Lester ordered his crew to take the three new prisoners and stash them in the cell where the two female Dirks were already held captive. When things were settled on the dock, Lester headed up to his father's office to report the day's events.

Blackwell smiled as Lester strode across the expansive office floor.

"Ah, my favorite son! Tell me, lad, what do you have for me today?"

"Actually, I'm your only son," Lester corrected before beginning to weave his tale.

"Nazis huh? That could be undesirable. I've known of the reestablishment of the organization for some time now, even entered into a little business with them. They're not going to be happy about the massacre." Blackwell fell silent, thinking for the moment. "Well, we'll just have to deal with it, if and when it becomes a problem. They'll find out, for sure - I think they have a couple of our workers on their pay roll. All in all, it seems things turned bad." Torn between his doting admiration for his adopted son and his displeasure with Lester's irresponsible treatment of such a powerful group of people, he gazed sternly out the window. After a few minutes, the father in him overcame the shrewd businessman, and he offered Lester a few words of encouragement. "We should get a pretty penny from that yacht, though, and the broads too. My Asian friend is heading in this weekend - sounds like he's expanding his prostitution businesses based around Indochina." Blackwell retrieved another mission folder for Lester to review.

"You finally got the call from our guy in the Keys," Lester remarked as he scanned the documents contained within the folder. "Looks pretty simple. I assume you would like this accomplished as soon as possible?"

Blackwell confirmed the question.

Lester assembled his team for the fourth and hopefully final time that week. He was beat from all the activity and needed a good nights sleep, not to mention his crew. He decided to run the mission at night, allowing his crew to get some quality shut eye before they took off.

Lester's crew was already waiting in the briefing room when he arrived. His thoughts settled on the plan for the night's job, and he decided to utilize five of the battle-hardened mercenaries. He laid out the strategy, which was relatively simple. As a private island, the Spike would most likely be without law enforcement or any other kind of protection. According to the information contained in the manila briefing envelope, at this time only eleven people were on the island, and two of them were children under twelve.

Lester laid the satellite image of the island on the large center table in the briefing room and assigned two of his men to swing around to the rear side of the island on a Zodiac raft. Their job was to cut off any chance of the prey making an escape and to clear out any unknown, straggling inhabitants. One man was to stay behind and guard the motorized rubber raft.

The job of the three men remaining with Lester was to gain access to the island via a large, flat beach on its north side. Lester figured this would allow his men to move up on the main area of the settlement with as much stealth as possible. Ordering the men to grant no mercy - not that his henchmen would anyway - he reminded them that the only person to be kept alive was Ms. Jennifer Klein herself. Lester distributed pictures of the politician's daughter so that the men would be able to recognize her.

The briefing and outfitting of the mercenaries lasted for a large part of the day, and afterwards, the men retreated to their private rooms to get a little rest before they began. It wasn't until early evening that Lester and his crew set for the island known as the Spike, as usual piling into their beefy speedboat with a full arsenal of deadly weapons.

Just as the gray tones of dusk gave way to black night, the darker bulk of Spike Island rose up before the boat. The two-man crew launched the Zodiac off the back of the speedboat, sparked up the motor, and silently glided around to the back side of the island.

"This is going to be easier than I thought," Lester commented. While he was studying the layout of the beach, several figures and two small cars emerged from the jungle path and arranged a camp on the sandy beach. In a short time, the warm, bright glow of a blazing fire developed and Hector nudged Lester's elbow, saying, "I'll be damned! They're having themselves a little beach party."

Lester contacted the other party with a closed-transmission radio and informed them of the recently discovered information. An hour and a half later, Lester put his plan into action. The remaining mercenaries, including Hector, advanced on the beach in a second Zodiac while the young Crow remained behind to coordinate the attack and guard the large main vessel. Afterwards, they would sink the Zodiacs and high tail it back to the Crow's secret lagoon.

The two man team soon arrived at the opposite side of the island where high, rocky cliffs rose like a fortress. The mercenaries were looking for a breach in the stone when Lester contacted them with the latest update, and they received orders to hurry into position and communicate as soon as they were prepared to attack. It took another fifteen minutes for one of the mercenaries to scale the cliffs and get positioned for action. Once he reached the crest, he informed Lester of his status over the comlink.

On the opposite side of the island, Lester ordered the attack, and the remaining three men geared their Zodiac closer to the beach. The three men flattened themselves on the bottom of the raft as they shut off the motor about forty feet from shore. The unexpected beach folk partied on, unaware of the danger lurking a short distance away.

Chapter Eighteen

While the resort's guests spent another beautiful day enjoying the island, the Yorks prepared for the evening's beach party, transferring a range of party supplies from the resort's main compound to the site they chose on the edge of the sea. Rod prepared an old fifty-five gallon drum for its use as a grill, dug a shallow fire pit in the sand just out of reach of the evening's tide, and gave his oldest son, Tommy, the task of retrieving hearty logs of oak and maple from the carriage house to stock the bonfire's fuel. Meanwhile, Carolyn slaved away in the kitchen, preparing the side dishes that would accompany the night's meal of steak and lobster. After positioning a portable sound system, beach chairs, and a cooler of cold booze, the camp was ready for the young people to caravan down to the beach in golf carts.

"I think I saw that Ugh dude while I was out and about," Marcie mentioned over the quiet hum of the cart's engine.

"What was he up to?" the airman standing on the back bumper questioned the girl.

"Looked like he was running around with a dead fish hanging out of his mouth," Marcie answered with disgust.

"No way. That's too strange," Jennifer commented as the group arrived at the beach site.

Rod's makeshift grill cast an orange glow on the camp site while a large tub filled with rum punch sweated nearby. An old Clapton tune resonated from the sound system's speakers, and Rod positioned logs in the fire pit as Tommy dutifully handed him each one. All around the beach camp, tiki torches burned away with the scent of citronella amidst the strong, warm breeze that washed in from the sea.

After only an hour, everyone laid back with full bellies and enjoyed the sea wind. Katie distributed rolling papers stuffed to the hilt with ganja and the adults smoked while the children played in the surf.

"I'll be back in a few - I need to replenish my supply," Katie announced when the first round was cashed. She started one of the golf carts, and Bobby jumped up, offering to accompany her back to the main villa. He hoped the two of them could be alone together for a little action.

"Hey Kate, wait up. I need to run back myself," Melissa said, standing up and brushing the sand off of her skirt. Kate, disappointed, braked so Melissa could situate herself on the back seat of the cart.

Back at the villa the three headed into the building where Bobby and Katie stocked up on more buds and Melissa hit the powder room. She was in there for some time, so the other two jumped in the hot tub and sparked up another doobie while they waited for her. Melissa exited the villa just time to join in on the weed and slid her body into the hot, soothing bubbles. It felt good on the stiff muscles she had gotten from parasailing.

"Everything come out O.K.? You were in there for quite some time," Katie remarked snidely, irritated that her third-wheel friend even followed her and her man of the moment into the hot tub. After the joint had made a couple rounds, however, Katie forgot all about her annoyance and even thanked Melissa with utmost sincerity for coming along. In a short time the three were wrecked, and their conversation turned to sex.

"Isn't a fantasy of almost every man to get caught up in the middle of two women getting it on," Katie whispered seductively as she wrapped her arms around the airman.

"You don't say? Maybe we could get Melissa to join in," Bobby tried to respond, but succeeded only in stuttering a few unintelligible words. Melissa slid around to the other side of the tub right next to Bobby, and the two girls engaged in running their hands all over his torso. The girls' lips were about to make contact, but unfortunately for Bobby, his fantasy would never be fulfilled.

They never saw the figure emerging from the shadows. In a smooth, calculated motion, the intruder slit the throat of the US Airman, and a single shot from the pistol pierced the skulls of both women. All three laid bleeding as the figure disappeared into the dark night, and the tub's bubbling water took on a reddish hue.

Back on the beach, a black raft materialized in the surf, and the York children shouted for Rod's attention. Rod got up from his chair and walked to the raft, full of curiosity. Suddenly, three men dressed in black and armed with sub machineguns jumped from the craft and assumed strategic positions. Timmy was the only one to react to the situation; he grabbed one of the tiki torches, thinking to use it as a spear. Several blasts from one of the intruders cut him down and his body fell to the wet sand with a dull thud. The rest of the group stood still, not believing what they had just seen.

One of the intruders unleashed an entire magazine of bullets into the air above the heads of the scared party, saying, "Everyone lay down on the ground and don't make a move." The girls, Ricky, and Carolyn hit the ground while Rod pulled his two children close and crouched in the sand, shielding them with his body.

One of the intruders separated the males into one group and the females into another while a second one grabbed each woman by the hair and jerked her head up, examining her face.

"This is the one, Boss," one of the men stated after checking out Jennifer. The leader muttered something into the microphone of his headset and told the first man, "Cuff her and get her into the Zodiac."

"What should we do with rest?"

Walking over to the group of women, the boss leveled his pistol at Carolyn first and said, "Too old." He shot her directly in the forehead, then pointed the gun at Paulina, saying, "Too young." Paulina let loose a blood-curdling scream, then fell to the sand beside her mother.

"As for the men..." boss pointed a sub-machinegun at Rod, Ricky, and Tommy, pulled the trigger, and all three of them fell to ground. Slight moans issued from their writhing bodies, and the boss, acting as an executioner, drew his pistol and shot each one in the forehead.

"Take her back to the boat," he ordered. "We'll wait for the others and make sure the rest of the island is cleared. We'll keep this one here for now - we may want to have a little fun while we're waiting for the others." Jennifer kicked and screamed as the Zodiac pulled away and Marcie trembled next to the prone bodies of Carolyn and Paulina.

In a short time two men in another Zodiac appeared on the beach. One of the newcomers reported, "The rest of the place is clear." He then turned and looked in Marcie's direction. The girl was still lying face-down in the wet sand, crying. The man walked towards the poor girl, feeling satisfied with yet another successful mission. Lester should reward him well. Everything had gone according to the plans - up until then, anyway.

Chapter Nineteen

Early in the morning after the night of gambling with Jeri and Keri, Eddie awakened to the smell of smoke. At first, he thought he was dreaming when he saw the white smoke pouring under the door of his cabin, but when he had buried his head still deeper in the covers and found it more difficult to breathe, his instincts spurred him to action. He pulled himself out of bed with unnatural weariness - it felt as though every muscle in his body had gone numb - and drug himself down the hall to the galley. He thought perhaps Frank had started breakfast and dozed off on the couch while it cooked.

Approaching the galley, he saw that the situation was much more serious than just over-cooked sausage. Flames licked the inside wall, greedy for destruction, and smoke threatened to choke him. He remembered the location of the tug's fire extinguisher and quickly put it to work, all the while feeling as though he should just lie down and take a quick nap. His weakened arms could barely withstand the weight of the extinguisher. Acting mechanically according to his training, he managed to stay awake long enough to put the fire out. As soon as he felt sure the flames would not rekindle, he settled down in the hallway, fast asleep.

Moments later, he felt someone's arms grasping him under his armpits and dragging him along the boat's floor. He came to in the gray morning on the dock, where he lay on his back and saw two paramedics, as well as several of the resort's tan-clad workers, hovering over him with concern. Then he went back to sleep for a long time.

*

Late morning sun broke through the hospital windows, calling Eddie to wakefulness. Pulling himself up in the bed, he tried to make sense of what had happened to him in the last twenty-four hours. He noticed an IV in his arm, and his clothes had been replaced with a hospital gown. At first, he couldn't be sure what happened, but gradually, he recalled the scene with the fire on the boat. He stared at the metal bars of his hospital bed for awhile, wondering what had happened to Frank.

A nurse entered his room with a thermometer and a glass of orange juice, and she took Eddie's temperature while she explained that he didn't have any injuries.

"It was just the high level of narcotics in your blood that worried us. You could have overdosed."

Eddie was taken aback. "Narcotics? I don't use drugs at all. I don't know what you're talking about."

The nurse finished taking Eddie's blood pressure and recorded her findings on his chart. "I know," she said, "your record is impeccable. An investigator will be in to see you shortly - the police suspect that someone attempted to murder you."

Moments later, a dry-looking man in a beige suit came to sit beside Eddie's hospital bed. He explained that the fire on the boat had been rigged. Also, the blood tests showed that Eddie and Frank had both been drugged.

"I don't know what made you wake up in time - you should've slept like a baby," the investigator said. "It's a good thing you did, though, because you wouldn't be here to think about it if you hadn't. The resort's patrol guards had just changed shifts, and there was nobody to help you. Do you remember anything about last night?"

Eddie told him about Jeri and Keri and learned that the two women had been long gone before the fire started. The investigator was interested to hear every detail of what occurred in the bar, at the casino, and on the boat.

When Eddie finished his account, the investigator leaned back in his chair and said, "It sounds like you ran into a pair of America's most notorious assassins. Your description fits their profile, and I'm sure your testimony will be helpful in tracking them down. Even now, we have the police force and the Coast Guard on full alert." He handed Eddie a business card and said, "If you remember any additional details you think might be relevant in locating these two vixens, give me a call. Otherwise, we'll be in contact with you. I'll leave you now, because I'm sure you need your rest. Thank you very much, Mr. Gilbert." He stood and shook Eddie's hand before taking his leave.

As soon as the investigator departed, Eddie felt an irresistible longing to get up from the hospital bed, put on his own clothes, and get moving again. He pulled the IV tube out of his arm and headed for the nurse's station, demanding to be checked out. The flustered nurse agreed that there was no reason to keep him in the hospital overnight, so after he filled out numerous insurance forms, Eddie was a free man.

His first mission was to find Frank, who, he learned, had also been visited by the investigator. When he came to his room, he found Frank picking half-heartedly at a tray of Jell-o and imitation mashed potatoes.

"C'mon, man, let's get out of here," Eddie said, "They just had to keep us here to check us out and make sure we're O.K. I'm ready to get going again, how about you?"

By three in the afternoon, the two men left the hospital and returned to the dock to find out how much damage the tug had suffered in the course of the last evening's events. Her galley would never be the same again, but as a whole, the boat pulled through remarkably well. The floor was sound, and there was absolutely no danger of any leaks. Happily, they found that the refrigerator still worked, although the stove didn't look safe to use.

Island Bound

Filled with the sense of adventure, Eddie suggested that they continue according to plans. His vacation was working out exactly the way he wanted it to, and he had no intention of stopping it and returning to Chicago's drudgery. "You comin', Frank?" he asked, knowing what the answer would be.

"You kidding? We almost got killed. We've got a boat with a burnt-up galley, and we've got no idea where we're going...Of course I'm coming," the big man said as he settled into a deck chair with a beer, opening it with a half-melted bottle opener.

Eddie studied the navigation charts after about two hours of cruising, "I've got an idea where we're going," he contradicted. "We're going to Spike Island."

"Spike Island? What's that?" Frank asked.

"You know that girl who called back in Key West?"

"Yeah."

"I found the name and location of the island in my wallet last night. I didn't tell you, 'cause I found it when we were at the restaurant with Jeri and Keri the night before last."

The sun fell quickly as the tug traversed the open sea, and the two men hoped they would make it to the island at a decent hour. "It should be right around here somewhere," Eddie said, squinting into the black ocean ahead of the tug. "Unless Marcie sent us out on a wild goose hunt. There are a few smaller islands on the chart; we might have to pull in somewhere tomorrow and get some directions."

"You're up for staying out on the water tonight?" Frank asked. The Bourbon Trader floated in calm waters close to a couple of islands that looked as though they were sparsely inhabited, if anyone lived on them at all.

"Sounds good to me. We'll set the anchor and break out the booze. Looks like we're not the only ones planning a sleep over," Eddie remarked, drawing Frank's attention to another large vessel in the distance.

Ed and Frank settled down in the captain chairs located on the rear deck of the tug with a couple of cool ones in their hands. They were in the middle of a heated discussion about who had won a wrestling match back in elementary school when a strange, unexpected sound invaded the night's air. To Eddie, it sounded like a whole brick of firecrackers ignited at the same time, a trail of loud reports followed one after another.

"Dude, that's gunfire." The police officer's ear recognized the familiar crack of small arms fire. "As a matter of fact, can you make out the flashes over there on that beach?"

Eddie wanted to doubt his friend's knowledge, but the truth was that he knew from his own experience Frank was right. A debate erupted about whether or not they should do something, and if so, then what. It only took a minute or two to decide. As civil servants it was in both of their natures to investigate and mitigate life-threatening circumstances. The two men quickly threw a plan together.

The high tech tug's communication systems were equipped with an emergency alert system that would transmit an emergency call on every frequency until it was either deactivated or the tug's batteries failed. Frank hit the alarm system's big red button while Eddie grabbed the firearms. Frank had just finished launching the tug's dinghy when Eddie stepped out of the cabin and handed him his 9-mm duty pistol with two magazines containing sixteen shells apiece. Checking the Winchester, Eddie found it was fully loaded with eight large-caliber, high-power shells. A pair of bandoliers crossed his body giving him the look of a bandito out of the old spaghetti westerns adding forty rounds to the eight already in the rifle. His smith hung at his hip, but Eddie left the boat forgetting to grab extra shells for the .357.

The small engine came to life, and Eddie steered for a small opening in the island's jungle foliage. The clearing was far enough away from the beach and the gunfire to hopefully allow the two to approach the area undetected.

"Almost like playing army when we were younger," Frank murmured.

"Yeah, sort of. Now we're using real bullets," Eddie said, a little nervous about the whole situation.

The plant life was thick, making it difficult to traverse the ground beneath their feet. It took longer to reach the area from which they had heard gunshots than the two of them had expected, and by the time Ed and Frank reached the outskirts, several lifeless forms scattered the beach. Four men dressed in dark clothing stood over a figure spread out in the sand, and Ed noticed a raft beached about thirty feet away. A large bonfire and yellow flames from several tiki torches provided enough light to survey the whole area, and the smell of gunpowder and grilled meats hung in the air. Eddie's eye caught another raft making its way out towards the vessel he noted earlier, and he identified the figure lying in the sand as a female. He didn't like the looks of the four men and what they had planned.

Eddie raised the Winchester to his shoulder and pulled the trigger, and the gun's loud bang was followed by several smaller cracks as Frank rapidly fired his 9-mm pistol. Almost every one of the slugs reached their mark, and one of the bad guys toppled over. Eddie dropped a second one with a chest shot from the Winchester.

The remaining two men left standing returned fire with two long bursts from the sub-machineguns they carried. Frank reloaded his weapon while the Winchester cracked again. It was another hit, but unfortunately, Eddie's target would survive. The darkly clad man took the round in his shoulder.

With that, one of the dark-clad figures aided the injured one to jump into the beached Zodiac and make their escape. The boat skimmed the surface of the water covering the distance between the beach and the boat within a minute's time as Eddie and Frank stepped out from their jungle cover and fired after it.

When the boat had disappeared into the murky darkness, Eddie cautiously strode to the middle of the beach, motioning for Frank to stay behind and cover his back. Approaching the women on the ground, he was surprised to find that he knew her. It was Marcie. She was terribly upset, but appeared to be unharmed.

"Marcie, it's Eddie. What the hell is going on here?"

"I don't know. These guys came out of nowhere and started killing everybody. They took Jennifer." Marcie hugged the fireman, sobbing as she spoke. Confused, Eddie looked out towards the boat where he was able to make out several figures scrambling over the side and back into the Zodiacs, obviously reorganized by whoever was calling the shots. He knew they had to high tail it or endure the same fate as the rest of the people littering the ground.

Eddie led the frightened women by the hand into the thick island jungle. He would have to wait until later to hear Marcie's story. The Zodiacs bore down on the beach with frightening speed, each craft carrying a couple of mean-looking fellows. Prior to leaving the beach, Ed scooped up one of the small machineguns discarded by the invaders and pointed the weapon in the direction of the approaching boats. Ed unleashed any remaining lead contained within the weapon's magazine. The bullets ripped through the humid Caribbean air. Eddie wasn't sure if the rounds found their mark. He figured it would give the bad guys something to think about during their short trip to the beach. Frank was reloaded and ready for action when Ed returned.

Slightly out of breath, Eddie felt it would be rude not to make some quick introductions. "Marcie, Frank. Frank, Marcie," he said as he stood aside and motioned for the other two to head into the jungle.

"What the hell is going on, Ed?" Frank asked, not expecting an answer.

The bad guys were sure to have reached the beach again by now. The most important issue facing Eddie, Frank, and Marcie was to escape with their lives still intact.

"We have to find the others - they were up at the villa when this happened. Why did they take Jennifer?" Marcie began sobbing again.

"Do you know the route back to the villa," Eddie asked, not even sure what the villa was.

Marcie led them to a gravel path, which the darkness hid from sight. All three cautiously made their way down the path towards the villa, listening to the group of invaders in the background. Another sound entered the night - a small internal combustion engine running at maximum power.

"Oh, they've got the golf carts. It's going to be impossible to out run them," Marcie wailed. Eddie remembered seeing the vehicles parked down by the beach and cursed himself for not thinking of taking them.

"We'll have to set up an ambush and fight them - it's our only chance." Eddie was busy examining the surrounding area when a short, squatty figure suddenly stepped out of the jungle and onto the path. Eddie damn near jumped out of his skin and shot the newcomer, but held back when he noticed that the figure waved a white cloth. He uttered an unrecognizable word and motioned for the group to follow.

"That must be Ugh. Let's follow him," Marcie suggested. Eddie didn't know anything about this Ugh guy, but figured this was no time for questions. The three followed the short man back into the jungle, and moments after leaving the path, the carts whizzed past. That was a close call. Ugh led them another fifty feet to a small cave entrance hidden by a large rock and thick plants. Everyone slipped into the crevasse, although Frank had a rough time wiggling his body through the opening. Once inside the cave, Frank was relieved to find a wide corridor and tall ceilings.

"Where are you taking us?" Eddie asked.

"Ugh," was the only response from the short man. He pointed once again down the corridor.

Holding hands in the dark corridor and trusting their strange guide, the group stopped for a moment. A creaking sound filled the chamber around them, and suddenly light invaded the area. Eddie could now see a thick half-opened wooden door, and past the door, a large, clean, well furnished apartment complete with a kitchen, washroom, and wet bar. A very large screen television set rested in one corner right in front of an overstuffed recliner. In another corner, Marcie spied an L-shaped computer counsel. Another wooden door concealed more mysteries at the other end of the hall. Ugh reached up to scratch his scraggly mop top, but instead of scratching it, he pulled it off altogether, revealing a horseshoe balding pattern of closely-cut, well groomed hair. The scraggly item in his right hand turned out to be a wig.

"What's up with this shit?" Frank voiced what the rest were thinking.

"First of all, my name isn't Ugh. It's actually Doug, and I play this little role to keep people away from the mining business I operate here. Behind that door is another corridor leading to my diamond mine and my own little dock." Ugh, or actually now, Doug explained.

Years ago Doug had been a hard-core fan of punk music. As a teenager, he even traveled to Great Britain to follow his favorite bands and found it impossible to refuse the offer when a bassist asked him to come along on a visit to his band's island retreat. After they arrived on the island, Doug had a grand time swilling beer and painting graffiti on the villa's marble columns. Soon, however, he grew tired of the band's hedonistic lifestyle and ignorant support of anarchy, and since he couldn't get home until the bassist arranged transportation for him, and the bassist had long ago shut himself up in one of the bedrooms with a large package of heroine, Doug took to exploring alone the many deep caves buried in the island's cliffs.

One day, he found the entrance to a small cave that looked different from all the others. Venturing inside, he found large chunks of diamonds strewn about the floor as if a goddess used the cave for a jewelry box. Intrigued more by their beauty than by the prices they would fetch, Doug left Great Britain and punk music and social revolution behind and decided to remain on the island to mine diamonds.

"What about Katie, Bobby, and Melissa? Are they alright?" Marcie asked, worried about her friends.

"Fuck no. Sorry, but they never had a chance. Two guys pulled up on that side first and smashed their brains in." Doug's punk background had taught him to speak directly and without gentleness.

Marcie stared at her knees.

"Well, I suggest you folks hang here for a little while," Doug concluded. "Let those buggars out there settle down. I've got some beer in the fridge, but now I have some things to tend to. I'll be back in a little while." With that, the short man put the wig back on his head and exited through one of the room's large wooden doors. The survivors stared at one another, waiting for someone to break the silence. Eddie spoke up first.

"I'm gonna trust the little guy," Eddie stated, walking towards the fridge in the other room. He returned with a couple of Coronas, a few limes, and a can of Coke. Marcie claimed one of the Coronas, Frank grabbed the Coke, and Eddie popped the top off the remaining beer.

The large TV came to life and the next hour was spent watching a recorded broadcast of a recent Chicago Bears game. Evidently this Ugh or Doug character had a satellite system for his television. The Chicago team was playing at home and snow cascaded across the screen, as the players were huddled about the sidelines blanketed in heavy garments. Unfortunately, the Bears were losing.

Doug returned to the cave in a little more than an hour's time.

"Did you have a tugboat?" he asked Eddie with concern.

Eddie nodded.

"Well, I hope you have insurance. Those assholes took off with it. The good news is I managed to save your dinghy. Nice little jet boat - I have one myself."

Doug led the three a short way to a camouflaged dock area where the tug's runabout floated beside two other watercrafts.

"You've got yourself a real Bat Cave operation here," Frank said, referring to the old comic hero.

"Everything but fuckin' Wayne manor," Doug laughed. He offered the three what little help he could but insisted that they promise to keep his diamond mine a secret. He wanted to keep the Ugh persona alive.

The original plan called for Eddie to head to one of the local island authorities to report the situation and seek immediate aid while Frank headed north with Marcie in the hopes of locating the United States Coast Guard or some other first-world police force. However, Marcie wouldn't hear of it. Since Jennifer was one of her best friends, she demanded to be included in Eddie's duties.

In the end, as usual, the female won out. Frank loaded up a boat Doug loaned him and prepared to go north. In addition to his transportation, Doug provided him with food, fresh water, fuel, and several maps, while Eddie lent him most of the weaponry. The only gun Eddie kept was his .357 revolver because he figured showing up on the shores of a banana republic with a full arsenal on his back was not such a great idea.

Frank exchanged a firm handshake with their odd sort of savior, promising once again to remain silent of the mining operation. Marcie gave him a big hug, and Eddie promised the two of them would get pizza together when it was all over. The others stood by, watching Frank as he maneuvered the boat away from the hidden dock. "I hope he finds a safe port," Eddie remarked as they headed back inside Doug's cave to talk over the rest of the plan.

Chapter Twenty

"What the hell happened out there?" Lester inquired of the two men scrambling over the side of the getaway boat.

"I'm not sure. Someone started shooting out of the trees, and we split - Becker and Spend are out." Hector answered, helping his injured coworker into Lester's boat.

"We're not going to spend a lot of time here. We've got what we came for." Lester said, pointing at the young girl lying bound and gagged in the bottom of the boat. "I saw another boat pull up in the distance. You're wounded, so you'll stay with me. Hector, take the rest of these guys and head back. Kill any one you come across. If you can't find anyone, sink any vessel you come across and destroy any communication materials - it'll be some time before anyone heads out to this island again." The mercenaries commenced to following out Lester's orders while he engaged the motor and cruised towards the small vessel anchored in the distance.

Hector and the three remaining uninjured mercenaries loaded back into the Zodiacs. He could see one of the unknown gunmen enter the beach lighted by the still burning bonfire, picking up a weapon and firing in the direction of the Zodiacs. The rounds flew harmlessly overhead, and the figure and the girl disappeared beneath the jungle canopy. All four men cautiously advanced over the sand of the beach, then scouted out the surrounding jungle.

When the search didn't turn up any of the surprise gunmen, Hector said, "Let's check the main housing area. We'll use the golf carts." He pointed to the two unoccupied carts nearby, and soon the carts followed the winding path, eventually arriving at the island's villa. No sign of life was to be found. The mercenaries quickly cut all the phone lines connected to the villa, cottage, and stable.

The posse searched in vain for the next hour until Lester radioed for the men to return to the ship. Just before leaving the island, the marauders stopped off at the resort's pier where several boats bobbed in the evening tides. The crew scuttled the vessels and returned to the awaiting Zodiacs. Once safely aboard, Hector reported the situation on the island.

"We'll just head back - our main objective has been met. Without transportation or communication, it'll be quite some time before any one hears from those meddling gunmen." Lester sent two men over to pilot the newly acquired vessel back home, and the two crafts made good time on the run back to the Crow's criminal headquarters.

As usual, once returning home Lester headed straight to Blackwell's office to report, leading his captive up the stairs. Typically the crook would place the girl in one of the rocky, damp cells, but his father had expressed an interest in personally welcoming the Klein girl to Crow Island.

"My son, I see you have our special guest with you," Blackwell said with an eager, strained grimace. Frightened and in shock after seeing the recent murders, Jennifer submitted meekly when Blackwell ordered his son to the set the girl in a chair in front of his large mahogany deck.

"I see by the confusion in your eyes that you have no idea what this is all about," Blackwell began. When Jennifer shook her head, he offered, "Let me explain."

Blackwell went into the story about his difficulties with her father and his enterprises, telling her about Bruce Klein's plant somewhere within the Crow organization. The plant informed him of deals the Crows negotiated, then Klein would use his political influence to cause all sorts of complications.

"The way I figure it, little girl, your father owes me a ton of money and needs to be taught a lesson. I will ransom you, letting your father know not to interfere with my operations. However, if he persists, then he shall know that anytime I want I can apprehend yet another one of his family members. In the end you will most likely be disposed of." Jennifer started crying and protesting that she had nothing to do with her father's business or political affairs, but Blackwell waved his hand, indicating his son should take the girl away.

"Secure her in the hall closet just outside the door. Then return - we need to talk about this Nazi situation.

Lester returned and took his place in front of his father's desk, lighting one of the hand-rolled Cubans cigars contained within a desk-top humidor. One of Blackwell's servants provided the two men with snifters of a fine old English brandy.

"I have made contact with Baron Von Kettler, the leader of the new Nazi movement in South America. He was a bit disturbed upon hearing the news that his men had been killed so brutally. He offered to forget the whole thing because of our business liaisons if we simply arranged to return the women to him, but I'm not sure I trust him. In my opinion, the women aren't so valuable to him that he would be willing to overlook such a serious affront. It could be that he wants to take advantage of the women's transfer to take his revenge on us. I would be interested in hearing your opinion on this issue - since it was you who managed to bring us to this situation in the first place."

Lester scowled. "What's up with our buyer?" He was referring to the ringleader of the prostitution industry in Southeast Asia.

"Mr. Tomo will be here any day now to make an offer, and when I spoke with him, he expressed interest in everything we have to offer - including the Nazi yacht."

"Fuck the Nazi's, we could take them." Lester set his opinion down on the table.

"Very well. You should attempt to make contact with Klein, but first, let's briefly talk about this trouble on Spike Island."

"Everything went smoothly until the end, but just as Hector and the other men were preparing to leave the island with the captive, they were fired upon from the surrounding jungle."

Blackwell considered his son's account, then asked, "Is it possible that the men on the back side of the island could have missed any resort personnel?"

"No," Lester answered with certainty. "We are certain they came later, because we saw their boat. Other than that, I can't imagine who it could be. All the Air Force soldiers that accompanied the targets were present on the island during the attack, and soon after killed. Nobody else knew they were there - not even Bruce Klein." Lester shrugged in frustration. "I even took care of that fireman you were worried about."

The next afternoon the Crows met again in the big office, and Blackwell tossed another manila envelope to Lester.

"You took care of the fireman, eh? Strange, because the fireman is alive and well and presently visiting Capersdeed with the girl that you left behind on the island," the older Crow said. He kept his disappointment in check, because Lester usually accomplished his missions with the utmost care.

"You'll find in the envelope police reports and hospital records, including a fine testimony from our friend Mr. Gilbert that provides a complete description of two of our best assassins."

Lester looked at the reports in disbelief, wondering what could have gone wrong.

"You'll be happy to know that I also have good news. The police commandant of Capersdeed contacted me and wanted to know if we had anything to do with a massacre that took place on one of the nearby islands last night. Courteously, he has detained Mr. Gilbert and the girl and is holding them until we decide what we would like to do."

"I'll leave at once to settle this," Lester assured him as he stood up to leave the office.

Blackwell put up a hand to stop him. "No, I need you here, my son. Send your lieutenant. He should be in the disguise of an American diplomat."

"I'll send Hector out at once," Lester replied as he set out to brief his most trusted henchman. Sooner than later, Hector was dudded up in the dark suit of an American ambassador and sitting behind the wheel of Lester's pride and joy, the Crisscraft. The inboard engine rumbled, and Hector started out on his trip, briefcase in hand, to the small island of Capersdeed. Old Glory flailed in the breeze from a highly polished silver pendant.

One of the aspects of pirating Hector enjoyed most were the little side trips Lester gave him. They were usually tasks too big for someone of lower rank, but too small to concern Lester or the big boss. Today was a simple task: a short cruise to the island, a couple of drinks, then pick up a couple of kids who managed to skip out on the job last night. He would take them out real comfortable, like they were going back to mommy, just get the punks out on the water, pop a cap in to them, dump them, then scoot back home for a job well done. Routine shit.

Hector wiped the mixture of sweat and salt water from his brow to see four men on the pier waiting to gently tow the beautiful antique craft towards the wooden beams of the tattered public docking area. Two uniformed Capersdeed federal police officers waited to escort the United States Ambassador to the commandant's office where he would take possession of the US citizens being held for violating international laws.

The officers led Hector a short distance to where a black government car was waiting. Hector recognized the car as an older model, but still all tricked out, Mercedes Benz. One officer took the wheel while the other joined Hector in the back seat. After the car pulled out of the congestion of the harbor and onto a placid, empty road, the officer in the rear suddenly cried out, "There's something wrong with the diplomat. Pull over!"

Hector's body slumped over in the backseat, and the driver pulled the car to a stop on the shoulder of the road. Swiftly, the officer in the backseat plunged a syringe in the driver's neck, pushed him out of the car, and put two shots into the back of his head. The poor guy never knew what hit him.

After brushing off his suit and straightening his tie, the man sat at the wheel of the Mercedes and put it in gear.

Chapter Twenty-One

The environment inside Doug's hidden cave was cold and damp, and Marcie's teeth began to chatter. Eddie wanted to offer the girl something warmer to wear, but the fact was that he was slightly chilled himself, wearing only a pair of cutoff military pants and his favorite Cubs jersey.

"You wouldn't happen to have a warmer shirt we could borrow?" Eddie asked their unusual host, motioning towards the shivering girl. Doug nodded and headed back into the developed portion of the subterranean habitat, returning with an old, gray, hooded sweat shirt.

"This is the best I could do." The short man handed the shirt over to Marcie, who thankfully pulled the item over her head. "You can use my jet boat if you need to," Doug said. "You could travel north towards the Virgin Islands, but Capersdeed is much closer. I don't know how much help that will be, but the jet boat should be able to make it that far. Just do me a favor if you should decide to use it. Dock it in a safe place and call this number." Doug handed Eddie a card with a phone number. "Just leave a message as to where you left it, and I'll be over to pick it up sometime. Oh, and don't tell anyone about my little operation."

Doug insisted that Eddie and Marcie should rest in his cave before starting out, arguing that the office wouldn't open until the next morning anyway. They agreed, but both of them had trouble sleeping after the gruesome events of the evening. The next morning they set out just a little before sunrise.

The open sea was a little rough on the small jet boat, but Eddie held the craft at its top speed throughout the entire voyage. Due to Doug's guidance, a map, and compass, Eddie and Marcie managed to make it to the island nation of Capersdeed within a few hours. The jet boat's motor sputtered and coughed as Eddie maneuvered the craft into one of the slips in the island's public dock area. Thinking of Frank, who had set out on a much longer voyage, Eddie hoped for the best. Doug had assured them that the boat would be able to make the trip with fuel to spare.

Eddie tied off the boat, securing it to the wooden pier, then took a quick look around trying to figure out his next move. He didn't like the looks the of docks around him. Large yachts, hotels, and restaurants had occupied all the other docks he seen up to that point, but the harbor at Capersdeed was rundown, old and filthy, and decrepit fishing boats lined the creaking wooden planks. A bleached-out sign fixed above an old wooden shack at the end of the pier identified the building as the harbor master's office. Nearby, small crews of tanned men labored away among the vessels, paying Ed and Marcie very little attention as they passed by. Capersdeed was definitely a third world banana republic.

A slacked set of wires ran from the corner of the shack to a nearby telephone pole. On the face of the building, a lamp with a broken light bulb hung over a smoky glass window that housed a noisy air conditioning unit. Behind the window a dark skinned man in a tan uniform sat with his feet up on a small desk. The man had a long drooping, bushy mustache and a pair of mirrored sunglasses over his eyes. In the corner, a long bolt action rifle leaned against the wall. To Eddie, the guard appeared to be snoozing. Eddie shot a quizzical look at Marcie and noticed her brown hair was matted with salt water and flat against her face. She still looked good. Marcie silently motioned to Eddie to wake the man up, and hesitantly, Eddie knocked on the window. There was no response. Eddie knocked a little harder, and the guard stirred, rubbing the dark stubble on his face. The guard slid the window open, allowing cool air to escape and flow over Eddie's face as he leaned in closer to communicate with the man.

Eddie greeted him using his limited knowledge of the Spanish language.

"You gonna haf to talk in English if yo want me to understand you mon," the guard responded in the typical Caribbean accented English spoken in ex-colonies of the British Empire. Eddie had mistakenly assumed that the language of the island nation was going to be Spanish.

"We're Americans, and we need help." Eddie quickly proceeded to relate the story to the Capersdeed harbor master. After listening intently to the long story of the murders and their escape from seafaring gunmen, the man picked up the receiver of a desktop phone and rapidly dialed a set of numbers. Eddie couldn't make out what was said - it seemed the guard was almost mumbling on purpose in order to keep the gist of the conversation secret.

The harbor master hung up the phone, stood up, grabbed his rifle and exited the shack saying, "We'll wait here, mon. De commandant is sending a car fo' you." After taking a seat on the ground and leaning his back against the side of the building, the guard paid them no more attention and proceeded to light up a filterless cigarette.

Detecting a fine line of sweat trickling down the middle of his back, Eddie wished the guard would let them wait inside the office. After about ten minutes a tan Ford Bronco with its top cut off pulled up. Two more dark-skinned men clad in similar uniforms as the harbor master jumped out, and the three exchanged quick conversation. Eddie and Marcie were asked to take a seat in the Bronco, Eddie in back and Marcie in the front passenger seat. One of the soldiers joined Eddie in the back while the other piloted the vehicle.

"Not to worry mon, just a precaution." The armed man noticed Eddie's concerned look. "You want a smoke mon?" He offered Eddie a filterless Lucky Strike. After what he had been through the last couple of days, Eddie accepted the cigarette, its harsh smoke causing him to cough a few times until his lungs became accustomed to it. A short-lasting nicotine buzz hazed over Eddie's brain, but the smoke and the buzz were gone by the time the vehicle had reached a large

Island Bound

two-story brick building. The driver parked the vehicle in front of a large rectangular building beside a black four-door sedan. The building was constructed out of cement blocks which were painted white, and its roof consisted of long silver aluminum planks.

Marcie and Eddie were escorted up a short set of wooden stairs to a heavy pair of doors made out of a light shaded wood. The doors opened to reveal a large, bright room. Planks of well-polished wood stretched throughout the room's interior, and a set of ceiling fans swirling overhead kept the room at a surprisingly comfortable temperature. A young Latino girl sat fanning herself while pecking away at an old typewriter with a single finger in front of a row of black metal filing cabinets. Above another set of double doors, a sign read "The Commandant."

"Is the commandant in?" asked one of the guards. The girl glanced up and nodded, so the officer opened one of the doors and motioned for Marcie and Eddie to enter the office. The officer secured the door behind as he entered while the driver lingered in the first room, striking up a conversation with the young office girl.

The commandant sat behind a large desk cluttered with various office materials and equipment, sifting through a pile of papers. He was a thin man with dark hair and Latin features, and his tan uniform was adorned with gold and lace. Black and gold epaulettes decorated the tops of his shoulders, and he wore a bright gold badge and several metals on the left side of his chest. Numerous plaques, framed certificates, and awards covered the back wall between two more uniformed guards posted attentively to the left and right of the commandant. Everyone remained standing except for the commandant, who raised his brow knowingly at his visitors.

"My men tell me you ran into some trouble last night. Why don't you run through the story for me, and we'll see what we can do to help." The commandant sat back in his chair, tapping the palm of his right hand with the tip of a long, thin, letter opener. An arrogant and skeptical expression dominated his facial features as Eddie began with the attempt made on his life and ended with his departure with Marcie for Capersdeed, dutifully leaving out Doug's role in their escape. Eddie wasn't sure why, but he also withheld any information about Frank's presence or his mission to seek out and locate the Coast Guard. He had a bad feeling in his gut about this whole situation.

"Escort them to the waiting room outside," the commandant ordered, then turned his attention to Eddie and Marcie. "I need to look into this. It sounds like the work of a rebellious, guerilla organization." The officer escorted the Americans back out to the lobby and sat them down on a long, wooden bench similar to the design of an old church pew. He returned to the commandant's office, not noticing or perhaps just not acknowledging the absence of the guard and the office girl. The smell of burning rope drifted into the room from a screened window in back of the girl's desk.

Eddie and Marcie sat on that hard bench for about thirty minutes before the officer emerged from the confines of the commandant's office.

"The commandant is ready for the two of you," the officer announced as he sniffed, drawing the scent of the room into his nostrils. "Where's the other officer and the girl?"

Eddie pointed to the rear of the building, then the officer ushered the two back into the office. With that, he quickly excused himself and headed out the door, then joined the office girl and the first officer behind the building.

"I've got my people working on this situation. A search party will be sent out shortly. I'm afraid there will not be much hope of finding your friend, but every effort will be made. In the meantime, I need to see your passports." The commandant spoke with a mild British accent.

"You want our passports? I told you, they stole my boat, and my passport was on it." Marcie nodded in agreement due to the fact that she had not even taken her passport with her from Florida. The girls never planned on leaving US soil.

"We'll get this all straightened out," the commandant assured them. "I've already contacted the nearest US Embassy, and they're going to send someone shortly. He should be here in a few hours. I'm sorry, but until that time, due to the laws of Capersdeed, I must arrest you and keep you detained." The commandant ordered one of the officers to arrest the Americans and lock them up in the jail, then responded to the confused looks on the faces of his prisoners. "Do not be alarmed. This is just standard procedure. You will be released as soon as your diplomat arrives."

The officer frisked both captives. During the search, Eddie nervously remembered the .357 stashed in one of the large cargo pockets of his cutoff fatigues. Unbelievably, the officer missed the weapon. The guy must have taken a trip behind the building as well at some point time during the day.

The officer led the couple back out into the main reception area, then to another door on the opposite side of the room. The uniformed man took a key ring attached to his leather gun belt and unlocked the door. All three descended into a dark, damp cellar. The room was rather large. The floor was brick, the walls stone, and the roof of the same wood as the floor upstairs. Four cells and a desk furnished the room, and each cell contained a thin mattress on the floor as a bed. The cellar was lit by several bulbs suspended from the ceiling by single wires since the only natural light snuck in through small windows near the ceiling and against the back walls of the cells. The windows had no screens, but rather, sturdy iron bars.

The officer secured the two in separate cells. Marcie was hesitant to sit down, not knowing who had occupied the space before her. Fortunately for the pair, no other cell was occupied. Eddie leaned with both elbows on the frame of the cage in front of him.

"This really sucks!" He exclaimed.

Chapter Twenty-Two

"All across the nation from coast to coast, people always ask me what I like most. I don't like to brag, I don't like to boast. I just tell 'em I like toast," Frank bellowed cheerfully over the sound of the boat's engine. Since he left Doug's cave, he had run through The Star Spangled Banner six times, had sung 99 Bottles of Beer on the Wall from beginning to end, and now busied himself rehashing old rhymes from childhood. The large jet boat had provided Frank a relatively comfortable ride, and his only problem was navigation. It was a big ocean out there.

If all was well and his navigation was accurate, Frank should be arriving soon in the US port on the map Doug gave him. The island was supposed to house one of the local US Coast Guard satellite stations.

After about an hour and half, Frank was still in out in open water, scanning the horizon. Fear settled on him when he realized that there weren't any signs of civilization and the small yellow light on the control counsel warned him that the boat had almost run out of fuel. Frank crossed his fingers and kept going, but ten minutes later the engine sputtered and died. Frank was at the mercy of the sea's currents.

When the sun's first rays peeked over the horizon, Frank started to get worried. Although its light helped him to stay awake, its appearance meant Frank must have gotten far off his course - it was rising on the left side of the boat instead of the right side where it should have been if he had been heading north. Checking his provisions to see how long he could survive on the open sea, he found a bottle of water, several pieces of fruit, and a slightly melted candy bar. That would get him through the next few hours. Fortunately, the boat also held a flare gun. Loading a flare into the barrel, Frank kept a sharp eye out for any other vessels.

The sun had traveled beyond its crest at noon and now had made a good dent in its return journey to the sea when Frank spied a small interruption of the horizon's straight curve. It became larger and larger, and by the time the sun had almost set, Frank could easily make out the shape of a small vessel. He fired the gun over his head, expending all his flares, then watched with tremendous satisfaction as the boat approached him and he made out the writing on her helm.

Frank had set out to find the United States Coast Guard. As it turned out, and completely by chance, the Coast Guard had found Frank.

Chapter Twenty-Three

Eddie was beginning to think that the diplomat would never show up. It had been several hours since he and Marcie had been locked into the cells, and now as it grew dark outside Eddie was getting nervous.

Finally the door at the top of the stairs opened, and two people descended the steps. An officer guided a man wearing a light-colored suit down the stairwell.

"Dese are de Americans, mon. The commandant said to turn dem over to you and offer any assistance." The guard unlocked both of the jail cells and the diplomat held his hand up to stop Eddie and Marcie from going into their story again. The guard, prisoners, and diplomat all ascended the stairs and exited to the front of the building where the black Mercedes was waiting. The car was empty, and the single guard asked, "Where be da two officers dat picked you up, mon?"

"I don't know, they were here when I entered the building," the diplomat responded. As if he had just thought of it, he said to the officer, "Y'know, we're kind of in a hurry - considering the situation, as you well know. Think you can give us a ride down to the docks?"

The island man nodded affirmative, sliding into the driver's seat. The diplomat sat in back with Eddie, and Marcie was upfront.

The diplomat looked Eddie in the face and held his left index finger to his lips, then reached down to his ankle where a small pistol was holstered. Attached to the front of the weapon was what Eddie assumed was a silencer. One of the roads leading to the docks was long and relatively desolate with only a few small shacks lining it on either side. Saying that he needed to relieve himself, the diplomat asked the driver to pull to the side of the road for a moment. The driver hesitated, considering the unusual request, but eventually pulled over next to a large bush. When the driver placed the vehicle's transmission in park, a quiet chirp emitted from the handheld weapon. The driver's head fell forward, activating the car's horn. The diplomat quickly pulled the man away from the steering wheel to silence the horn, then exited the car and dragged the lifeless form behind the bush. When he returned to the car, he took the driver's seat and drove off from the scene, taking a route away from the dock area. Eddie and Marcie regarded the diplomat with shock.

"Sorry to scare you folks. My name is Brighton Sparks, and I work for Mr. Klien, Jennifer's father. You all walked into a big ol' basket of shit, but you should just stay calm for now. I'll explain everything shortly." Brighton briefly enlightened his passengers as he steered the car along various back roads. He explained that one of Mr. Klien's spies within the Crow's criminal organization caught wind of the kidnapping plot and contacted him. Brighton was sent down to protect the millionaire's daughter. Unfortunately, the information was a little slow in coming, and Jennifer had already been snatched by the time he arrived. One of Brighton's contacts informed him that one of the other girls on the island had escaped and it wasn't long before Klein's sources located them in Capersdeed. Brighton hoped Marcie or Eddie might remember some details about that night that would help him in tracking down his employer's daughter.

"So you know of these guys, but you don't know where their hideout is?" Eddie asked.

"I will shortly," Brighton stated as he pulled the Mercedes onto a small airstrip where a familiar Cessna aircraft sat at the end of the field. The propeller was a blur, turning too fast for the human eye to make out the blades. Brighton pulled the black car over behind the aircraft, and all three got out. A door on the side of the plane popped open, and Eddie was surprised to see a stocky figure with a cheerful face.

"Is that you, Marvin?" Eddie asked when he placed the pilot's familiar face with a name.

"Ya mon. You be dat fireman I flew down to de Keys las' week." The flight seemed like a year ago to Eddie.

Eddie, Marcie, and Brighton entered the small seating area of the plane where a bound and gagged man occupied one of the seats. The pilot increased the throttle of the aircraft, causing the plane to run down the airstrip. The plane left the ground and headed into the evening sky.

After only twenty minutes, Marvin landed the small Cessna on a desolate airstrip. The plane was taxied and parked in front of a single wooden shack that looked to be deserted.

Ignoring Eddie and Marcie for a moment, Brighton took the man roughly and pushed him into the shack where he strip-searched him and tied him to a chair. When Eddie and Marcie timidly followed Marvin into the dark doorway, they saw that the figure in the chair was dressed in black socks, bikini briefs, and a dago tee shirt. His long black hair was tied back in a pony tail, and gold chains hung around the man's neck and wrists.

"You may want to hang outside. We need to get some info outta this guy. We worked him over a little earlier, but he wouldn't talk so we're going to have to use some more extreme methods," Brighton explained.

Eddie and Marcie stepped outside and pondered over the whole situation. They were both hungry - neither of them had had a bite to eat for almost twenty-four hours. Screams and taunts escaped through the cracks of the old building before Marvin reappeared, looking a tad haggard. He mentioned that they got what they needed and would be ready to head out soon.

"How did you get mixed up in all this, Marvin?" Eddie asked the pilot.

"How does anyone, mon. I do a little work for Mistah Klein from time d'time."

Island Bound

Brighton's extreme measures turned out to be successful and he now knew the location of the Crow's base of operations. Eddie naturally suggested contacting the authorities, but Brighton wouldn't hear of it. Momentarily, Eddie wondered if Bruce Klein himself might be engaged in a few activities he wouldn't like to be disclosed to the police.

"Why don't you folks get back in the plane, and Marvin will take you back to Miami?" Brighton suggested.

Brighton instructed them to contact Mr. Klein and fill him in on all the trouble down in paradise.

"Wait, wait, wait," Eddie protested. "I'm going with you, Brighton, even if I have to swim behind your boat. What are you going to do, attack them alone?"

After checking him out with a shrewd eye, Brighton handed Eddie a gun and asked if he was familiar with the workings of a firearm. Eddie fished the .357 from his cargo pocket and displayed the weapon.

"I never leave home without it," Eddie said.

"I see," Brighton said. "Do you know how to use it?"

"Sure."

After considering the matter for some time, Brighton agreed that Eddie could be a tremendous help. "I just hope you realize that this could be a life-threatening situation. Are you sure you don't want to just go back to Miami and relax on the beach? I don't want you backing out on me."

Eddie watched as the Cessna left the runway, carrying Marvin and Marcie back to Miami. When the plane became a black dot in the sky, Brighton led Eddie down a footpath overgrown with jungle foliage. Eventually the two exited the jungle canopy and found themselves on a small rocky beach. A boat was waiting in rolling surf a safe distance from the sharp rocks jutting from the beach and into the shallow water.

The boat did not fit the image that Eddie had in mind. It was simply an old recreational boat constructed mainly of fiberglass. It was the kind of boat that the cool dads from the old 1970's sitcoms would have parked in their suburban driveways. The hull was sun faded, but had originally been the color of sand. The rest of the boat was white with a slight yellow discoloration.

"We figure a boat like this one would have a better chance of not drawing any unwanted attention," Brighton explained. Eddie thought that made sense.

The Crow's island hideaway was much farther south than Brighton had hoped. The shortest route would still take the night to cover, and unfortunately would take them close to Capersdeed. The commandant would certainly be aware of the escape by then, and had probably sent out a team of patrol boats to recover the prisoners. It was quite obvious that the man was in cahoots with the Crow organization.

There was no time to waste in avoiding Capersdeed. Brighton planned to extinguish all the boat's running lights and hope they could slip silently past the island during the night. By his reckoning, Brighton estimated their time of arrival to be in the neighborhood of six o'clock in the morning - a good time to sneak in and sneak out. Hopefully the Crow's security force would still be wiping the sleep from their eyes by the time Jennifer was tucked safely in the boat.

Brighton slapped a fishing hat on top of Eddie's head and stashed the weapons where they would be out of sight. The boat turned out to be a sleeper, and the inboard engine propelled the craft at a surprising rate.

Eddie was dozing off on the floor of the boat when Brighton laid a heavy hand on his shoulder. "Capersdeed patrol boat," he whispered, pointing over the port side of the old boat. Luckily for the two, patches of steamy fog were settling around the island for the evening. Brighton had shut down the boat's motor and was allowing the craft to drift with the sea's currents. A searchlight from the patrol craft circulated from a point on the enemy vessel. Taking a sniper rifle for himself, Brighton slid a mini-14 across the floor to Eddie. Eddie assumed Brighton's weapon was mounted with some sort of night targeting sight. Shouldering the gun, Brighton followed the progress of the stalking patrol boat.

Eddie liked his new ally, figuring the lean, weatherworn man should be about ten years older than he was. He kept his brown hair cut down in a neat flat top, and Eddie thought the man spoke with some sort of German accent. By now Brighton had exchanged the costume of a diplomat for the costume of a mild-mannered fishing man. Eddie improvised with the hat Brighton gave him and a vest he found in the boat. The fishing get up would hopefully allow the two men to get close enough to Crow Island to find a hole in the island's security. When Eddie posed questions to the man during the early part of the boat ride, he found Brighton was friendly but standoffish.

An hour after the boat set out for Crow Island, Eddie began to ponder why he decided to go with Brighton. He was on safe ground. Why didn't he just get on the plane with Marcie and head back to civilization? He was supposed to be on vacation, after all, and Brighton was sure to be more than capable of retrieving Jennifer alone. Eddie didn't have an answer for himself. He figured it was just in his make up not to back down from a challenge. After a few minutes Eddie had dozed off, not waking until he felt Brighton's hand upon his shoulder.

The patrol boat was so close Eddie could hear the voices of the men onboard; a chuckle followed by the stink of a cigar drifted across the water. The patrol boat's beacon began its circular motion back towards the old sport boat. The bright beam passed the old girl's decks and, for a moment, passed on to continue its rotation. Suddenly, it returned and laid on the side of the sport boat.

"This is the Capersdeed Shore Patrol." A harsh voice amplified by a loudspeaker replaced the chuckles of the men on board. "Identify yourself and prepare to be inspected."

Island Bound

Brighton identified himself as a person not to be crossed. There was a loud crack and a splash, then the beam of light pointed up into the fog of the late evening sky. Brighton had used the infrared scope to mark the man operating the search light, then aimed at a man standing behind a mounted machinegun.

The second shot missed and the remaining crew returned fire. In the haze and confusion of combat, the crew's barrage was sporadic and off target, but a low, slow, banging rumble identified the use of a heavier caliber machinegun. The crackle of small arms joined in to the symphony.

Eddie kept his head down low, feeling the streaking, heated lead slamming home on the sides of the old boat. Ed and Brighton were fortunate that none of the rounds did any critical damage to the boat or themselves.

"Hey kid! You gonna work for your money? How about sending a little lead back at them?" Brighton screamed, jumping into the pilot seat of the boat. Eddie could feel the engine unsuccessfully trying to turn over.

"I'm getting paid for this? Let me see the cash!" Eddie retorted as he lifted the mini-14 to his shoulder. He rapidly pulled the trigger, sending a hail of return fire in the direction of the patrol boat. It was difficult to visualize the craft itself, so he concentrated his aim on the muzzle flashes of the enemies weapons. Up in front, Brighton couldn't get the engine to start up; it must have been hit. Dead in the water in a fiberglass boat fighting against adversaries with the power of heavy weapons, things didn't look all that good for the would-be rescuers. Brighton removed himself from the control seat.

"I guess it is time for plan B," Brighton stated as Eddie was slamming a fresh magazine into the mini-14. Brighton appeared on Eddie's left with a disposable rocket launcher that Eddie recognized as an antitank weapon from his days in the reserves. The patrol boat had moved in to an uncomfortably close range, and its outline was easily discernable behind the fog. A streak of fire careened from Brighton's shoulder, and the explosive shell slammed into the patrol craft. Then, all went silent and the smoking hulk of the patrol craft drifted by. Her decks appeared to be lifeless, and the boat was already lying low in the water.

Brighton went to work on the boat's motor. Since he had been the one to outfit the vessel with its inboard, he was familiar with the mechanics. After about twenty minutes, the two were once again on their way. Brighton explained that the damage was easily repaired - a problem with a couple of fuel lines was easy to fix.

The new day's sun was showing itself when the two fishermen made their mark. The information collected during the interrogation proved to be accurate. Brighton and Eddie sat in the boat, two fishing lines dangling into the warm salt water. Only a mile away, the Crow Island rose menacingly from the sea. For the most part, the surrounding waters were empty, and they had only seen a couple of other boats in the distance since the sun rose. From far away, no one could guess that these two gentle old fishermen calmly casting their lines meanwhile made plans to thwart the intentions of a multi-national crime ring.

Chapter Twenty-Four

The sun of a new day was rising as Blackwell and his son shared a steaming, freshly brewed pot of joe. They were enjoying the morning on the verandah built on the east side of Blackwell's large plantation home, Blackwell reading the *Miami Times* as he puffed away on one of his hand-rolled Cubans, Lester quietly nibbling at a still warm, morning-baked cinnamon roll. In the courtyard just below the verandah, some of their workers readied a helicopter pad for the arrival of a Crow family business acquaintance. Mr. Tomo was flying in for the day to inspect the recently acquired merchandise. At each of the four corners of the landing pad, Crow security men stood poised, dressed lightly in tan uniforms with sub-machineguns strapped across their backs. With dark glasses and hair cropped short, the guards were a picture of detached military might.

"Looks like the Marlins should have a good team this year," Blackwell concluded as he neatly folded the sports section of the newspaper.

"Did we have to get up so early for this?" Lester muttered as he gazed crossly at the helicopter pad below. He had not slept much over the past few days, and he didn't see why it was so important for him to be present for the proceedings that morning.

"One can never start a profitable day too early," Blackwell pointed out. "I want to get that livestock in the pen downstairs moved. They're beginning to cost money to maintain, and the stink is just unbearable. Have one of the men hose them down before Mr. Tomo has a chance to inspect them."

"I'll see to it at once, Father." Lester excused himself from the table and exited the verandah as the sound of rotor blades chopping through the morning's air could be heard in the distance. Blackwell continued to read as he awaited the arrival of the helicopter, and the guards around the landing pad remained silent.

Soon a dark gray helicopter appeared over the space of the verandah and the courtyard below, and Blackwell found it necessary to put his coffee cup on top of the newspaper to keep it from scattering all over the room as the vehicle's rotating blades created a small windstorm. The guards lining the pad took a step back away from the descending aircraft as the landing gear touched down and rested on the pad's painted surface. The hum of the engine quieted, and the blades slowed and eventually stopped. A door behind the pilot's seat slid back towards the tail, and a squat-looking Oriental gent decked out in a dark suit and sunglasses exited the vehicle. His black hair was kept in a spiked-up flattop with a long back spread over his broad shoulders. The tan-skinned man was short, but the Japanese bodyguard was a powerhouse of tight, massive muscles. The bulge of a large caliber handgun holstered beneath his pricey silk suit let spectators know that he meant business.

Once he stepped out of the helicopter, the bodyguard turned to assist the frail, aged Mr. Tomo from the helicopter. The trusted bodyguard wasn't aware of Mr. Tomo's agenda for the day, but he imagined it would be a routine visit between old business partners.

Blackwell and Mr. Tomo, who had first met as young men, had been business acquaintances for many years now. Although Mr. Tomo was only ten years senior to Blackwell, the passing years had not been as good to the Japanese man as they had been to the island dweller. The two crime bosses first discovered a mutually beneficial relationship when a broker in Hawaii introduced them on a private golf course. Blackwell needed an unusually large shipment of opium for a customer in the States, and Tomo needed a little muscle to take care of a problem with one of his competitors based in Central America. They worked together to solve their individual conflicts and found out quickly that they possessed compatible business ethics. Since then, they maintained a supportive, enduring, and happy relationship of murder and unwholesome profit.

That morning Mr. Tomo chose to wear a silk multi-colored Hawaiian shirt tucked into a pair of tan linen pants. His gray thin hair was greased up, slicked over, and parted on the right side, one section painstakingly combed across a bald spot on his crown. Thin leather sandals protected his feet from the warm ground beneath, and his right hand carried a brown leather briefcase. Tomo and his guard were guided by one of the Crow security personnel to Blackwell's office while the other three Crow men remained in their positions around the landing pad.

Lester had once again joined his father on the verandah by the time Mr. Tomo presented himself.

"Mr.Tomo, it is very good to see you, my old friend. It has been too long." Blackwell rose from his seat to greet the old man and show him the proper respect he deserved. Lester stood as well, setting his cup of coffee down on to the tabletop. Setting the briefcase down, Mr. Tomo accepted Blackwell's hand. He nodded at Lester, and all three sat down. The Oriental bodyguard remained near the French doors that led back into the house from the verandah. The Crow's guard took a position on the verandah opposite the bodyguard.

The three men spent the first hour of their visit enjoying the fresh baked cinnamon rolls, tea and coffee. Mr. Tomo started the day's business.

"Before we get started, I have an announcement to make," Mr. Tomo declared.

"Well, do tell, my trusted friend," Blackwell replied.

"I am retiring," he said as he set his briefcase on the table with finality. "I'm old, rich and tired. But not to worry - Mr. Han-sun will be taking my place." Mr. Tomo called his trusted guard over and introduced the man to the Crows. Mr. Han-sun was surprised to hear of his elevation of position in the crime society.

Island Bound

Mr. Tomo had blood relatives in the business, and the guard had always assumed control of the organization would go to one of them.

"Well Mr. Han-sun, welcome to the club." Blackwell shook the man's hand, noticing his iron grip.

"I will let you know when the change has officially taken shape. As for now, there is business at hand. Please take your prior position Mr. Han-sun." Mr. Tomo subtly informed the man that the promotion had not taken effect. Tomo was still the boss and Han-sun was still a guard.

Understanding his old associate's to-the-point manner, Blackwell led the Asian pimp into a second room without further ado. The highly polished wood floor gleamed in the morning light, its purity unmarred by the clutter of furniture. In the center of the room, a line of women stood before two Crow guards armed with Russian AK-47 assault rifles. Lester had ordered the women to be hosed down, cleaned up, and dressed for presentation. Now, they all wore white, loose-fitting shirts and pants similar to hospital scrubs. The youngest of the group, a child less than five years of age, whimpered slightly and tried to wrap her arms around her mother's leg for security. One of the guards abruptly separated them. A young woman, deeply tanned, was in the middle of the group.

"Have them remove their clothing." Mr. Tomo asked. The guards prompted any shyness by using the stocks of their assault rifles to make their point, and the cotton garments dropped to the ground along with two blondes in the line-up who resisted.

"Excellent specimens, every one of them. The tall blondes make a handsome addition to the collection, and the child should blossom nicely. I'll take them all. Mr. Han, call for the boat and bring the shackles up. The blondes seem fiesty, but we'll take care of that before long." Mr. Han-sun left the room.

"The girl with the brown hair, in the middle. She will not be available for a little while. She is the daughter of an American politician," Blackwell interrupted. "You have heard of my troubles with Mr. Klein. He will be taught a lesson very soon, but after that, we will deliver the girl to you." Jennifer looked beaten, her face was drawn, and her eyes hinted that she had been drugged.

Blackwell and his guest returned to the warm morning air and the verandah to complete the business. First they would set a price, then they needed to arrange the details of exchanging the goods. They took their seats at a long mahogany conference table, and Blackwell poured two glasses of ice water from a crystal pitcher. Just then, far off in the distance, they heard the distinctive sounds of gunfire. Blackwell ordered Lester to investigate the noises then continued his discussion with Tomo.

Demanding an explanation from one of the Crow watchmen, Lester learned that several high-speed boats had entered the lagoon and dropped off a party of armed men. Lester ordered one of the guards with an AK-47 to retrieve two of the remaining guards at the helipad then to report to the rear garden area where several guards were already engaged with the intruders. A second guard remained with the prisoners and helped Mr. Han-sun in shackling them while Lester went to join in the conflict. Before he left, he pushed Jennifer into the room where Tomo and Blackwell sat.

As Blackwell and Tomo struck their deal for the merchandise, two of the remaining men below went off to assist in suppressing the battle that was raging behind the large main house. The helicopter pilot and the final guard stayed behind to protect the two bosses, casually puffing on British cigarettes and making conversation.

Mr. Tomo opened his briefcase and withdrew several large stacks of US currency.

"That's one million now, and one hundred thousand when the final girl is delivered," he clarified as he relinquished the cash. Blackwell accepted the bills and temporarily secured them in a small compartment built into the bottom of the table.

"With that done, Blackwell, and considering the fact I do not wish to get caught up in your troubles, I will thank you and excuse myself. Mr. Han-sun will stay behind to secure the shipment." Blackwell ordered the guard assisting Han-sun to escort his guest to the helipad. The two had finished securing the group of women. Blackwell asked Jennifer to sit with him and join him in a cup of coffee. Jennifer, filled with fear and confusion, hesitated but did not resist as Blackwell poured her a cup of coffee and, placing it on a table beside her, drew his chair so that he could sit facing her.

Mr. Tomo was nearing the landing sight when a bullet screamed from the brush surrounding the helipad. The hot lead slammed into the aircraft's windshield causing a large star to form on the glass. The pilot and the guard dropped to the ground for cover behind the helicopter, and the pilot withdrew an automatic pistol from his shoulder holster. The guard escorting the Japanese man asked the crime lord to wait in the relative safety of the entrance just off of the launch sight, then he joined the two men at their position behind the helicopter from which they returned fire to their unseen attackers.

Blackwell left Jennifer momentarily to secure the doors of the verandah, then led her with a pistol at her back to the room where Han-sun and the prisoners waited for the conflict to cool down. The room that Blackwell used to entertain clients coming to do business on the island was as safe as any within the main house. A single stairwell and verandah doors made of bulletproof glass were the only access points for the entire room. The door opening onto the stairway was bulletproof as well and featured built-in firing slits so that a gunman could stand behind their protection and still repel intruders.

The only disadvantage of the room was that it did not offer a view of the landing pad. Thus, Blackwell didn't see his three men stormed and overrun by the invaders. Shortly after Blackwell retreated to the security of his reception room, the three Crow guards lay wounded or dead in company of a few corpses from the attacking party. Armed with German assault rifles, men dressed in gray uniforms left their dead behind and entered the main building.

Minutes later, two soaking wet, armed fishermen followed behind the invading storm troopers.

*

By the time Lester arrived at the back of the main building the invaders had fought their way into the large garden area. Lester immediately coordinated a defense strategy and called up reinforcements from the bowels of the Crow installation. A breathless guard reported to Lester.

"Four speed boats penetrated the lagoon. They dropped about sixteen troopers down by the docks and knocked down the guards there in no time. We struck back right away from the main house, but there were just too many of them." He stood at attention and waited for Lester to issue orders.

Lester assessed the situation while reinforcements, numbering approximately twenty, emerged from the basement barracks and reported. The invaders held positions in and around the garden area, which was crisscrossed with brick paths and stone-walled flowerbeds. Lester caught a momentary glimpse at one of the invaders as the person left one spot to advance to another and noticed the figure wore a dark gray battle uniform with a red band strapped around his upper arm. The bullets were raining in on the main house with constant fury.

The scene behind the mansion home turned into a bloody carnage as the Crows' skillful mercenaries turned the tide of the battle. The tan uniformed men moved away from the safety of the building. The covering fire for the advancing soldiers was so heavy the invaders had no choice but to withdraw and try to redirect their firepower. Out of the mansion's windows and doorways, two men worked high-powered sniper rifles, surgically picking their targets. Another team peppered the garden area randomly with a belt-fed 30-caliber machinegun while loud explosions from a grenade launcher terrorized the attackers physically and psychologically. Meanwhile, small arms added a persistent, rhythmic crackle to the violent scene.

The combat proceeded steadily, the Crow army advancing, the invaders retreating. Finally, the battle found its way to the edge of the docks, and the only retreat still available to the invaders was a wet one. The boats in which they had arrived were nowhere to be seen - the crafts had either been sunk or the drivers had been too cowardly to stick around. Of the original sixteen invaders, only two remained. Throwing their weapons to the ground, they waved a white handkerchief in the air.

A smile parted Lester's lips and he ordered a ceasefire. Yelling to the attackers to show themselves and move forward into position, Lester approached the men who had dared to attack Crow Island. Two men, tall, lean, and uniformed from head to toe in dark gray stood up unarmed and surrendered themselves to Lester and his band of cutthroats.

"You two come with me," Lester instructed one of his men. "The rest of you guys, keep us covered." Lester and two Crow soldiers cautiously walked towards the gray-clad men, and sure enough, their red arm bands were decorated with a black swastika. One of the men was breathing heavy, and blood stained the fabric around his left shoulder. The other man appeared to be unharmed. Both stood silently, their arms stretched above their heads submissively.

"Well, well, what do we have here? Nazis, huh?" Lester exclaimed. The AK-47 cradled in Lester's arms was still warm and smoking, and he used it to plant a round into the forehead of the wounded Nazi. "Sorry about that, but I'm afraid we don't have the proper medical facilities to accommodate wounded dogs." Lester ordered his men to pick up their mess, thinking how the old man would be angry when he saw the damage to his beloved flower garden. Taking two soldiers with him, as well as the Nazi prisoner, Lester returned to the helipad and verandah area to check on his father, the merchandise and Mr. Tomo. He was relatively certain that the attack came from more than one point, and he hoped another party of invaders had not pillaged the main house while he fought near the docks.

While en route to the other end of the mansion Lester ordered one of his men to take the Nazi and lock him up in the cells by the subterranean docks. Then, Lester and the second man continued on their way. When they reached their destination both men were surprised by what they discovered.

Lying in a bloody heap in the center of the hallway leading to the landing pad was Mr. Tomo. Through the hall's open doorway, Lester could make out one of his men writhing in agony from his wounds beneath the dormant chopper. Three more gray-uniformed men lay dead in the stairwell, their blood slowly dripping down the stairs and staining the wood of the floor below. The security door at the top of the flight of stairs was badly damaged and stood wide open. Noticing that the bodies were unarmed, Lester wondered why they didn't carry the same German assault rifles the rest of the attackers had used.

Lester and his man cautiously advanced up the stairwell to investigate, the subordinate soldier taking the point position. After entering the room, the two men found a more disturbing sight. Three of the prisoners had disappeared and Mr. Han-sun seemed to have taken quite a beating. Worst of all, Blackwell, handcuffed upright on one of the chairs from the verandah, stared lifelessly at the ceiling. A trickle of blood drained from a small hole in the middle of his forehead.

"What the fuck happened here?" Lester's screamed at the shackled Nazi women. They remained silent, too stubborn, or perhaps too frightened, to reply.

Lester shot one of the women in the head, splashing her companions with bloody pieces and parts. Once again, Lester phrased his question.

"Our men were attempting a rescue," the young woman answered with a Brazilian accent. "That Jap fought them off. Then, two more guys - they weren't our men - came in, and one of them got into it with the Jap. They released three of us and headed out." As if the woman had reconciled herself to her imminent death, she added scornfully, "Before they left, the girl with the brown hair shot your asshole father with his own fucking pistol."

When she had finished, Lester shot her in the head as well - punishment for calling his father an asshole.

Furious about his father's death, Lester organized a posse. He didn't want to admit it, but he realized the two independent invaders were most likely the same people who fouled up the action on Spike Island.

Chapter Twenty-Five

Brighton surveyed the island with his binoculars, telling Eddie what he saw. "On that small beach over there, there's a boat grounded on the sand, probably a patrol boat. Looks like a 50-caliber machinegun mounted on her deck."

The small, secluded beach would make an ideal sight to attempt to breech the island's security, but they would need to get past the patrol boat.

"So, Ed. You know how to SCUBA dive?" Brighton asked matter-of-factly. When Eddie replied in the affirmative, Brighton opened the lid on a large tackle box and removed SCUBA gear for two, a couple of grenades, two waterproof rifle cases, and a large watertight storage bag.

The long arms, Brighton's sniper rifle, and Eddie's mini-14 were secured in the cases, and Brighton stuffed the carryall with the grenades, a pair of two-way radios, the binoculars, both pairs of the men's shoes and their floppy, hook-covered fishing hats. Once they attached the air packs and equipment to their bodies, they jumped in the water and headed towards the beach. The environment below the surface was so beautiful Eddie found it hard to believe what kind of shit was going on above. He should be diving for sport, not for combat.

The two men emerged near the beach and proceeded to flipper walk onto the shore, cautiously approaching the patrol boat. They were surprised that no one fired at them, but when they got closer, they saw the boat was deserted. As they passed it, Brighton recognized the boat to be a craft manufactured by a company based in Argentina.

Under a bush at the edge of the beach, the men stashed their SCUBA equipment and prepared their weapons for attack. When they were all locked and loaded, Brighton distributed the grenades between himself and Eddie.

"Did you spend any time in the military?' Brighton quietly inquired as he handed Eddie a fragmentation grenade.

"Navy," Eddie nodded.

"Do you know how to use these?"

"Yup."

The men stealthily made their way into the jungle foliage behind the beach and a brief reconnaissance revealed five battle-dressed, heavily armed men. Brighton and Eddie waited to see what they were up to, and Brighton used the time to scan the area with the binoculars.

"I don't know what's up, but Jennifer's up on that verandah," Brighton whispered, handing Eddie the binoculars. "See that guy sitting across from her? I think that's Blackwell. I've never seen him in person, but I've seen pictures."

"We've got to figure out something soon; Jennifer isn't looking too good," Eddie remarked.

Island Bound

The sound of distant gunfire echoed across the island, and the five men in gray opened fire. The volley was short. The five men stormed an area where a few men established defensive positions around a stationary helicopter, and Brighton looked up and noticed that the verandah where he had spotted Jennifer and Blackwell was now empty. Several dead and injured bodies littered the ground around the helicopter, and the last three troopers disappeared through a doorway beneath the verandah. Sounds of a struggle emitted from the open doorway, but a distant din of explosions indicated that a real battle raged somewhere else on the island.

"I don't know what's up, Ed, but whatever it is, we can use the confusion to our advantage. I'm heading to the door. You cover me. I'll wave up when I feel the area is clear," Brighton planned.

Three loud explosions followed by more small arms fire came to their ears from the room the five men had entered, then there was almost complete silence except for the sounds of the jungle and a few quiet moans from the injured. Brighton waved Eddie on and proceeded into the building.

Eddie carried on an inner dialogue, "This place is huge - we got lucky to find Jen so quickly. I must be an idiot to offer to come along on this. I'm no warrior; I'm a firefighter, for God's sake."

Checking his mind's bitching when Brighton silently beckoned him to approach, Eddie entered the opening. A thin, frail, Oriental man lay on the floor not breathing, blood pooling around him.

"Right around this corner is a stairway, and its angle and direction cause me to believe that it leads to a room off of that deck out back. Those three guys bought the farm. They're all lying on the stairs. I'll pick up one of these." Brighton displayed the German assault rifle. "This should be more appropriate for the next job at hand."

"And what would that be?" Eddie interjected.

"We're going to walk in and introduce ourselves," Brighton smiled, motioning for Eddie to follow behind. Brighton casually proceeded up the stairs, and Eddie followed at a safe distance.

Brighton exited the stairway to find several women and a girl huddled in a corner. A large dark-skinned guy was playing with a stun-gun, shocking the women for his entertainment as Blackwell looked on with amusement. Apparently they weren't expecting any more hostile visitations. Eddie entered the room and planted his eyes on Jennifer. Her face came alive with recognition.

"Sorry to barge in like this, but you've got something we want," Brighton calmly greeted the evil men. The oriental and Blackwell both attempted to respond, but Eddie and Brighton both leveled their weapons in their direction. With automatic weapons in their faces, the captors became captives. Kneeling beside Jennifer while Brighton covered him, Eddie unlocked the pair of handcuffs that were binding her wrists.

"We've got to take them as well," Jennifer said, referring to a woman and a little child. "These are the Dirks, and they went missing a few weeks ago. The others are Nazi bitches - I guess that's what's going on here, they're trying to spring their women."

Eddie was bewildered. "Nazis?"

Just as Eddie moved over to the Dirks to free them, the Oriental man sprung across the room, knocking Brighton to the floor. The two men grappled for control of the rifle. Eddie went to aid his friend, but out of the corner of his eye he saw Blackwell rising from his chair with a small pistol in his hand. A single tug on the mini-14's trigger released a round from the barrel, and a bullet grazed Blackwell's hand. The pistol fell to the floor, and Eddie covered the crime lord while Jennifer locked him up with the same cuffs that had bound her wrists earlier.

Eddie was going to make another attempt at assisting his ally, but by then, Brighton had things under control. Brighton had forced the man towards the women in the corner, and one of the Nazi women tripped him as he passed. His stumble allowed Brighton just enough time to gain the advantage. He pinned the man against the wall and planted blow after blow onto his face. When the Japanese man had ceased to move, Brighton dragged the heavy body away from the group of women, giving the guy a swift kick to the stomach just for added measure.

Eddie had by now released the Dirks and was ready to high tail it on out before anyone else showed up. Just before leaving the room, however, Jennifer moved in close to the restrained crime lord. She bent over and picked up his discarded pistol, pointing it at the man's head.

"This is for all the shit you have put me through the last few days!" she screamed as she pulled the trigger. The bullet's aftermath would haunt her for years to come, but at that time she was thirsty for revenge and nothing could have stopped her.

Brighton and Eddie led the Dirks and Jennifer out the way they came, and Eddie grabbed the brown briefcase lying near the body of the Oriental man.

"What are you doing with that?" Brighton asked.

"I don't know. It might have something important inside."

The group reached the landing pad.

"We should take the high road out of this place." Still clutching the German assault rifle, Brighton took a seat in the cockpit. The rest scrambled in behind as Brighton attempted to get the machine going.

After a few tries, Brighton turned around to the others and said, "This is just a waste of time. The engine must have been hit."

As Eddie exited the aircraft, he noticed dark figures moving about by the stairwell inside. He mentioned the fact to Brighton, and the group picked up their pace. The trip back to the beach was long, and Jessica Dirk was having a hard time with her child who was too big to carry and too small to run as fast as the others. Eddie stopped long enough to scoop the child into his arms and heard sounds of people tramping through the bushes behind them. They reached the beach with only a couple of minutes to spare.

"All right folks, we're not out of this yet." Brighton inflated the buoyancy control jackets of each set of SCUBA equipment for the women to use as floats, and Eddie led them into the water.

"I'll cover you, and when you reach the boat, I'll head out myself," Brighton shouted.

Halfway to the boat Eddie heard gunfire erupt on the beach, but the only thing to do was continue on to the boat with the women and children. Once they arrived Eddie helped the child into the boat first, then the women, and at last himself. He turned to look at the beach to check Brighton's progress and saw he was standing chest-deep in water, blood staining the sea around him.

Leveling the mini-14 towards the figures pursuing Brighton into the surf, Eddie pulled the trigger in rapid procession. The pursuers hunkered down into the saltwater, and the temporary reprieve allowed Brighton the opportunity to make his way out to the safety of the boat, a crimson trail marking his course in the water. Jennifer helped the wounded man into the old boat while Eddie continued to fire at their pursuers. Once Brighton made it onboard, Eddie hit the throttle and jetted out of the lagoon, setting his course for Spike Island. He hoped the boat carried enough fuel to reach their destination. If luck were on his side today, perhaps Frank would have already arrived at the prearranged destination with the US Coast Guard or some other respectable law enforcement agency. The pirates would certainly pursue them to avenge the death of their leader.

"Eddie, this guy is bleeding pretty bad," Jennifer yelled over the sound of the boat's motor.

Looking behind him, he agreed with her. "Jenny, take control of the boat. You're gonna have to haul it - I'm sure our friends won't be far behind." Eddie pointed the girl in the direction of Spike Island, then crawled to the back of the boat to check Brighton's injuries. Two bullets nested themselves in his body - one in his left forearm, the other in his right shoulder. Back home, on the job, Eddie would easily have been able to treat both injuries, but with limited supplies on the bouncing speedboat, that task would be much more difficult.

Brighton struggled to raise his head, saying "Beneath the steering is a small toggle switch. That switch allows fuel from an extra source to enter the system." Eddie tried to interrupt, but Brighton waved him off. "I'm feeling pretty weak, let me finish - just in case I'm not around to help later. There is one more rocket tucked beneath the rail opposite of where I grabbed the last one. Take this," Brighton handed Eddie a little black box with a button and red light.

"This is a homing beacon," he explained. "I've already activated the signal, and if your friend didn't make it, hold out as long as possible on Spike Island. Mr. Klein should have an extraction team around here soon."

Brighton finally stopped talking long enough for Eddie to get a word into the conversation. "Hey, don't be so negative, man. Eddie Gilbert's on the scene, buddy. Paramedic extraordinare. I'm gonna take good care of you."

Eddie opened a small first aid kit from the boat's storage box and cut the front of Brighton's shirt, which was saturated with his blood. Puddles of the life-sustaining liquid dripped onto the deck around his chest. Eddie set out to treat Brighton as best as possible.

Brighton's skin whitened, his breathing grew shallow, and his pulse became weak and rapid. Frothy pink blood gurgled from the man's lips with each exhalation, and Eddie knew at least one of Brighton's lungs was filling with blood. Without proper treatment, Brighton would soon slip away. Eddie laid his patient back to make him more comfortable, knowing the best he could do would be to bandage the wounds and attempt to control the bleeding.

Moments later, Eddie watched as the life drained out of the warrior's body. Jessica Dirk and her daughter broke down and began sobbing, and Eddie sat silent for a moment before covering Brighton's face with the fishing hat still plastered to his head. Then he went to relieve Jennifer of the responsibility of piloting the craft.

"Jen, Brighton's dead," Eddie told her when he reached her side. "I'll take over here, but you should keep a sharp eye out for any bad guys trying to catch up."

Jennifer joined the Dirks in the back of the boat, trying to avoid the lifeless form of Brighton. The speed of the boat washed sprays of salt water over the side, and Jennifer could taste the salt on her lips.

*

Back on Crow Island, Lester and his army had finished mopping up the failed Nazi attack. Assuming his father's role, the new crime boss assembled a hunting party to head out and catch up to the escaped prisoners and their rescuers. Immediately upon discovering the grizzly scene and his dead father, Lester had ordered one man to follow the escaping boat at a safe distance and to report their location when contacted. Lester planned to the lead the expedition himself, taking along twenty of his minions.

An unusual flood of emotions taxed Lester's thoughts. His father had been killed, a profitable and long-lived business partner was dead, and someone had gotten away with his merchandise. His entire being was geared for vengeance. Lester contacted his scout inquiring about his progress and listened as the man reported his location. Lester smiled at the good fortune, assembled his men, and headed out.

*

A half hour away from Spike Island and almost out of fuel, Eddie felt someone shaking his shoulder. He turned his head to see Jennifer standing before him.

"I think we're being followed," she said, holding her hair from blowing in the wind and glancing nervously behind. "The same boat has been hanging out in the distance for the past two hours."

Eddie wasn't surprised; he had expected the kidnappers to try and catch his rag tag little crew. The fireman had been pondering strategies throughout the entire trip, hoping he wouldn't have to use any of them in the case that Frank had summoned the authorities and they would all be waiting on the island. They had no such luck.

Once the island resort was in sight, Eddie circled the entire island searching for the presence of the cavalry but was disappointed to find nothing but open water. Eddie parked the boat on the same small beach that he and Frank used to sneak their way onto the island just a couple of days ago, although it seemed like it had been an eternity. The little party gathered their arms and equipment before leaving the beached vessel. At first, Jessica refused the firearms that Ed offered, but in the end she submitted to carrying an automatic 12-gauge shotgun similar to the weapons used in the circles of law enforcement. Two bandoliers of shot shells hung from her shoulders, and she could have passed for a Mexican bandito out of the old westerns. Jennifer accepted the mini-14, and Eddie loaded himself with Brighton's rifle, the rocket launcher, and a variety of grenades. Brighton would have to be left back in the boat for now.

Eddie led his group through the jungle foliage and out to the dirt path where he hoped Doug would show himself and, once again, take them into the safety of his hidden caverns. If that didn't happen, his plan was to make it to the main house and try to radio for some assistance. If they were lucky, they might have time to come up with a defense plan as well.

They covered the distance between the beach and the main house in a short time, but Doug never appeared. Eddie tried to find the hidden entrance to the cave, but it had been so dark that night, and his mind hadn't been clear enough after the gunfight on the beach to remember anything.

Moving out from under the cover of the jungle, the group stumbled forward into the hot sun of the main clearing where the reek of dead bodies spilled from the hot tub where Jennifer's lifeless friends still posed in the same positions they held when they were slaughtered. Jennifer's face went white and she held a hand in front of her mouth, stricken speechless. Eddie held Molly's head against his shoulder so she wouldn't see and quickly moved the women beyond the ghastly scene.

"There's a phone somewhere in the main building, I assume?" Eddie asked.

"Yes, but you have to use a code, and Katie was the only one who had it memorized. Let's try the keeper's house." Jennifer pointed in the direction of the cottage-like home near the edge of the clearing. As the company picked their keeper's house, a shot rang out from the edge of the jungle. Eddie felt the wind from the projectile pass over his head.

Looking up, he noticed several large boulders half way between the cottage and their current position. They were the best cover available, so he led Jennifer and the Dirks behind them.

"We'll take cover here. Everyone stay down, and I'll see if I can find this guy."

"Is it those bad guys?" Molly spoke for the first time since Eddie had seen her.

"Yeah, I imagine it is," Eddie answered, surprised to hear her pipe up. Addressing Jennifer and Jessica, he spoke in a more adult tone. "It's probably the one who was following us. If we get him, we may be able to head out of here. Hopefully, the rest of them are still far behind." Eddie peeked over the crest of the largest boulder and settled the stock of the rifle into his shoulder. Setting his eye to the rifle's scope and scanning the tree line, Eddie unfortunately didn't see anything remarkable. Still searching the undergrowth for the hidden gunman, he instructed his companions to head to the cottage one after another and enter the building.

Jennifer was the first to set out. She was running her heart out when another crack filled the air. This time, Eddie caught a glimpse of the weapon's muzzle flash and fired off two rounds in the direction of where he had seen it. He still couldn't pin down the person operating the weapon.

Jessica took her daughter in her arms and ran for the cover of the house, and Eddie fired off two more rounds. This time there was no more return fire. It was now Eddie's turn to make the trip. He fired off the last round in the rifle's magazine, turned away from the rock, and sprinted for the door of the cottage, the report of several rounds echoing in his ears. Eddie saw rough holes form in the front of the cottage where the lead smacked into its surface as he bounded up the few stairs onto the covered porch and into the living room of the cottage. Eddie reloaded the rifle.

"The phones aren't working and the radio is smashed up," Jennifer stuttered in fear.

"Shit, I should've thought of that. They trashed any chance of communication during their last attack. We're going to have to find Doug or else make our way back to the boat. Maybe we could use the resort's boats...No, they sunk those I'm sure," Eddie thought out loud.

Eddie checked out the back of the building. Once on the back porch, he found a small yard with a shed and a swing set. The yard butted up to the thick tropical foliage, and a small stone path trailed off towards the large central villa. The sounds of several weapons firing in the distance made their way to Ed's eardrums as they struck the front of the house. Eddie returned to the rest of the group in the front of the house.

Jennifer took control while Eddie was gone. She had the Dirks lying flat on the ground while she took up a position by the window, pointing the mini-14 in the direction of the dirt pathway. Eddie kneeled beside her.

"The rest have shown up. I've seen a few of them stick their heads out of the jungle, checking things out from time to time. They got here awfully quick," Jennifer commented. Eddie could tell the girl was frightened. The pistol handle of the mini-14 was tucked into a firm, white grip. Eddie was full of fear himself.

"Our only way out will be through the jungle behind the house. It looks pretty thick, though," Eddie said as he lifted the sniper rifle to his shoulder yet another time. This time he was welcomed with the sight of a figure behind the scope's crosshairs. He could also make out a group of several people huddled together in conversation. The crosshairs settled on another body, and Eddie pulled the trigger. The figure slumped over, and the rest of the group unleashed a barrage of return gunfire, causing Eddie and Jennifer to join the Dirks lying flat on the ground.

"Let's give them something to think about," Eddie said as he prepared the rocket for use. The apparatus popped out to twice its size, and Ed flipped up the small sighting instrument, making sure the space behind him was clear. He shouldered the weapon and returned to the opened window to see several figures advancing across the open space of the clearing. Eddie aimed for the middle of the column and activated the trigger. The missile streaked across the field like a comet in the night sky, its explosive ammunition impacting the ground close to three of the advancing men. The ground rocked and three of the men toppled over while the third lost his footing for a moment and dove for cover. Gunfire erupted from the tree line beyond the attacking men, and Eddie expended the last five rounds of ammunition for the sniper rifle. When his weapon fell silent, all four of the approaching men lay dead.

Eddie discarded the rifle and retrieved the 12-gauge automatic from Mrs. Dirk, strapping the bandito ammunition carries around his torso. The shotgun was fully loaded, holding eight slugs. Eddie considered his next move, knowing that if they stayed in the cottage they would meet death soon. Packing up his crew of vacation refugees, he headed to rear of the cottage. The yard was empty and its surrounding vegetation formed a dense barrier. Stumbling through the thick undergrowth would be slow, but they had no choice. Eddie took the first step into the foliage, separating a small path with his body. The women followed behind like children being led about by their teacher on a grammar school field trip. The brush ensnared Eddie's feet with each step, and the humid atmosphere caused sweat to seep from every pore.

By the time the jungle parted to reveal a path, their bodies were covered with nicks, scratches, and bug bites. During the ten-minute walk, Eddie heard occasional gunshots and the shouts of the men hunting for their prey. As the four stepped onto the path they could hear the sound of bodies thrashing through the jungle behind them indicating that the hunters had found their trail. Eddie popped two rounds in to the direction of the noise, and automatic gunfire crackled in response. Eddie followed the path on its downhill trend, hopefully away from the villa and towards the beaches of the island's lower elevation.

Eddie really didn't have a plan to follow. They were trapped on a relatively small island with no way off and no way to call for help. Sure that the mobsters had sunk the boat as soon as they arrived, Eddie figured his straggling group faced only two chances for survival, Doug or the personnel Frank was supposed to assemble. They could only elude their pursuers for so long. Eddie kept his eyes wide open for a sign of one of the camouflaged mine entrances, but the jungle skirting the path remained thick.

As the group rounded a curve in the path, Eddie could see the tan sand of the beach - the same beach where this all began just a few days ago. They were out of space, and the sound of boots pounding on the packed earth became louder with each passing second as the enemy behind drew up closer and closer. They had no choice but to fight it out. Eddie sent the Dirks down to the beach to locate a final hiding place. As Jessica scurried onto the sand with her child in her arms, searching desperately for some place to hide on the vast, naked shore, Molly still clutched to the same teddy bear. Eddie felt a great surge of compassion for the little thing; she had been through more in the past few days than most people would during their whole life, but she bore it all with more calm than any of the adults.

Eddie and Jennifer stepped into the bushes on opposite sides of the path, and Eddie used an old phrase to instruct his fellow defender: "Don't fire until you see the whites of their eyes." He remembered his high school history teacher's lesson on the Battle of Bunker Hill and how he had been stricken by the simplicity of the advice. "I'll spark up the first shot."

The two unintentional warriors hunkered down and waited for their visitors, and Eddie shouldered the shotgun, his trusty .357 revolver tucked into the waist of his fishing pants. Eddie thought about Brighton, wondering what the bad guys had done with his body when they found the old boat. Glancing at the girl just across the way, Eddie thought, "That Jennifer's a real trooper." As Eddie gazed at the woman, she removed her hand from the stock of the mini-14 to wipe a puddle of sweat off her brow, then repositioned her hold on the weapon and waited, ready for the fight.

Ed made out the sound of several heavy feet plodding down the trail. The mercenaries were moving along the path with confidence in their ability to overcome the meddling amateurs. When Eddie saw the first man move into his field of view, he held himself steady. Two more men rounded the curve, walking slightly hunched-over as they glued their attention to the sides of the path. The point man approached to within twenty feet of Eddie's hiding spot, and Eddie pulled the trigger of the semiautomatic shot gun twice. The heavy lead slugs slammed into the chest of the approaching victim, knocking him off his feet. He fell with thud to the packed earth below. From the other side of the path, Eddie recognized the higher pitched sound of the mini-14 going off, and the second man in the column dropped to the ground with a grunt. Ed could see the man trying to crawl back beyond the curve in the path, but Jennifer finished him off with another pull of the trigger.

All was silent for a moment except for the light chirps of jungle birds and the buzz of large Caribbean insects. The path remained empty.

"You're cutoff. You have no choice but to give up and make it easier on yourselves," a voice shouted. "There are twenty of us and more coming. If you surrender, your deaths will be swift and painless. However, if you make us fight you out…well, let's just say you won't appreciate our behavior." Eddie didn't know it, but the voice he heard was that of Lester Crow himself.

Eddie thought for a moment and responded, "Yeah! Well fuck you buddy!"

Jennifer suddenly opened fire aiming off to her right side. It seems the bad guys were attempting to flank her while the man offered his deal. Meanwhile, two more men attempted to round the curve in the path. Eddie let the remaining bullets stored in the shotgun's magazine streak up the pathway, slamming into another of the attackers. The second man continued to advance, but quickly this time, almost at a sprint. Eddie found it difficult to draw his .357 in time to greet his attacker. Only an arm's-length away, the advancing man felt the bite of the pistol's ammunition. The figure stumbled forward, ramming into Eddie, and the fireman lost his balance and fell out into the path with the man on top of him. The Smith was buried in the man's stomach, and Eddie pulled the trigger again ensuring the end of the man's life. Two more men rushed around the curve, and this time, Jennifer fired the last two rounds in the rifle's magazine. She missed her target but still slipped a fresh clip into the bottom of the rifle.

Eddie pushed the lifeless form off and crawled back into the bushes. The two men were forcing their way through the plant life surrounding Jennifer. Slipping a couple of shotgun shells from one of the bandoliers strapped around his torso, Eddie reloaded his gun and aimed the weapon at the back of one of the men. The first slug knocked the man forward. It was a direct hit to the center of the man's backside. Jennifer placed a lucky blow onto the face of the second man with the butt of the semi-automatic rifle, and the attack phased the man long enough for her to pound two more of the fierce blows to the center of his head. This man fell, joining his comrades on the jungle floor.

Eddie tugged at one of the grenades he had placed in the large side pocket of his fishing trousers. Just beyond the curve of the path, the remaining attackers opened fire, sending a hail of bullets in the defender's direction. A sharp sting slapped across Eddie's right cheek, and when his hand came away from his face, he saw blood on the tips of his fingers. It didn't hurt much, so Eddie assumed the bullet had just grazed him. As only the Duke could, Eddie grasped the pin of a smoke grenade between his teeth and pulled the bomb away. When Eddie tossed the object as far away as possible, a bright green smoked billowed about. Ed and Jennifer retreated to the beach at the end of the path and turned back to see the cloud swirling around, lifting above the heights of the palm trees surrounding the beach and the pathway.

Eddie reached deep in his pocket for another, his final, grenade. In large yellow letters Eddie read the word 'Fragmentation" applied to its smooth surface. After tossing the bomb up the pathway, an explosion rocked the ground, but bullets continued to carry on in the direction of the beach as the smoke from the first grenade began to disperse. Eddie and Jennifer continued to return fire, both knowing the end was near. They were almost out of ammunition, and they were both losing spirit.

Somehow, above the rumble of the gunfire, the faint sound of a horn entered Eddie's eardrums. Eddie turned around and laid his eyes on the beautiful sight of a United States Coast Guard fighting ship. The gray helmet of a sailor was visible, popping out of a center of a formidable machinegun turret, its barrels trained in the direction of the beach. Frank stood behind the helmeted man on the back of the turret, his tall frame towering above. A long plastic horn stretched from his lips and above the head of the turrets gunner. It was a toy trumpet, and Frank took advantage of times when he ran out of breath to wave it excitedly over his head. Almost as if in competition, the captain of the fighting ship activated the vessel's air horn, its high-pitched sound drowning out all other noises about the beach.

Despite the welcome sight of the Coast Guard ship, the gunfire from the jungle pathway increased in its intensity, forcing Eddie, Jennifer, and the Dirks into the breakers. As the women waded in the direction of the Coast Guard vessel, Eddie shuffled into the surf backwards, anticipating the need to fend off the attackers until the Coast Guard could affect a successful rescue of the women in his party. Eddie wished he had the mini-14 that Jennifer was still clutching onto because the rifle had a better range than the slug-throwing shotgun.

Eddie was chest deep in saltwater when several men emerged from the pathway, assaulting the now abandoned beach. Eddie blasted away with the shotgun while the sailor in the weapons turret worked the large dual machineguns. The guns displayed no prejudice, beating down everything on the beach with high-powered ammunition. Most of the aggressors returned to the safety of the jungle path, but a few of the bad guys dropped to the wet earth, blood gushing from large wounds staining the sand where their bodies fell.

The cavalry had finally arrived.

Chapter Twenty-Six

Eddie, Jennifer and the Dirks rested safely in the confines of the Coast Guard infirmary while shore teams attempted to apprehend the outlaws still on the island.

"You know any good plastic surgeons? That wound on you cheek is a real humdinger," a medic said frankly. Eddie hadn't heard the word 'humdinger' since his childhood. "You're lucky you didn't take that hit anymore to the right - you wouldn't be here right now," he went on.

The stitches would have to wait. The ship's size didn't warrant a full-fledged medical doctor, so the infirmary was staffed by medics.

"I used to be a corpsman in the Navy," Eddie said, making small talk.

"No shit, what was your job?" The medic inquired.

"I served as a medic for the Marine Corps infantry companies." The two men exchanged stories while they waited for news from the operation taking place on the island.

The Dirks were out cold, enjoying their first good sleep since they were captured by Lester and his goons. Eddie was all patched up and Jennifer sat with her head propped on her right arm. She looked to be deep in thought, keeping to herself. She wasn't ready to be social, after losing two of her best friends and taking a few lives herself. Those facts were going to take a while for her to accept.

They had been off the island for almost two hours when the captain presented himself. Eddie immediately stood up out of respect for the officer's position, an old habit he had picked up from the Navy.

"No, no, please sit down. I'm Captain Tower. I hope you're all being taken care of."

Eddie nodded in approval.

The captain spoke with a southern twang and wore wire-rimmed glasses along with an immaculately clean uniform, everything buffed and polished.

"I just dropped by to update you on the situation. Those guys were going to fight to the end. They refused to give themselves up, and unfortunately, most of them got away. I would appreciate it if someone filled me in on the particulars."

Eddie narrated the story from the beginning.

"Hey I need to make a phone call," Jennifer piped up. "I need to call my father."

The captain ordered one of his crew to assist the young lady, and as the two ventured off to some other part of the ship, Eddie finished his story.

"Well before we pull out I've got to see what the big brass has got to say about this," the captain concluded. "It seems that girl has some connections. We're only going to hang around here for a few more minutes - we got things settled out there. It's a sad state of affairs, so many young innocents losing their lives like that. I was ordered to leave their bodies where they were fell because there's going to be an investigation."

Before he left, Eddie asked him if anyone had seen a strange character who hobbled around, lived in the caves, and said ugh all the time. The captain didn't fully comprehend the issue but assured Eddie that he would look into it. Eddie continued with one more request, asking the captain to retrieve Brighton's body from the bottom of the old boat. The captain agreed to make certain all the affairs were settled, then excused himself, leaving Eddie to his own devices.

Eddie left the infirmary in search of Frank and found him still hanging around the front gun turret. When Eddie approached, Frank was trying to get the gunner to allow him to fire off the weapon. The crewman kept saying no.

"Hey buddy, long time no see!" Eddie cried as he grabbed the big man around the waist and twirled him around a couple times. Frank's bulk was so overpowering that the two of them almost landed flat on the deck.

"Eddie," Frank said, his face beaming. "I thought you were dead for sure. What happened to your face, man? You look terrible."

Eddie waved Frank's hand away as he reached up to see what was under the bandage on the right side of his face. "You're tellin' me."

The two were about to go below decks to see if they could locate a few sodas and to talk about their recent adventures when the captain strode across the deck in their direction.

"We're going to take you all to Key West where a private jet will be waiting for you. The girl's father is a prominent politician, so you can be sure you'll have excellent service. We have to keep those political types happy, after all. You all have to be hungry. Can I get you guys anything?" Captain Tower offered. Frank naturally accepted the offer.

"You got any Key Lime pie laying around here?" Eddie asked with a slight grin cracking from the side of his mouth.

"No, but we do have apple." Eddie accepted the offer, and Frank asked for a whole pie.

The ship docked at the naval station based on the island of Key West and a military police vehicle transported Jessica and Molly Dirk, Jennifer, Frank, and Eddie to the tiny Key West International Airport. The Dirks remained on the base to make their own arrangements. Hugs, phone numbers, and addresses were exchanged with the promise of keeping in touch, then the three remaining survivors of the Crows' evil plot climbed into a twin-engine leer jet that was parked on the runway near the terminal. The engines were running, and the flight crew intended to take off as soon as their passengers arrived.

Jennifer, the first one onboard, was surprised to see Marcie already seated in the plane. The two long time friends embraced, the tears began to flow.

"What are you doing here, crazy?" Jennifer asked. "I thought you'd be home by now."

"You kidding? I wasn't about to leave until I found out what happened to you," Marcie replied warmly.

The flight was relatively short, and when the leer touched down in Tampa, a stretch limo was waiting. In a short time, the luxury automobile delivered the group on to the doorstep of Mr. Bruce Klein's Florida home where the business tycoon stood waiting with several other family members. The homecoming turned out to be quite an event.

The next few weeks took on a depressing state of affairs. The captain was as good as his word, and he sent a report to Eddie detailing the situation on the island after the Coast Guard drove away the Crow fighters. Behind the technical language of the brief, Eddie came to realize that the mercenaries had found Doug's hideout and killed him after ransacking his mines. Brighton's body, on the other hand, was nowhere to be found, and the report officially declared him a missing person. Afterwards, Eddie almost questioned whether or not Brighton had really been dead, although he knew it was virtually impossible to lose that much blood and still be strong enough to survive without hospitalization. The only other possibility was that the Crow forces had done something to hide his remains.

In addition to the troubling news about Doug and the vaguely hopeful mystery of Brighton's fate, several government agencies called daily to pick the brains of the survivors. No one had ever been successful in getting so close to the Crow organization, and the investigators felt Eddie and his friends held the key to putting the evil enterprise out of business forever.

The worst part of the aftermath, especially for Jennifer and Marcie, was confronting the deaths of their friends. The weeks after their return were filled with funerals and heart-wrenching meetings with the deceased's family members.

All of the survivors, apart from Jessica and her daughter, Molly, spent a few weeks recuperating at the Klein's large, plantation-like estate in North Carolina. Bruce and his family were very gracious and wanted to show their gratitude to everyone involved in the rescue of his daughter. He told everyone to stay as long as they felt they needed to, and when they decided to go home, he would fly each one home.

Frank left after a few days, saying that he needed to get back on duty. The two old friends parted with a great deal of emotion, which they concealed behind jokes and teasing. Eddie remained behind to finish the rest of his vacation since he needed a little break from adventuring and wouldn't even consider setting sail on the Caribbean again any time soon.

One Wednesday afternoon Mr. Klein approached Eddie as he sunned himself by the pool with Jennifer and Marcie.

Island Bound

"Ed, I'd like to have word with you," he said, drawing Eddie aside to where they could talk privately. "You seem like the kind of guy who could be very resourceful, and I've got a place in my personal security force for you, if you're interested."

Eddie slowly shook his head from side to side, in essence declining the offer.

"Well, you think about it. The spot will always be open. The starting pay would be around one hundred grand a year." Mr. Klien handed Eddie a business card with his private number, instructing Ed to call him if he chose to reconsider. Eddie liked the sum but was still unsure.

"Thanks Mr. Klien, but I'm a firefighter, not a cop or security professional. I appreciate the offer, though."

After their conversation Eddie decided to head back home the next day. He wanted to get things settled before returning to work. As a final gesture, Bruce Klein pulled some strings and arranged for Eddie to receive a large sum of cash for his heroic behavior. The award wasn't so much a gift for returning Klein's daughter to him as it was for turning in the briefcase he had acquired while sneaking around on Crow island. As it turned out, that Mr. Tomo was also quite a counterfeiter.

The next morning Eddie packed his bags, said his good-byes, which turned into another emotional scene, and headed out for the airport. Marcie gave him a ride, telling him she'd like to come up and visit some time soon. Eddie was quite fond of the young lady and welcomed the suggestion. He did need some time to settle affairs first, but they planned to hook up within the month.

Nearly four hours later Eddie's plane touched down at O'Hare airport in beautiful Chicago, Illinois. The smooth Mr. Klien had provided Eddie with first-class tickets. He traveled with a carry-on only because he had last all his belongings when the tug had been stolen. He even lost the tug. Mr. Klein graciously settled the account with the yacht broker on Eddie's behalf.

Eddie stepped out of the sliding doors located on the lower level near the arrivals pick up area. The February wind was cold and bit down hard on Eddie's deeply tanned skin. Ed inhaled deeply, and as the crisp air entered his lungs, it actually felt good to him. He missed Chicago, as well as work. Rather than to force any of his friends or family to come out in such cold weather, Eddie decided to jump a cab. He needed some time alone.

The cab deposited Eddie at the front door of his building, and the door man opened the rear door of the taxi. Eddie paid the driver, greeted the doorman, and entered the lobby. One other person was waiting for the elevator, a young woman Eddie had never met. The two exchanged glances.

"What happened to you?" she asked.

Eddie had almost forgotten about the various visible injuries that were in the process of healing over.

J.D. Gordon

"I went on vacation and had a rough time of it. Unexpected trouble," Eddie responded.

The elevator door opened, revealing the corridor leading to Eddie's unit. The two riders nodded at each other, a silent good bye. Having bummed a set of keys off the doorman since he had lost his own, Ed opened the door and stepped into his home, sweet home. Occasionally, just sometimes, its feels good to come home.

Afterword

    Eddie sat under the hot sun, tiny beads of perspiration forming on his upper lip. Although he had taken the time to smear suntan lotion on his exposed nose and arms, the burn was still going to be bad. Eddie's face was already as red as a lobster. That was the one and only draw back, but to Eddie it was worth it. There was nothing quite like sitting in the bleachers at Wrigley among close friends while enjoying the afternoon with the Cubbies. The crowd was getting a little out of hand, but it was nothing unusual for a pack of bleacher bums. The Cubs were playing the Brewers, and up until a couple of minutes ago, the Brewers were winning four to two. The game was in its seventh inning, the bases were loaded, and Sammy was batting. The count was one ball and two strikes with two outs. The smell of mustard and hot dogs, cheap beer and roasted peanuts hung in the air, and Eddie had his half-empty beer in his lap, wedged between his legs. Half in the bag with one, two, or three beers too many, Eddie was in the process of slipping his shirt back on to avoid the possibility of several days of discomfort with his sunburn rubbing up on sheets, shirt, blankets and towels.

    Eddie heard the distinctive crack of the bat against the ball and popped up in the moment of silence, accidentally spilling his beer on a guy sitting in front of him. The bum was sporting ripped clothes and baggy pants. Eddie watched the ball as it streaked overhead, over the bleachers, and onto Waveland Avenue, bouncing into the hands of a fourteen year old kid waiting patiently for ball to reach the street, as that one just had. The crowed cheered as the ball player ran the bases.

    Eddie had just finished a forty-eight hour shift at the fire department because he covered for another firefighter who needed the time off but had already burned through all his vacation time. The shift seemed as if it would never end. Eddie was assigned to the ambulance for the entire forty-eight hours, and both nights were busy, preventing Eddie from resting up. He had worked two structure fires and lost three patients.

    Eddie started to think about the troubles he had encountered while on his vacation. The incident took place only six months ago, but now it seemed like it had been years since he was fighting and dodging bandits. For the most part everyone involved kept their promises of staying in touch, but Eddie saw Marcie the most since she visited on a semi-regular basis.

    Eddie wiped the thoughts from his mind for the time being. The Cubs, for once, were kicking some ass. After the game Eddie and his friends hit the joints and saloons surrounding the ballpark, their night ending at Wrigleyville Dogs where they consumed hideous amounts of greasy foods. Afterwards, Eddie cabbed to Union station and bought a ticket for the first train, which ran right through the town of Salt Creek. The town's stop was a short walk from Eddie's building.

Eddie dozed off on one of the benches in the station, and a security officer prodded Ed to life shortly before the first train departed for the western suburbs. Eddie arrived home around seven-thirty in the morning, spent time cleaning himself up, and prepared to hit the sack. The hangover hit hard, and he needed rest desperately.

There was one more thing Ed wanted to take care of before hitting the mattress. Grabbing his cordless phone, he dialed a set of ten numbers and listened as the phone rang on the other end of the line.

"Mr. Klein, This is Eddie - Eddie Gilbert."

"Hey Ed, it's good to hear from you. What's up?" The man replied.

"I think I may be interested in that job you were talking about."

About the Author

Jimmy (J.D.) Gordon is a native of the Midwest. He developed an appreciation for the finer things in life and growing up in Chicago. Jimmy considers "finer things" to include pan pizza, six-string music, and Cubs baseball. Living in the Windy City, Jimmy has developed the need and desire to occasionally search for warmer climates. He now lives with his wife in the Village of Glen Ellyn, a suburb west of Chicago. Jimmy has been a professional firefighter and paramedic for the past nine years. He is a first-time author.